SEIZE

Other Books in the Magnus Blackwell Series

Blackwell: The Prequel (A Magnus Blackwell Novel, Book 1)
Damned (A Magnus Blackwell Novel, Book 2)
Bound (A Magnus Blackwell Novel, Book 3)

By Alexandrea Weis and Lucas Astor
Death by the River (A St. Benedict Novel, Book 1)

By Alexandrea Weis
Realm

Forthcoming from Vesuvian Books

By Alexandrea Weis
The Secret Brokers

By Alexandrea Weis with Lucas Astor
The Chimera Effect
4 for the Devil
A River of Secrets (A St. Benedict Novel, Book 2)

SEIZE

A MAGNUS BLACKWELL NOVEL: BOOK FOUR

Alexandrea Weis With Lucas Astor

Seize
A Magnus Blackwell Novel, Book III

This is a work of fiction. Names, characters, places, and incidents either are the product
of the author's imagination or are used fictitiously.
Any resemblance to actual persons, living or dead, or locales is entirely coincidental.

Cover Credit: Original Illustration by Sam Shearon
www.ghliterary.com/clients/sam-shearon/

Title Treatment and design layout by Michael J. Canales
www.MJCImageworks.com

ISBN: 978-1-944109-88-2

VESUVIAN BOOKS
Published by Vesuvian Books
www.vesuvianbooks.com

Printed in the United States

10 9 8 7 6 5 4 3 2 1

Praise for the Magnus Blackwell Series

Awards

2018 American Fiction Awards
Winner—Horror: Supernatural/Paranormal—Blackwell

2018 Feathered Quill Book Awards
Gold (1st Place) Winner—Mystery—Blackwell
Silver (2nd Place Winner—Adult Fiction—Blackwell

2018 Readers' Favorite
Finalist—Fiction: Paranormal—Damned

2017 FOREWORD REVIEWS: Indies Book of the Year
Bronze Winner—Horror—Blackwell

2017 International Book Awards
Finalist—Blackwell

2017 Readers' Favorite
Honorable Mention—Fiction—Supernatural—Blackwell

2017 Best Book Awards
Finalist: Horror—Damned

Praise

"I love the storyline … The author throws fire on many pages
through vibrant dialogue and fantastic scene writing … far from
predictable, and so satisfying and rewarding."
~*Feathered Quill Book Awards* Judges' Comments

AND THE DEAD SHALL RISE

Chapter One

The dead were everywhere.

Bathed in late afternoon rays of sunlight, Magnus stood on a patch of land surrounded by algae-covered swamp and cursed. Why had he and Lexie been dragged to this godforsaken hellhole again? The songs of cicadas welcoming the coming twilight played in the background while the black eyes of the dead stared at him from the water.

Scarred, bruised, with fresh gaping wounds, the ghosts of men, women, and children lingered above the water. Some missing limbs and even heads, the apparitions glared at him. He preferred things the way they had been before when he'd depended on Lexie to tell him what the dead wanted. He feared her gift firmly entrenched in his center.

Lexie spoke in hushed tones to Detective Emile Glapion. Emile understood Lexie's gift having been raised by a voodoo priestess. Several officers from the St. John The Baptist Parish Sheriff's Department waited around them, peering into the water at the naked victim.

"Otis Landry was a good man." Emile's voice carried in the humid, sticky air. "I know how hard this must be for you, but can you think of any reason why anyone would cut up your landlord like that?"

Otis's bloated corpse had strange symbols carved across his torso and arms. Magnus recognized the geometric shapes and wavy lines of the devouring spell used on Renee. Her murder, as well as others' in the city covered with the same carvings, remained unsolved. By the rate the bodies were piling up, Magnus doubted the police would ever get a handle on the killings.

He floated closer to Lexie, unseen by the others, eager to eavesdrop on more of her conversation. These days, Magnus found his charge hard to read. It was as if the black inside her blocked him. He used to be able to glean her every thought, sense her feelings, and guess her next move, but now, she was a mystery—much like other women he'd known.

An image of the lovely Frances floated across his mind. But as soon as he pictured her delicate face and honey-blonde hair, he remembered the way she screamed as he pushed her over the cliff behind his family home.

He didn't like reliving that moment. It was one of many he wished to forget.

"I know Otis was related to Renee in some way." Lexie pouted her pink lips. "She called him family once."

"Distant second cousins. Not close blood. But what could Mr. Landry, Gus Favaro, and Renee have in common?" Emile asked. "They all had the same spell carved into them, but were from different worlds."

"Were they?" Lexie's knuckles shone white against her dragon cane. "They all had businesses in the French Quarter. Renee had her shop, Gus Favaro had a restaurant or two there, and Otis Landry owned several residences."

Very good. He liked it when she used her head. But what about motive?

"We know Renee had dealings with the thugs who served Bloody Mary, and she was killed inside the prison, so it had to be someone with ties to the prison or the city." Lexie shifted her gaze to the dead man. "Perhaps Otis knew the same men Renee did since they were related."

Emile rested his hands on his hips, the shiny silver badge of an NOPD detective attached to his belt. "I don't see it. As far as I can get from his records, he was a law-abiding citizen with no priors, no outstanding tickets, and up-to-date on his taxes. His maid said he was a quiet man, divorced, and lived alone with no previous run-ins with the law. Gus Favaro had no criminal history either."

"Excuse me, but this search for justice could go on and on ..." Magnus waved his cane at the restless souls. "Meanwhile, others are waiting to speak with you."

Emile stooped to investigate the water's edge while Lexie peered into the swamp.

Magnus noted the change in her face. She saw them.

"There are so many."

"So many what?" Emile asked, standing up.

Lexie tapped her fingers on the dragon's head. "The dead. They're here."

Emile scrubbed his face with his hands. "Are we talking spirits in general, or your Mr. Blackwell." Emile's gaze darted around the shoreline. "Is he here? I bet he's here."

The question brought a grin to his lips. Being a ghost did have its advantages.

Lexie casually nodded to her right. "He never leaves my side."

"That must make for fun times with Will."

Magnus blew out an aggravated breath. "Would you please tell the detective I'm a spirit guide, not a peeping Tom."

A strange howl cut through the air. Magnus reached out with his power, searching the area. Coyote? Wolf? But nothing came back to him.

Lexie stood motionless. "What was that?"

Emile chuckled at her reaction. "It's nothing. Lots of wild dogs, coyotes, even a few gray wolves out here." He scoured the dense green brush and cypress trees surrounding the water. "Unless it's the *rougarou*." He grinned. "Local Cajun legends say their kind live in these swamps."

Lexie's gaze tore into the detective. "Tell me you just made that up."

"All the books you've been reading lately and you've never run across the legend of the *rougarou*? It's a half-man, half-wolf creature that roams the swamps and kills those who wander into its territory. Perhaps you should get a book on the subject."

"Detective?" an officer called a few feet away.

Emile pointed at the ground. "Stay here and don't touch anything. Same goes for your ghost." He hurried away.

Magnus snorted as he passed. "I hope he's joking."

Lexie motioned to the apparitions crowding the water. "Is this what you saw at Kalila's home?"

"Unfortunately, yes."

She glanced back at a white shell-covered road. "We're not far from her place. Maybe these are her spirits, the ones she held captive."

"No. The ghosts haunting her swamp were different. Different faces, different clothes from different eras. These people all look to be from the same period in history."

"Then who are they, Magnus?"

He took in the dead wafting over the water as if stirred by an undetectable breeze. Their vacuous stares and tattered clothing all looked the same. Then one face in the rear caught his attention.

"There." He gestured to a lone standout among the apparitions.

With black eyes and blank stare resembling the others, Otis Landry bobbed in the water.

"Otis Landry is among them."

Magnus pressed his lips together. He didn't like what he felt coming off the murky marsh. The darkness in the ribbon connecting him to Lexie throbbed as if pleased with his discomfort.

He watched Lexie, anxious to see if she registered the change. She sucked in a deep breath and closed her eyes. Her energy bloomed like a waterspout on Lake Pontchartrain during a fierce storm. Their ribbon pulsated, and its blackness expanded. He wished to shut it off, but if he did, he would lose Lexie and his ability to stay in her world. He was here to protect her, and a little discomfort was worth it as long as he knew she was safe.

"They all died here at once," she murmured. "They're all speaking at the same time, whispering about the great storm."

"Storm?" Magnus rested against his cane. "Intriguing. Picking up anything from our victim?"

She opened her eyes. "He's telling me how much he liked me. How sorry he is I have to see him this way." She turned to Magnus.

"And to get out of here while we still can. She is coming."

"Who is—?"

"What have you picked up?" Emile's question cut Magnus off as he returned to Lexie's side. "I was hoping your skills would help us out."

Magnus sensed Lexie's hesitation. *This is a bad sign.*

Anytime she withheld information, she was up to something. He'd seen her do it with her husband, Emile, and even him, even though he could tell when she was lying.

"I'm not sure what to tell you."

Emile's sullen frown let Magnus know that wasn't what he wanted to hear. "You know I'm going out on a limb with my department. I promised my captain you could help." He wiped the sweat from his forehead. "He's been reluctant to have you consult on cases. He's getting pressure from the higher-ups to keep you out."

This wasn't news. Opposition to her appointment as mambo had haunted her from the night she'd won her title at the *haute défi.*

"I can guess who is pressuring them," Magnus told her. "His tactics must be stopped."

Emile rubbed behind his neck, sizing her up as if debating what to disclose. "Harold's politically connected. He's making things difficult for you."

Magnus flinched, knowing how much the information would hurt Lexie. Harold Forneaux, her biggest opponent and the man gunning for her job, had been out to discredit her at every turn.

"He's been speaking out against me, pushing the council to vote me out. I hear what he tells other priestesses about me. Claims I'm a fake mambo." Lexie let the air out of her lungs in one long hiss. "He wants my baton juju." She rubbed her thumb over the handle of her cane.

Emile leaned closer and lowered his voice, but Magnus could still hear him.

"Then tell me something I can use to take back to my boss and impress him."

Lexie relaxed her shoulders and offered a sad smile. "Otis died here, or close by. His body was dumped in the swamp. He's sorry I had to see him like this."

Emile grimaced. "Anything on who killed him or why?"

"That's it." She shrugged. "Wish I had more."

"Lexie. I need solid leads, not random stuff that won't help us. I'm giving you a chance here; don't blow it."

Magnus detected her apprehension. It made her blackness bloom. When she was confident, happy, smiling, or with Will, her white side prevailed. She wasn't the vibrant woman he cared for when the darkness took her over. In those times, she reminded him of the evil spirit who held her soul—the diabolical Kalfu.

"There are others with him," she said softly. "Others in the water. They died here. Violently. They're keeping him from getting through. Perhaps if I knew who they were or where they come—"

"Others?" Emile furrowed his brow.

"Ask him about the past." Magnus raised his nose in the air. "The storm they mentioned. See if he knows."

"What about a storm here, a long time ago? Was there one?"

Emile stared at her.

Magnus couldn't decide if he was confused or dumbfounded.

Emile mopped his damp brow with his tie. "Yeah, there was a storm, a big one—the New Orleans Hurricane of 1915. It killed over a hundred people in a small town that used to be around here—Frenier. They buried everyone in a cemetery nearby."

The wind suddenly changed direction, making the apparitions bob and sway. Magnus sensed the charge in the air.

Lexie turned to Magnus. "We should go there."

It was not what Magnus wanted to hear. How could he keep Lexie safe when she always insisted on pursuing such escapades?

Emile held up his hands. "Hold on. You can only get there by boat, and even then, it's private land. No one is allowed in the cemetery. And it has nothing to do with our investigation."

Lexie frowned, obstinacy glistening in her eyes.

Why can't she take no for an answer?

"Who owns the land?" A hint of irritation deepened her voice. "Can we get their permission to visit?"

"If you're going to be mambo, you should get to know the local legends." Emile paused as he rubbed his chin. "The land used to belong to the famous voodoo priestess, Julie Brown. No one goes to the property because she haunts it and the owners don't want anyone getting hurt or disappearing. Dozens of people have vanished from that cemetery through the years. They say it's because Julie Brown doesn't take kindly to strangers."

"She won't hurt me."

Magnus refrained from groaning. Lexie's confidence had swelled since she'd first accepted her baton juju a few months ago, but he feared her magical powers sometimes blinded her to the dangers of her job.

"Are you out of your mind?" Emile tossed up his hands. "I'd never let you go there alone."

"I can handle myself," she asserted with a perturbed lilt. "I'm not afraid of Julie Brown's ghost."

Emile's shoulders drooped. "You're not going anywhere near those swamps without me. It's too dangerous. Bloody Mary had a lot of pull around these parts, and some of her people might be out for revenge."

Magnus clenched his fists. That was the wrong thing to say to Lexie. Damned woman thrived on danger.

Emile opened his mouth to continue when an officer in Sheriff's Department dress blues came up to him.

"Excuse me, Detective. We're about to pull the victim out of the water. Thought you might want to get a better look."

Emile glanced from the officer to Lexie and then raised his finger to her. "The answer is no. If I feel we need to go to the cemetery, I will go through the proper legal channels and get men to go with us. You're not to go there alone."

He left her to join the other officers.

Lexie picked up her dragon cane and inspected the different colored eyes—one black and one white, representing her power.

"Magnus?" she called in the sweetest voice. "Can you help me find a boat?"

Chapter Two

Late afternoon light trickled through tree limbs arching over their flatbed boat. Lexie and Magnus circumvented the murky depths of the narrow bayou, cutting through the greenish, foul-smelling water. Magnus stared into the inhospitable landscape while the play of light created intricate patterns on the land. He chastised himself for going along with Lexie's plan. How could he protect her way out here?

Magnus checked on the man he'd enlisted to take them through the swamp. He sat at the back of the boat, wearing a camo jumper and brown hat stitched with Ned's Fishing, his hand on the engine's throttle.

"Why are we here?"

Seated on the board across the middle of the boat, Lexie kept her eyes ahead. "The spirits on the water said I needed to visit the cemetery."

"Why didn't you tell me that?" he asked indignantly.

"Because you would have told me not to. They said 'what I seek is here. She is here.' I intend to find out who she is and what I can learn from her."

Magnus didn't like that. "Do you think she is that Julie Brown woman?"

Lexie shrugged and said nothing. He could feel she was hiding something but decided not to press her. Since the moment she'd embraced Kalfu's darkness, he'd learned not to push for answers. Things got heated between them when he did.

He returned his attention to the water. "I hate boats."

"How can you hate boats? You're a ghost."

"Unfortunately, being dead does not mean you give up your fears." He used the tip of his cane to push around a few fishing nets at the bottom of the boat. "My father dragged me out on one once when I was small. I fell in and almost drowned. I've detested them ever since."

"You could have stayed on the dock."

He motioned to their mesmerized pilot. "And how would you have convinced our Mr. Ned to take you to the cemetery without me?"

A slight sneer lifted her lips. It wasn't much, but he noticed it. His Lexie had never sneered before the darkness had possessed her. Sometimes when she made that face, Magnus swore he saw Kalfu staring back at him. The voodoo god of darkness seemed to haunt her at times—in a look, a smile, the way she moved.

"I could have done it without you whispering in his ear." She turned her attention to the banks of dense green foliage and cypress trees. "My powers are much stronger now."

"But at what cost?" he muttered.

11

She spun around to face him. "Are you questioning my choices? You know I had none."

Magnus didn't need a reminder of the hellish nightmare they'd endured because of Emily's obsession with him.

He tempered his annoyance by rubbing the handle of his cane. He couldn't feel the wood against his fingertips, but he could sense the strength residing inside the piece—the power of Damballah.

The engine cut off. Magnus was about to whisper to the fisherman when he spotted something ahead.

The brush cleared and revealed a spot of grassy land. Cypress trees circled it, their branches hanging low in a protective embrace. Small white crosses dotted the landscape, and a crooked, little, black iron fence encircled the cemetery.

Streams of sunlight showed how far back the graves went into the trees. The wood crosses and the occasional headstones jutted from the land. Eventually, a line of thick brush blocked his view.

An eerie quiet rose as they approached the shore. The cicadas, birds, and breeze all stilled when the tip of their flat-bottom boat touched land. The ability he'd received from Lexie came to life, setting off a firestorm of warnings. A black, heavy tension jabbed at him, sweeping away the quaint charm of the surroundings. Evil lived in the cemetery.

"I don't like this."

Ignoring his concerns, Lexie climbed from the boat, letting her baton juju and the hem of her white dress drag through the shallow water as she proceeded to the shore.

"You feel the pull of the place, Magnus. We're meant to be here."

He did feel it, but his recent experiences with Lexie had taught him such feelings usually led to something dangerous.

A small waterspout formed where her cane touched the water. It spread, riding the ripples made by the magical staff outward into the small bayou. A mist ascended from the ripples. Lexie didn't seem to notice the growing white fog hugging the surface, but Magnus did.

This is no ordinary cemetery.

Lexie hurried ahead, infuriating him.

"Stay," he whispered in the ear of their boatman.

Ned sat back and dropped the brim of his cap over his eyes.

Magnus leaped onto the shore, making sure not to let his ethereal being touch the smoke-covered water gathering around the boat.

His every instinct told him to leave, but he felt as compelled as Lexie to find out what had guided them to the spooky place. Magnus just prayed they had not walked into a trap.

When he reached her, waiting by the cemetery gate, she seemed intrigued by an arch of wood above the entrance—the date 1915 carved into it.

He gestured to the lock on the gate. "How do you plan on getting in?"

She dropped her cane on the other side of the fence. "Didn't you ever break into places when you were a kid?"

To his amazement, she went to the side of the gate where the iron fence dipped and swung her leg over. With a small hop, she landed on the other side.

"I never dared embarrass my family name." Magnus floated through the gate and waited. "My father would have had my hide."

Lexie picked up her cane. "Sounds like you had a pretty boring childhood."

"It was a different time. Childhood was something to survive, not enjoy."

"Want to talk about it?" she asked, sounding like the warm, fun-loving Lexie he adored.

He glowered at her. "No."

Numerous water oaks, their branches draped with long tendrils of Spanish moss, surrounded the land strewn with white wooden crosses. Sprays of plastic flowers dulled by sunlight adorned some of the crosses, but the names carved into them had eroded.

He followed Lexie from the gate, her feet crunching the twigs and dead leaves on the ground.

She stopped at a crooked wooden cross and wiped the moss from the nameplate. He peered over her shoulder, not caring who was laid to rest on the spot. One grave was as empty as another to him. The dead didn't dwell on their patches of the earth but remained close to the people they had once loved. Life attracted spirits, not dirt.

Lexie strolled ahead, heading deeper into the shade offered by the Spanish moss. The farther they traveled, the more uncomfortable Magnus felt.

It was a weird sensation as if the trees watched their every move.

When the area opened up, a small patch of land carpeted in inviting green moss brought a respite from the dreariness of the cemetery. Light came and went through the swaying branches, offering an almost fairylike atmosphere. Perhaps the place wasn't as foreboding as it seemed.

They headed across the soft ground, and Lexie's footfalls faded. Shadows appeared, popping out from behind every bush and tree trunk. They moved and shifted as if caught up in a frenzied dance, but there wasn't a breath of wind around them. Their contortions reminded him of the wild activity he'd seen on the banks of Bayou St. John when he and Oscar had witnessed a voodoo ritual. The comparison sent a shiver through his being. Then the last traces of sunlight receded as the gnarled canopy of branches threaded together until they became engulfed in a bone-chilling shade.

Along the edge of the clearing, the grave markers changed from white wooden crosses to upright square-shaped stone slabs. Some tilted to the side, some had turned over completely, and one had been swallowed up by the trunk of a tree, allowing only a portion of the stone to peek through the bark.

"This must be the section before the 1915 storm." Lexie went to a stone slab and read the name. "M. Brown, died 1875."

Magnus went to another slab. "L. Brown, died 1901." He checked out another. "J. Brown, died 1915."

"Same family?" Lexie perused the headstones. "Perhaps Julie Brown's?"

A stiff breeze came out of nowhere and whipped past them, rustling the Spanish moss above. The wind created an ominous rustling sound. It echoed across the enclosed space like the whisper of a thousand voices urging them forward. There was something else in the wind, a darkness he'd not detected before.

He was about to tell Lexie about it when a light surfaced to the right. Though dull at first, like a weak flashlight, it grew in intensity until it almost blinded. Something was in it—the shape of a woman. He held up his hand, shading his eyes. He wanted to go to Lexie, but he couldn't move. Magnus was glued to the ground, unable to budge.

"The priestess you speak of was named Julie Brown, Mambo,

and she worked for me."

The voice was feminine and had an accent. Irish? Magnus remembered the musical cadence of his friend Oscar Wilde. The way she spoke sounded the same.

A woman with creamy skin and emerald-green eyes stepped out from the light. She wore a black velvet gown that dragged the ground. Magnus stared at the folds of the dress, swearing he saw movement. Human skulls rose from the fabric as if crying out for help, and then sank back into the velvet.

"Who are you?" Lexie asked.

Magnus admired the spirit's wavy, red-gold hair hung about her shoulders. In her hand, she carried a baton juju shaped like a rooster. The handle was a large cockscomb. Along the shaft, feathers had been carved into the wood and shimmered in the light. The tip resembled claws, with sharp talons.

"I'm glad you received my message." Her strident voice echoed across the clearing. "I thought it time you and I meet."

"Your message?" Lexie approached the tall woman. "You're the one the spirits sent me to see?"

The black baton juju tapped the ground. The staff vibrated. Shiny black feathers popped out all over, covering the cane. The shaft plumped, the black legs of the rooster jutted out, its talons catching the light. The head bent and twisted. The rigid wooden comb flopped over as it became flesh. The rooster wings spread open and flapped. Its black beak and coal eyes were the last parts of the cane to come to life. The creature stretched its neck and let out a shrill crow while flapping its wings.

Magnus stared at the hideous beast. "Who are you?"

"I'm Maman Brigitte, Mr. Blackwell. My husband, Baron Samedi, told me about you. He said you were a special spirit. One held in high esteem by Damballah. But I'll be damned if I can figure out why."

Lexie rested against her cane. "You're the one who speaks through the Chez twins, Helen and Corinne. I've seen what they can do. Their ability is impressive."

"I don't speak through fools," Maman Brigitte argued. "The words coming out of their damn mouths aren't mine. They're manipulative little shits who bow to anyone for a price. Be careful of them. They're out for their ends."

Her warning bothered him. He wanted to question the spirit, but Lexie must have sensed his displeasure and cast a threatening gaze his way.

"So, you sent for me?" Lexie kept the hint of cool indifference in her voice. "Are you the one who killed Mr. Landry?"

Maman Brigitte rocked her head back and cackled. The ground beneath them rumbled. Tombstones shook, the Spanish moss in the trees swayed violently, and the rooster at her feet crowed.

The cacophony jarred Magnus.

So much for the dead having any peace.

The shaking took a few unsteady headstones to the ground. Even the tree trunks seemed to shift as the earthquake continued. Magnus felt certain the ground would split open and swallow Lexie whole. He reached for Lexie, but the stern frown on her face remained unchanged.

Then the earth went still. The sudden quiet took Magnus by surprise.

"I'm simply one woman helping another. In a world where men think they own us, we should stick together." Maman Brigitte walked toward Lexie. The rooster at her feet dutifully followed. "I've grown weary of being told what to do by the bastards, and I feel that you have too."

Magnus wanted to put in his two cents but decided against it.

"Forgive me, Maman." Lexie lowered her head, hiding her grin. "But don't you serve a more powerful spirit of the dead, like I do. Kalfu casts a wide net over your world and mine."

"You haven't learned shit about the history of the gods you serve, have you?" she snapped. "Part of being a mambo is knowing where you come from and knowing the gods to which you owe your power. I require sacrifice to be appeased and can give you so much if you only pay me what I'm due."

Lexie held her ground, not backing away. "What do you feel you are owed?"

Maman Brigitte smiled and then pointed at Magnus. "Him, for starters. That son of a bitch is dead, and his ass technically belongs to me."

"If that were the case, dear lady, I would be in your realm now." He grinned at her, driving his point home. "As you can see, I am not. If I belong to anyone, it's Lexie Arden."

Like a shot, the ghoulish woman stood in front of him, her scrawny black bird ruffling its feathers.

"Careful, Mr. Blackwell. Piss me off, and I could snuff you out with a snap of my finger. I have the power to reclaim the souls of the dead, and yours is just aching for it."

"But it's not in your power to do that," Lexie declared from behind the spirit. "You're the protector of tombstones and graves like your husband. But you're called on by your devotees in matters involving healing and to punish the wicked. When people are sick, you can either ease their suffering or heal them. You do not have the power to claim the dead."

Maman Brigitte faced her with a wide-eyed expression of

surprise.

Magnus refrained from snickering.

Lexie inched closer to the spirit. "You're the only fair-skinned member of the voodoo gods, your origins are considered to be part of the Irish migration of women who were sent to New Orleans for crimes like prostitution, and ended up working as slaves. You see, Maman Brigitte, I have read up on the gods and know exactly who you are and what you can do. And you can't touch my ghost."

The tension in the air teased Magnus. He wasn't sure if it was a good sign or a bad one.

Then Maman Brigitte clapped her hands. "Well done, Mambo."

She snapped her finger. The rooster at her feet stood at attention, and the neck of the black creature stretched upward. It elongated to such a point that Magnus was sure it would snap, but instead, the animal's neck pulled and shifted until it took on the appearance of black rope. The body of the bird then lengthened, and its feathers retreated under its skin, leaving only a black shiny surface. The entire body extended and no longer resembled an animal but a thick black staff of knotty wood. The neck curved into a handle and the talons pointed downward, forming the tip of a cane. Feathers cropped up, carved along the surface of the staff while the beak in the handle shimmered as if encased in black metal. The cane, taking on its last magical changes, rose from the ground and the handle slid under Maman Brigitte's open hand.

Maman Brigitte gripped her baton juju. "But you have questions still, don't you, Lexie Arden? About our power and how we can use it. I can answer those questions. Come."

Maman Brigitte set out from the graveyard, heading for a row of dense brush along the shoreline.

Magnus glided up to Lexie, more alarmed than before. "What is going on?"

Lexie sucked in a deep breath. "She wants us to follow her."

"Into the swamp?" He thumped his cane on the ground, but it didn't make a sound. "It's getting dark, and you should be heading back."

"But maybe she has a clue about the murders, can give us a name or a place to start. Don't you want to know why she brought us here?"

Magnus snorted with indignation. "Since when have any of these spirits ever lifted a finger to help you or anyone. They speak in riddles and leave it for you to figure things out. This is no different. She probably wants something precious like Kalfu did. How much more are you going to give to these creatures until there is nothing left of yourself?"

Lexie stopped at the brush. "It's my duty as mambo to do everything I can, learn everything I can, from the spirts. How else am I to help anyone, save anyone, heal anyone? The queen did everything she could for her people, and so must I. The cost doesn't matter."

"Think about what you are doing," he begged.

She glared at him with all the resolve he had felt from her since the first day he had seen her at Altmover Manor.

"This is something I have to do."

He wanted to hold her back as she stepped up to the brush, but he couldn't stop her. That was the problem with being a spirit guide—he could advise, cajole, and worry for her, but he couldn't save her from her fate. Even the foul-mouthed voodoo goddess leading her deeper into the swamps couldn't change Lexie Arden's destiny.

Chapter Three

Green leaves heavy with dew slapped Lexie's face as she negotiated the thick brush, following the strange woman with the wild red hair. She was proud of herself for standing up to the goddess. Before her run-ins with Kalfu and Damballah, she would have shaken like a leaf in the woman's presence. Now, she was intrigued by what she could learn from her.

If her studies of voodoo and its dysfunctional gods had taught her anything, it was they had a rational side best approached in a no-nonsense manner. She had to remain calm no matter what Maman Brigitte professed she could do.

A glimmer came through the brush, lighting the way out. Lexie breathed a sigh of relief.

She parted the last of the leaves and paused, overcome.

Ethereal balls like the dim display of the fireflies she'd chased as a child hovered above a smooth body of dark water. They resembled small round lanterns hanging from invisible cords, but there were thousands of them. Set at odd angles, they lit up the broaching evening with a warm glow. A gentle spring breeze blew across the water, making the bizarre formations sway.

"Now, this is interesting," Magnus said next to her.

Lexie gazed out at the water, a sense of profound peace filling her. The white ribbon in her chest swirled with contentment, dousing the strength of the black like rain on a forest fire. She calmed, and all her restlessness and doubt ceased. Her confidence soared, and the negative thoughts plaguing her sank into a pool of undulating white silk. She'd forgotten what it felt like to be free of the darkness, free of Kalfu's oppression.

"What is this place?"

"The people of these swamps call them *Le Feu Follet.*" Maman Brigitte waved her cane over the mesmerizing display. "I may be the goddess of death, Mambo, but I'm also the goddess of fertility and birth. And these souls are those waiting to be born."

A swell of grief came over Lexie. None of the lights gently swaying on the water would come to her. She'd given up her chance at having a child the moment she'd given her loyalty to Kalfu. She wanted to cry out, but she held it in.

Maman Brigitte moved closer to the water's edge. The nearest orb, as if detecting her presence, wafted toward her. She held out her hand, and the anomaly danced.

"There is no heaven or hell in our world, there is only life in its many forms, and this is its purest. I'm the keeper of this place. It's one of the few spots on your Earth where Kalfu's obnoxious ass can't reach."

Lexie took in the lake, luxuriating in the calm embracing her. "Why bring me here?"

The spirit turned, a hint of a smile on her lips. "Because we needed to speak without that pesky shit butting in. I know he took something precious from you, but I can give it back."

Could she do that? Having a baby had been all she'd thought about since sacrificing her fertility to Kalfu. She ached for a chance to carry a child.

Magnus was at her side. "This is a trick, dear girl."

"Not a trick; a bribe." Maman Brigitte eased her way closer, the tap of her black rooster cane causing ripples in the still water.

Lexie squeezed her cane, the power of Damballah from the magical baton juju surged to life, filling her with a euphoric zing of energy.

"You can't be considering her offer?" Magnus grumbled in her ear.

She ignored him and cocked her head, eyeing the woman.
Okay. I'll bite.

"What do you want?"

The smile on Maman Brigitte's face widened, and the lights from the lake danced in her eyes.

"For you to work with me."

The disclosure stumped Lexie. "Why?"

"I need you to right the imbalance Kalfu has created. I will reward you when your task is complete."

Lexie pressed her fingertips to her brow, befuddled. "I don't understand. I belong to Kalfu, and he is—"

"And you belong to Damballah." Maman Brigitte pointed the tip of her cane at Lexie's chest. "The light and dark compete inside you. Everyone in my world knows about it. What I'm asking is for you to help me teach Kalfu a lesson."

This was not what Lexie had expected. "Lesson? What lesson?"

The goddess sighed as she rested her hands on her cane. "The others among us are not happy. We had agreed you were not to be approached until you learned more about your ability and our ways. One of the reasons why Damballah never revealed himself to you until after Kalfu had stolen part of your soul. You were to be able to choose which of us you wanted to claim as your own, but you were tricked. But that asshole Kalfu coerced your allegiance by giving power to a dead spirit—a spirit he stole from my world and used to force your hand. The rest of the gods are upset, and want him disciplined." She touched her chest. "That's why I'm here. When justice is needed against those who disrespect the living and the dead, I'm called on to make things right."

"You plan on using me to discipline him? Why not have Damballah do it? He's the leader of your kind."

Maman Brigitte's hearty laugh created choppy waves on the tranquil lagoon next to them. "Despite what all your fancy books say, Mambo, our world is very much like yours. Occasionally, some of our kind grab for power they're not entitled to. Black and white forces must coexist, and the scales of life must remain balanced. Kalfu has upset this balance. By plotting for control of you, and releasing the shadow spirits on the world, he has skewed the powers of light and dark. Such disparity is dangerous for your world and mine."

Lexie gaped at the spirit in utter disbelief. It was one thing to hold the power of light and dark in her being, but the ramifications of such responsibility had not hit her until that moment.

"What do you want me to do?"

"Do? That will be revealed in time." Maman Brigitte walked back toward the wall of foliage, and then she stopped. "And when Kalfu comes to you again, keep this encounter from your mind."

SEIZE

Lexie pictured the handsome blue-eyed man who filled her dreams. "How? He knows my every thought, my every wish."

"Wish for something he can never give you, and the white inside of you will grow stronger. Push away his darkness by thinking of the light. It will keep the bastard weak."

She stepped into the brush. It wrapped around her like a cloak, and then swallowed her.

"Lexie, you need to be very careful."

Magnus's voice intruded on her bliss. There was a spark of hope for a future with Will. The days of living in fear that Will would discover her secret would come to an end.

"Kalfu will destroy you if he gets wind of this." Magnus moved in front of her, drawing her attention. "He could destroy both of us."

She glowered at her ghost. "And you don't think it's worth risking everything to get rid of this filth inside me. I regret every day I gave myself to that monster, but I had no choice. I had to save Will."

"And to solve your problems, will you trade one monster for another?" His green eyes burned into her. "Think about this. You are mambo; your job is to work with the gods of voodoo, not be controlled by them."

She chuckled. "Where did you learn that?"

Magnus shifted his gaze to the lights on the water. "There's not much to do in your store all day but read about voodoo."

The ribbon of light between them, all white and pulsating, opened the door to his feelings. Images of their time together came to her—the laughter and friendship.

"Can you feel it, Magnus? The ribbon between us is white again. All the black is gone."

25

"I felt the change the moment we came here." He raised his head to the sky. "The power of the place is overwhelming."

The last fingertips of sunlight retreated across the horizon and the edge of night crept closer to their spot on the shore.

"We need to go," he insisted. "Our boatman has to get back to his family, and you need to get home to Will. He's worried."

Part of Lexie wanted to stay, but her love for her husband sent her to the thick hedge leading back to the cemetery.

When the first green leaf touched her face, the blackness returned. It started as a single spot on a swirling base of white, and then spread, bleeding into the white and interlacing with the ribbon attached to Magnus. The special place had protected her, but beyond its border, darkness owned her soul. Her limbs dragged as Lexie pushed on through the brush, anxious to make her way home. She closed her eyes and fought her desire to return to the place where Kalfu's blackness could not control her anymore.

Chapter Four

Lexie eased her shoulder into the thick canvas of green leaves while Magnus waited behind her. He glanced back at the water, the uncanny lights still floating above. He'd forgotten how much he missed the white light pulsating inside him.

His respite over, Magnus was about to will himself back to the cemetery and join Lexie when a funny sensation overtook him.

A familiar voice buzzed in his ear. "You think you've made something of yourself, don't you?"

He froze, paralyzed by fear.

Magnus spun around, searching the small patch of land at the edge of the mystical lagoon. "Where are you?"

A glittering cylinder of light rose from the boggy ground. Its twinkling shot upward, and then morphed into the shape of a man. Flesh and the details of a tuxedo and white tie quickly emerged.

The spirit had his same fair hair, intrusive green eyes, and chiseled features. A cold swath of dread raced through Magnus's soul.

Reynolds Blackwell stood before him, looking as he had the day Magnus had seen him at The Hastings Gentleman's Club.

Magnus stared at the man. "What is the meaning of this?"

Reynolds flicked the ash off his cigar. "Is that the best you can do after all this time?"

He stumbled backward. The coldness in his father's voice hadn't changed. The hateful gleam in his eye was just as Magnus remembered.

"Why are you here?"

Reynolds went around his son, inspecting his attire and cane, a trail of cigar smoke following him.

"For years, I've waited in silence, watching you conduct your life, and afterlife, with the same careless disregard. You never made anything of yourself. You were such a disappointment and still are."

Magnus's anger awakened the same compulsion he'd always felt around his father—to run away and never return. He'd spent his life trying to please the ruthless man and had found a reprieve when the son of a bitch had died. But the sight of Reynolds, standing beside him, broke open the dam of frustration he'd harbored his entire existence.

"You said you've been watching me? How?"

Reynolds's evil grin sickened him.

"I was in a river of milky white with no cares, no concerns. I was at peace, and then something woke me from my rest. I found myself back in the land of the living, and the first person I wanted to see was you."

Why has he come back now?

"Don't come to me again. We have nothing to discuss." He snapped up his cane, about to disappear. "I will make sure you return to your eternal sleep if it's the last thing I do."

"And will you be joining me?" Reynolds flicked his cigar. "You should be with your kind, not the living."

Reynolds faded into a cloud of cigar smoke.

Enraged that his father got in the last word, Magnus punched at the foliage next to him, picturing his father's face and wishing, like he had a thousand times before, that he'd stood up to the insufferable man.

Then his father's words echoed in his mind. *"You should be with your own kind, not the living."*

Someone is sending me a message. And I'm going to find out why.

Mosquitos buzzed around her but never touched her skin. A swarm of black bugs sent her to the other side of the flat-bottom boat where she waited for Magnus. The craft rocked as she settled into her seat. She needed Magnus to give poor Ned instructions to head back to the dock where she'd parked her car. She'd tried several times to coax the man, even used her power on him, but Ned remained reclined against the outboard motor, his cap over his head, not moving a muscle.

"Where are you?" Lexie whispered, glancing back at the cemetery.

A nudge came from her darkness. He was near. Then the scent of fresh-cut grass, green with spring, wafted past her nose.

"Don't tell me your Mr. Blackwell has disappeared again."

The smoky voice instantly sent a shiver down her spine.

A mist rose from the water, covering the swamp with an eerie light. She turned to Ned's spot in the boat, but he was no longer there. The cold around her intensified. Then the chirping crickets, hooting owls, and sounds of the motor stilled. The lack of any noise unraveled her. The frigid air penetrated her bones, and she hugged herself, waiting.

A shadow developed on the surface of the water. Unrecognizable at first, it quickly took on more depth and came toward her boat. He strutted in his casual way, traversing the clouds hovering above the water. His faded jeans, snug white T-shirt, and Ned's fishing cap on his head came into view. When he smiled, his chiseled features lifted, accentuating his high cheekbones and pointed chin. But it was the gleam in his uncanny blue eyes that disturbed her the most. It meant Kalfu was up to something.

"Why are you here, Kalfu?"

"Kal, remember." He playfully frowned and took a seat at the back near the engine. "Since you work for me, we should be on a first name basis."

"Why are you in my boat?"

He leaned across to her. "Why were you meeting with that foul-mouthed she-devil? I know she's plotting against me."

"I didn't meet with her." Lexie brushed her arms, wanting to get out of the swamp. "I went to a cemetery to search for clues on a murder, and she was there."

"Yes, you've been in demand by everyone in the city since we made our little pact. Working with the police on murder cases, appointments throughout the day with clients wishing to commune with the dead—you've made a name for yourself. How do you like the success I gave you?"

Success? What he had given her was far from success; it was a curse. She struggled every day to keep the opposing forces inside her from overpowering her soul. Lexie despised him for what he'd done to her, but she was at his mercy until she found a way to free herself.

"What makes you think you have anything to do with my success? They come to see me, consult with me, use my power to help them—"

"My power," he corrected in a sinister tone. "I made you stronger, and better able to help all those people you care about. Perhaps one day you will explain to me why you do not cast them aside." He stood in the boat, but it didn't list. "Now tell me why Maman Brigitte summoned you?"

Lexie remembered the fiery redhead's words. "*Wish for something he can never give you, and the white inside of you will grow stronger.*"

Lexie envisioned a child, a girl, wrapped in pink, her tiny hand grasping Will's thumb. The love in her husband's eyes awakened her white power. The black, aroused by Kalfu's presence, cooled and retreated.

"What are you doing?" He stared at the center of her chest. "Why are you pushing me aside?"

Lexie kept up the picture of the child in her mind, not allowing him to get to her.

"Where is Magnus? I want to go home."

Kalfu snapped his finger and the boat engine revved to life.

"You don't need that fool. I can take you back."

"And the fisherman?" She looked around, but no one was guiding the boat. "Where is he?"

"Safe." Kalfu pointed at his chest. "In me."

The thought disturbed her. She had been where poor Ned dwelled, and it still gave her nightmares.

Kalfu knelt before her as she sat on the wooden beam across the center of the boat. The cold drifting off his presence circled her and settled into her bones. The mist on the water around them thickened, a sure sign of his growing impatience.

"What did Maman Brigitte promise you? Your dearest wish?"

The musical sound of his voice did little to appease her fear. Every time he came to her, Lexie wondered if he had tired of her as he had with Emily Mann. Each time she looked into his eyes, she imagined him sending her across the bridge to blackness.

"You can't give into her no matter what she says she can do. She's a liar, just like her worthless husband. What good is guarding the dead, I ask you, if you don't have any use for them."

The mist above the water swayed and danced, reminding her of storm clouds rolling across the sky. The black in her fought to rise, but she kept Kalfu at bay.

He shook his head, a frustrated grimace on his lips. "Continue to test me, and I will make sure your husband has a nasty accident. Perhaps even lose his sight. He won't be much good as an architect then, will he?"

The threat shook her, knotting her stomach. Every day she questioned why she had joined with Kalfu.

"The gods are angry with you for stealing me. They want revenge."

He clapped and stood, the boat never registering his movement as it glided down the waterway.

"So that's what she told you. Clever little cow."

Kalfu's face dimmed, but despite the coming night, she could see his anger, shimmering like a full moon.

"And I never stole you, Alexis. A deal is a deal; you are mine. Nothing Maman Brigitte can do will change that."

Ahead, a single lamp from the dock broke through the darkness. She concentrated on the glowing lantern, relieved to have something human, something normal, to pull her out of Kalfu's world. The unease brought on by his appearance dissipated as the boat drifted closer to the dock. She was almost free.

"Go home to your husband. He's wondering where you are." Kalfu glimpsed the dock. "We will talk again."

Ned reappeared in the back of the boat, his hand on the throttle, and the same blank expression on his face.

The mist around the boat dissipated as if swept away by an invisible hand. The temperature rose, warming her skin. The sounds of the swamp returned. The noise shocked her, even the roar of the engine caused her to flinch.

Ned never broke from his spell as he navigated the green flatboat to the dock. The exact way he secured the craft to the old wooden pier while still in his trance set her nerves on edge. The entire journey had not gone as she expected, and Magnus's departure had left her feeling vulnerable. She'd never realized how safe he'd made her feel before.

"How did you get him to bring you back?" Magnus showed up, displaying a caustic frown. "I went to the shore by the cemetery and you were gone. I tried to join you, but something blocked me."

Her ghost's handsome face settled her shaking. The lights from the dock chased away the last vestiges of her fear.

"It was Kalfu." She gripped her cane, saddened to feel the two sides of her power competing inside her once more. "He questioned me about our meeting with Maman Brigitte."

"I figured as much. It seems he was playing both of us." He faced the fisherman still sitting in the boat. "Thank you, my good man. Go home."

Lexie glanced back as Ned roused from his trance. "What is it?"

The fisherman blinked his eyes as if trying to focus.

Magnus tapped his baton juju on the dock. "My father's spirit came to me. The same loathsome man he was in life. He told me he was adrift in a river of white and something disturbed his slumber."

"The River of Shadows." Lexie rocked her head back, suddenly beat. "He must be one of the spirits taken from there when Emily turned the city upside down. They've been seen by many since then, including me."

"Hey, do y'all know how I got in this boat?" Ned called while adjusting his cap. "I wasn't in no boat before, was I?"

"Taken from there to distract me, no doubt, while Kalfu toyed with you." Magnus motioned to Will's BMW, which was parked beneath a street lamp. "We must go."

Lexie stepped from the dock to the oyster shells on the parking lot. The crunching under her feet grounded her.

They both ignored a frantic Ned struggling from the small boat and onto the dock.

Lexie hit the remote on Will's car. The amber lights flashed.

"But how could Kalfu send your father to a place he couldn't enter? And why would Maman Brigitte bother? She brought us there so Kalfu couldn't overhear our conversation. Dredging up your father makes no sense for either of them."

Magnus stopped at the driver's side door. "If not them, perhaps it was another spirit wanting to lure me away from you."

"Another spirit? Which one?"

A disturbing sense of foreboding tickled her belly. She eased into her seat, considering the question.

Magnus materialized in the passenger seat. "According to your books, there are many spirits to choose from."

She swallowed hard. Didn't she have enough spirits in her life? Lexie couldn't imagine encountering more of the diabolical personalities plaguing the pantheon of voodoo. She was already in over her head with Kalfu, Damballah, and now Maman Brigitte.

"What would any of them want with me?"

He tapped his finger on the head of his ghostly cane. "I don't know, but I have a feeling we will soon find out."

Chapter Five

Lexie flipped the switch as she walked through her front door, flooding the living room with yellow light. The rough-hewn beams, bricked walls, and large windows overlooking the Mississippi River were what had sold Will on the condo. She'd preferred the courtyard view from the balcony of their small French Quarter apartment. The character of their old place had suited her better.

The cool air conditioning brushed her skin, raising the hairs on her arms. The icy chill meant Will had set the thermostat too low again. In winter he kept it too warm, in spring too cold. Would she ever feel comfortable in the place?

Comfortable? The word struck her. This was her home, but for weeks she'd felt adrift in the massive space with its breathtaking views. She was like a ghost passing through with no sense of attachment to her surroundings.

She dropped her purse onto the antique wooden table Will had insisted they buy. She surveyed their spacious living room with its pricey leather and oak furniture—another expenditure Will had talked her into.

"What took you so long?"

A stunning man with an intimidating square jaw strutted into the room. Her gaze lingered on his broad bare chest and then she smiled at his blue pajama bottoms. Her Will still sent her heart racing, especially when he was half-naked with his thick brown hair haphazardly tossed about his head. No matter how crappy she felt, how vexing her day, or how bad her doldrums, just the sight of him lightened her burdens.

He came up to her, his brown eyes flickering with concern. "You said you'd only be gone an hour. That was three hours ago. Why didn't you call?"

The hint of annoyance in his voice distressed her. She had promised to return sooner, but the adventure at the cemetery had wiped all notion of calling him from her mind. She needed to do better.

"I stayed longer because I wanted to check out a nearby cemetery. Thought I might get some clues from the dead there." She rested the dragon head of her baton juju against the black granite kitchen countertop. "The murdered man was Otis Landry."

Will ran his hands through his hair. "Otis? Who would kill him? He was a nice, mild-mannered guy."

Lexie sagged against the counter, drained of strength. "I have no idea. It was horrible. He was cut up just like Renee. It was …"

He came up to her and wrapped her in his arms. "I'm sorry, baby. You shouldn't have to see such things."

She curled into his muscular chest, bolstered by his body heat. The only time she'd felt warm these past few weeks was when Will held her.

Lexie rested her head against him. "I kept looking at his body in the water and thinking is this because of me?"

Will arched away. "Don't be silly. Of course, it isn't your fault. He wasn't killed because he rented a shop to the mambo."

She retreated from his embrace, the cold engulfing her as soon as she turned away. "You never know."

His voice took on a hard edge. "I know a lot of people aren't happy about you being mambo, but killing your landlord is a strange way of showing it. All a new landlord can do is not give you another lease, or sell the building to a new owner who won't honor your existing lease." He rubbed his chin, his eyes narrowing on her. "Although, losing the shop might be good for you."

Lexie's anger surged. "Why would you say such a thing?"

"You spend all day at the store. Now with Emile asking you to help out the NOPD, you might never be around." He let out a long, haggard breath. "We've talked about your cutting back before. This might be the right time."

She ran her fingers over her brow, tensing at his condescending tone—the one that always grated on her nerves.

"I've busted my ass to get a shot with the NOPD. And I need the store to do my work as mambo. I have dozens of spiritual readings booked every day. Where do you expect me to do them? Here?"

"I'm just saying that you're pushing yourself too much. You haven't been yourself for weeks. When I talk to you, it's like you're not listening to anything I say. Like today, when I mentioned the new account I got with another big construction firm, you tuned me out."

Lexie concentrated on her center, trying to quiet her blackness. Part of her wanted to snap at her husband, but another part wanted to celebrate his good news.

"You've been getting a lot of new accounts lately."

He pulled her into his arms, and his warmth quieted her ire. "It's wonderful. Since I moved the firm to Poydras Avenue, we've been getting tons of referrals. I might even have to hire another architect soon."

His woodsy cologne elicited the same reaction it always did—guilt. Guilt over not telling him about her infertility, guilt over not sharing the darkness inside of her, so many things. She wanted to crumble into his arms and release all the pent-up feelings she had so closely guarded, anxious to share her upheaval. But fear held her back. What if he left her?

Will kissed her cheek. "I thought we could celebrate my new account this weekend?" He nipped her earlobe. "Go to your favorite Italian restaurant and top off the night the same way we celebrated when I got the Jordan Construction account. Remember?"

Their evening of frenzied lovemaking came back to her. She'd been amazed that her desire for Will had not faded once Kalfu's dark grip had settled over her. If anything, she'd craved Will's embrace even more. He kept her whole and sane, and sex was the one thing that quieted her guilt and sorrow.

"That sounds nice, but I can't think about the weekend yet. All I can see is poor Mr. Landry."

Lexie slipped out of his arms and went behind the breakfast bar. She opened their refrigerator, the ever-present dead stare of her landlord in her head.

"Do they have any idea who did it?" Will slid into a stool across the bar. "Was it like Emile said? Another ritual killing?"

She retrieved a can of soda and popped the lid. "Yep. They aren't sure if it happened in the swamp or at his home. His maid reported him missing."

Will banged his fist on the granite. "Damn. I hate to hear that. I know they say this city is getting dangerous, but why kill a good man like Otis?"

Lexie fingered the lid on her can, debating about how much to reveal. "This wasn't about him."

"How can you be so sure about that?" He held up his hand, his mouth slipping downward. "Wait, I get it. You picked up something."

She put the soda can on the counter, carefully choosing her words. "No, I didn't pick up anything about Otis's murder. That's just it. We have two murders of businessmen in the city, and one voodoo priestess and the only thing they have in common is they run businesses in The Quarter. Other than that, I haven't got a clue about why they were killed in such a gruesome manner."

Will got up from his stool. "You don't know what else these people were into. There might be another angle you're missing. New Orleans is a pretty dark place with lots of underworld activity."

She waited as he came up to her. "But if that's the case, who would benefit from their deaths?"

He eased his arm around her waist. "Leave that for Emile to figure out. You need to come to bed so we can get to work on my son and heir."

Lexie's stomach tightened. Every hour of every day, what she'd sacrificed plagued her.

"Do you have to say that every time we have sex? You're constantly going on about a baby."

"Not this again." He backed away, exasperation deepening the lines around his mouth. "I didn't mean anything by it. What is it with you lately? You're so moody."

Lexie wanted to defend herself, but her darkness nudged her to keep quiet. It was why she was moody. Hiding her inner turmoil made her life with Will comparable to walking on eggshells.

"Let's just go to bed and forget about it."

She was about to turn away when he seized her arm. "No, I don't want to forget about it or spend another night staying awake and figuring out what has gotten into you. Since we moved in here, you've been different. You don't talk to me anymore, tell me how you're feeling. It's like you're keeping secrets from me."

She flinched at the mention of secrets.

"When we moved in here, you never wanted to buy furniture, never wanted to decorate, never wanted to make any decisions about our new home." He folded his arms over his broad chest. "At our old place, you were constantly hunting for ways to make it feel like home, but not here. I want to know why."

Lexie gazed into his eyes and crumbled, but only on the inside. Outwardly, she remained the pinnacle of self-control. She had to protect him. She'd given up everything to save him, and he could never find out the price she'd paid for his life. If he did, her guilt would be his, and she would never want him to suffer as she had. Lexie always heard about the burdens of marriage, but until now, she'd never understood just how heavy those burdens could be.

"I'm sorry. I guess a lot has happened and after losing Titu and the mess we went through with Renee, I'm not quite myself."

The wrinkles in his brow softened. "Look, Lexie, I know how

horrible the whole encounter with Emily Mann was for all of us, including what's-his-name. But we survived it. We're together and we have to move on."

"What's-his-name? Really, Will."

He tossed his head to the side, grinning. "I can't help it. Meeting Magnus gave me some reassurances about your relationship, but I never want to run into him again."

Her ghost had promised to steer clear of their condo, giving them the privacy Will had demanded. But there were times she caught him staring through the windows of their living room.

"You won't run into him. When I'm here, he stays in his world."

Will kissed the tip of her nose. "Good thing. I want to be all alone with you."

He pulled her into his arms, and she melted. Before she could protest, he lifted her on the kitchen counter, plying her neck with kisses. She giggled at his enthusiasm, thankful they could come together. She gave in to him, her hands scouring the breadth of his back and the thick muscles of his chest. His smell, his demanding kisses, and her desire shut out the constant chatter in her head.

She reclined on the counter as he eagerly worked the hem of her white dress up her legs. She ran her fingers through his hair, dazzled by his sexy grin, the one that had won her over the first day they'd met.

He traced kisses up her thigh, sending the sweet hot tingle up her spine. Lost in sensation, she turned her head toward the wall of windows and was about to close her eyes when the blinking lights from the ships careening along the Mississippi River distracted her. Then a shadow darted across the window, muting the lights. The dark umbra, shaped like a man, had no face. It hovered outside the window several stories above the ground.

All the heat Will's kisses summoned fizzled out when she realized what she had witnessed—a shadow spirit. The escaped prisoners of the River of Shadows came and went, different figures every time, slipping in and out of her home, her shop, even her atelier. They had harassed her and others in the city since Emily Mann had set them loose on New Orleans. The number of sightings grew with every passing day. Lexie heard the rumblings from other priestesses in the city. It was another problem everyone expected her to deal with. Would it ever end?

"Hey?" Will turned her head to face him. His eyebrows pinched together. "You're somewhere else again."

Guilt blossomed in her chest. She ran through a list of excuses to explain her lack of interest.

"I'm with you. Just keep thinking of Mr. Landry. I can't get that image out of my head."

"I'm sorry, baby." He picked her up from the counter. "No more talk about ghosts or murders. Let's go to bed and forget about everything."

He carried her to the hallway leading to their bedroom, but as they passed the window, the black shadow shifted and changed. A gust of cold surrounded her, but Will didn't seem to sense it. She snuggled closer to his warmth, wanting to blot out the icy blast. She knew what it meant. He was there, watching her.

In the window, blue jeans and a white T-shirt came to light, and a face evolved from the darkness. Lexie's chagrin pinked her cheeks as Kalfu winked at her.

What does he want?

Before she could find out why he was floating outside her condo window, Will whisked her away to their bedroom.

Will nuzzled her neck as they turned in their bedroom door. *"I'll be waiting, Lexie Arden."*

The voice—another horrific side-effect of her darkness. It was male, smoky, and demanding. It seemed Kalfu had infiltrated even her deepest thoughts.

"Leave me alone," she shouted in her head.

"Never," he replied. *"You belong to me."*

Chapter Six

Streaks of sunlight snuck in through the open french doors of her shop on Royal Street. The breeze drifting in had hints of cumin and coriander from the new Indian restaurant a few doors down. Lexie's stomach rumbled, distracting her, and making her recount her inventory of voodoo doll keychains set up on a tabletop display.

Out of the corner, a shadow crossed the wall to a door marked *Private*.

Lexie almost dropped the tablet in her hand.

Before disappearing behind the door, the shadow glanced back at her as if to coax her away from her work.

What the hell?

They had never done that before. They had shown themselves at odd moments in her shop, skulking around corners or blending into the real shadows, but this was different. This was an invitation.

Lexie left the keychains and hurried to the door. She entered the short hall behind the main floor and held her breath, waiting to see if the shadow would reveal itself. She registered every creak of the old building while her heart pounded in her ears.

"They're everywhere." Magnus arrived and stood next to her.

She stuck her head in the storage room to the right. "I've been seeing them too. With no ties to bind them to a building or person in this world, they're free to wander where they like. One showed up in my condo last night. I'm glad Will didn't see it."

Magnus arched an eyebrow. "Are you any closer to getting rid of them?"

She groaned and started down the narrow hall. "No. I've read through every reference book I know. I have no idea how to return them to the River of Shadows."

"Seems to me you have all this power but no inkling of how to use it. You need a tutor to show you what to do."

Sorrow squeezed at Lexie's heart. "Titu was my tutor, but without her to guide me, I've had to rely on my books for my education."

His lips turned downward. "Perhaps in your profession, you should start applying yourself. Testing your limits. I'm sure the knowledge will come with time."

"I don't think voodoo works like that."

Lexie entered the small kitchen in the shop's rear. She stopped when she spotted the gray Maine coon cat sitting on the kitchen table, preening itself.

Magnus floated up to her side. "Ah, our furry friend is here."

The cane in Lexie's hand vibrated. The cat jumped from the table.

It sat in front of Lexie, staring up at her with its green eyes.

The white in her center pulsated in perfect rhythm with her cane.

A tendril of mist rose from the floor right next to the cat. It twirled, becoming a cyclone and surrounding the fluffy feline. The swirling cloud climbed into the air until it completely covered the creature. Then the twister darkened, turning a deep shade of gray. Black shapes moved inside the storm cloud. A hand, dark-skinned and thick, reached for Lexie. Then the sleeve of a white jacket followed. Slowly, a man's broad shoulder and chest eased out from the mystical mass.

When the rest of him stepped out, Lexie recognized his round face and jovial grin.

A *pop* sailed through the air. The mayhem of fog got sucked into the floor until the last of the churning haze evaporated.

"Good day, Mambo," Damballah greeted in his baritone voice.

Lexie slowly approached, studying the spirit's three-piece white suit. "This is a surprise. I seem to be getting a lot of attention from the loa of voodoo lately."

"A powerful lady requires a great deal of attention. But the gods of the dead will not have your best interests at heart. Never trust them. They will pour honey in your ears, but not keep their promises."

"You know what Kalfu and Maman Brigitte said to me. I should have known."

He chuckled, and the musical sound warmed the small kitchen, enveloping her with comfort.

"I wouldn't be a very good god if I didn't know. Rumblings are spreading through the land of the dead about your arrangement with Kalfu. Many want revenge. What upsets the dark half of our world upsets the light. The imbalance of the universe must be righted."

She arched closer to him, the white in her vibrating at his presence. "But you could stop all of this by returning the spirts to the River of Shadows."

"I cannot. Only you can do that, Lexie Arden. A spirit can release another spirit from our realm to the human world, but only a human can banish a spirit from your world back to ours."

She tossed up her hands, brimming with frustration. "So how do I do it?"

"You will find a place of knowledge. There you will find the answer."

The prediction curled her stomach into knots. "When will that happen?" she asked a bit too desperately.

"Soon enough." The spirit held up his open hand, urging her to remain calm. "And when it does, temper what you do with such wisdom."

"I don't understand why I have to send the shadow spirits back. Can't you find someone else more experienced with voodoo? I haven't been a mambo for very long."

"But you're the keeper of both our powers, and the mortal who is bound to us. You will decide how the world will be ruled— through light or dark." He toed a gouge in her brick floor with his white shoe. "Beware. Kalfu is a trickster. The devil likes you to think he's in control, but only you have the will and the ability to choose your fate. He cannot choose it for you."

Hearing her fears about Kalfu's evil expressed by the gracious spirit drove home the task ahead of her. Since the moment she'd received the baton juju at the *haute défi*, Lexie had felt overwhelmed by her new life. Now, she was drowning beneath the weight of her responsibilities and the burning hole in her stomach, the result of so many sleepless nights and nagging doubts, was about to swallow her whole.

She rubbed her arms, shivering. "He's like a sickness inside of me, changing me. I only want to be free of him. But how do I do that? How do I free myself from his grip?"

The bald man's beaming grin lit up his face, sending a pleasant trickle of joy through her. She became so calm in his presence, so free—unlike Kalfu, who made her feel buried under a mountain of self-loathing.

"Binding can be a funny thing. It can be used for good and bad. In your case, a little bit of both, but remember to free those bad binds, you might also have to release the good. Learn all you can before you seek a way to unbind yourself from Kalfu. But once you do, balance will be restored to the universe."

"But where is this place of knowledge?" She impatiently tapped her cane on the floor. "I've exhausted every library I can think of."

Damballah gave a dramatic flick of his wrist. "A good teacher never gives away the answers. He helps you find them. All in good time."

Mist slithered from the floor as if coaxed by a snake charmer's flute. It coiled around his legs, hugging him, then climbed upward to his hips and waist.

Panic raced through her. He couldn't go. She had other questions. He was the only lifeline she had to the good in her, and she didn't want to lose the peace he brought with him.

"And when I've done what you ask, will you give me what I want?"

The fog around his chest thickened and spread, covering every aspect of his being.

She stood back as the lights in the mist appeared, flashing like lightning around him. A mysterious breeze sailed through the kitchen. It swirled around the cone of mist, breaking it apart. In a violent *whoosh,* the cloud evaporated and took Damballah with it.

She stared at the spot where he had stood, and then dropped her gaze to the floor. The gray cat was back, its green eyes sparkling in the sunlight.

"Will anyone ever answer my questions?"

Magnus chuckled. "It's like dealing with a gypsy at a fair. You get no answers, just a lot of cryptic messages."

The creature on the floor raised its tail haughtily before trotting down the hall toward the shop.

"You never appear with all the theatrics. Why do they?" Lexie asked.

"My dear girl, any spirit choosing to be seen in such a god-awful white suit loves making an entrance. It's a matter of taste."

"I'm glad you're not like that." She walked to the counter and retrieved the half-full coffeepot from the warmer. "And what knowledge was he talking about? Where am I supposed to get it? From some random tourist? I've combed every book I can find to learn new spells, new ways to control the power within me, but there's nothing. What am I to do? I already have no life. I'm here all day, and at night I'm home with Will unless Emile calls me out on a case."

Magnus went to the counter. "Did you tell your husband about Maman Brigitte and our romp through the swamps?"

She selected a mug from a tray next to the coffeemaker. "I told him about the cemetery. Not the other stuff. You know how Will feels when I talk about spirits."

Magnus tapped his cane on the brick floor. "The same way he feels about me."

"Will likes you," she offered while pouring her coffee. "He's glad you're around to protect me."

"But he still doesn't know about Kalfu, does he?"

She added two packets of sugar, ignoring him.

"My dear girl, your husband needs to know he's sharing you with another. Sooner or later he will find out about your struggles, and he will be hurt that you never confided in him."

She furiously stirred sugar in her coffee. "I'm hoping to get rid of Kalfu before he finds out."

"How do you propose to *get rid of* something so—"

A rustling rose behind them at the kitchen entrance.

Madame Henri, with her wrinkled face and silvery hair, stood in the doorway, looking around the room.

"Your shop assistant told me you were back here."

Magnus scowled at Lexie and began to fade, but the older woman waved at him.

"Don't go on my account, Mr. Blackwell."

Lexie flinched and her coffee mug bobbled.

"I didn't realize you can see him."

Madame Henri's light laughter carried across the kitchen. "I wouldn't be a very good priestess if I couldn't see the dead."

Magnus snapped up his cane, bowed, and vanished.

Madame Henri approached a chair at the small table. "I came because I have news. Something is about to happen that could jeopardize your position as mambo."

Lexie tightened her grip on her mug and went to the table. "What, more rain, rats, shadowy spirits, or are we going to have to suffer locusts, frogs, and three days of darkness?"

Madame Henri settled in her chair. "Nothing so dramatic. Harold Forneaux is stirring the pot again. He's called an emergency meeting of the voodoo council day after tomorrow. He's not happy with your appointments to replace Titu and Jacques. He claims it's been too long since the last council meeting."

"It's only been a few months." With a shaky hand, Lexie set the mug on the table. "Why does he want another meeting right away?"

The lines in Madame Henri's brow deepened as she dropped her gaze to the table. "The shadow people are becoming a problem—one you haven't been able to fix. Followers in the city are going to him, claiming they live in fear of the shadow spirits. Some say they are causing havoc in their homes and hurting their businesses. Harold wants to exploit that and weaken your position as mambo."

"Yes, I know about Harold's plans to usurp me." The shaking in her hands spread, catapulting her insecurity to the stratosphere. "I've been searching for weeks how to send them back. I've combed every book I own, but there is so little known about the shadow spirits. There are no references I can find on how to deal with them; there are no spells on how to send them back."

Madame Henri held up a hand. "I know your predicament, but I must agree with Harold that something needs to be done and soon, before chaos descends on the city once again. At the meeting, Harold will call for a vote to appoint a new mambo—a seasoned practitioner who can bend the forces of the universe to her will."

"Her will? Not his will?"

Madame Henri gave her a curt nod. "Harold has someone he's going to propose as mambo, but I have no idea who. No one I've asked has a clue."

Lexie drummed her fingers on the table. "If Harold finds a new mambo, will I be challenged to another *haute défi*?"

"No." Madame Henri exhaled, and her shoulders sagged. "He's bragging this woman will destroy you before the *haute défi* ever happens."

A dagger of dread sliced through her. She'd been threatened before by Harold, but he'd never advocated physical violence. And who could he have who was stronger than Lexie?

"Could it be one of the Chez twins? They follow Harold around like puppies."

"Helen and Corinne would never be accepted as mambo by anyone in the city. No, he has someone else we know nothing about."

Lexie considered her conundrum. She'd accepted she would face challenges as mambo; she just hoped she would have more time to settle into her position. Since the day after the *haute défi* with Bloody Mary, she'd sensed the animosity of the voodoo community toward her. If Lexie didn't do something soon to silence her detractors, she wouldn't remain mambo for much longer.

"What do you know about the Chez Twins and their association with Maman Brigitte?"

"Maman Brigitte?" Madame Henri pursed her lips. "Why are you asking about her?"

Lexie peered into her coffee, remembering the pale spirit with the bright eyes.

"I met her in the swamps the other night. She guided me to this old cemetery outside the former city of Frenier."

"Ah, yes. Her old stomping ground." Madame Henri clasped her hands and rested them on the table. "There was a powerful priestess in that area called Julie Brown. Maman Brigitte used to speak through her. Julie Brown was a seer. She predicted the storm of 1915 and that the town of Frenier would die with her." She wrinkled her brow. "But why did Maman Brigitte speak to you?"

Lexie retrieved her mug, wanting to keep her fidgety hands occupied. "She wants me to pledge my loyalty to her, and she promises to help free me of Kalfu."

Madame Henri chuckled and stood. "Careful, child. You haven't had a lot of dealings with the gods of our world. You're mambo, and they will want to make themselves known to you. Just remember, the female deities are much craftier and more menacing than the men. Never attach yourself to a woman; they never let go." She placed her hand over Lexie's restless fingers. "I know you want to rid yourself of your darkness, but I would suggest holding off. You will need his power to help you keep your baton juju."

Lexie pulled her hand away. "I can't remain attached to Kalfu to hold on to my title. My sanity and my marriage aren't worth it. Sometimes I swear all I want to do is chuck this whole mambo thing out the window and live a normal life."

"But you don't, do you?" Madame Henri smiled up at her. "Because you know you have been given a great gift—one that can help many. Walking away from such a miracle isn't in you."

Lexie relaxed her hands as a happy memory came to her. "My grandmother always told me that what I have is meant to help others. She urged me to use it in any way I can. I don't walk away because of her. My grandmother would want me to be the best mambo I can."

"And you will be a great mambo." Madame Henri's soft smile faltered. "But there will be many trials before that day comes. Keep your grandmother's love in your heart when they begin. You will need her hope to guide you."

"That is why I must rid myself of Kalfu. For the faith my

grandmother and the queen placed in me. Queen Marie never embraced the dark side to remain mambo. She did it with her wits and skills. I shall do the same."

Madame Henri took a step back, avoiding Lexie's gaze. "But the queen lived in different times. Her power came from the community of poor and oppressed in the city. If you give up what Kalfu gave you, you will not be able to remain mambo."

Lexie's gut burned with indignation. "But I am the chosen one."

"But to remain the chosen one, you must utilize everything in your arsenal," she insisted in a firm tone. "See Harold and his followers shut down for good and then pursue cleansing yourself of your blackness."

Lexie stared into the woman's dark eyes. "And how would I cleanse myself? Is there some way to cast him out of me?"

"Casting out a dark spirit like Kalfu requires a sacrifice. Something greater than what you gave to join him." Madame Henri turned away, wringing her hands. "You still have much to lose, Lexie. Sometimes ridding yourself of the darkness can be just as painful as accepting it."

The warning put Lexie off. Was she willing to give up more to be free of Kalfu? Freedom in any form comes with a hefty price.

"I'm willing to take that chance."

Madame Henri stopped at the kitchen doorway. "But you could cast off Damballah in the process. You could lose all your power as well. Voodoo gods are fickle, have egos, and are susceptible to moments of irrational behavior. In the end, we must live with their decisions. Make sure you're ready for that."

"When you were released from the darkness, was it worth it?"

A sad shadow crossed Madame Henri's face. "I had a son once,

Jean Marc. Damballah took his soul as sacrifice to rid me of Kalfu. After my son died, Damballah left me." She flourished a hand down her black dress. "But here I stand. I once served two masters; now I serve none."

Lexie stepped closer. "Do you miss the power?"

Madame Henri hesitated and then nodded. "Very much. I wanted to be mambo of this city, but after the spirits left me, that wasn't possible. But at least my soul is my own. Remember that, Lexie Arden. Let your soul guide you in your decisions, not the power within." She gripped Lexie's hand. "I will see you at the council meeting."

After the older woman shuffled out of the kitchen, Lexie took her mug to the french doors and viewed the rippling water in the courtyard's fountain. She sipped her coffee and considered the trials ahead.

Harold Forneaux starting shit didn't surprise her. He'd always been a thorn in her side. Her bigger problem was Kalfu. Would he give her up?

She doubted it. Unlike Madame Henri, Lexie had power and influence as mambo that made her valuable to both Damballah and Kalfu. Even so, she wasn't about to stop searching for a way to get out from under his control.

The speaker on the wall phone beeped. The harsh noise almost made her drop her mug.

She hit the green button on the speaker. "Yes."

"I have a David Hutchins holding on the line for you," Nina said.

Lexie frowned. "Who?"

"He says he's an attorney and has to speak with you."

A hundred thoughts ran through her mind, the foremost

being that someone must want to sue her. But who?

Lexie picked up the receiver. "This is Lexie Bennett."

"Mrs. Bennett, my name is David Hutchins with Kinder, Archer, and Lance Law Firm. I'm an estate lawyer, and my client has just left you the bulk of her property and holdings. Can you come to our offices on Poydras Street at your earliest convenience?"

Her heart sped up. "Me?" Lexie frantically searched her memory. "Who is your client?"

"Her name was Kalila La Fay."

Magnus stood in his murky world, engulfed by a myriad of emotions as he watched Lexie on the phone. He couldn't fathom more unrest for her. She'd been through enough. That anyone would challenge her made him angry.

How could she consider giving up the power she possessed? The darkness in both of them he could do without, but what if the light went with it? The ties Damballah created binding him to her would be severed. An afterlife without Lexie was unimaginable. Going on without her would cast him into a dark despair from which he would never return.

Chapter Seven

Lexie walked along Poydras Avenue, tapping her baton juju on the sidewalk and studying the high-rise buildings of glistening glass and steel. Swaths of sunlight broke through the long shadows of the buildings, adding an odd play of light and dark—a reminder of her struggle.

"You should tell your husband," Magnus insisted.

"I did tell him, but I'm not sure he heard me. He didn't get home until late, and then he was half-asleep when I mentioned my meeting." She waved off Magnus's dour expression. "Let's see what she left me. It might just be a ring or something."

Magnus chuckled. "Whatever it is, there will be strings."

"What makes you say that?"

"When have there not been strings attached to anything in voodoo?" He eyed a pretty young woman in a slinky dress strutting by. "Everywhere you turn, someone or some spirit wants something from you. You need to stand up for yourself more."

At 650 Poydras, she stopped, brooding over his words. "I will. When my enemies are defeated, people will fear me."

"Is that Kalfu talking? Because it sure isn't Lexie." He floated into the building.

She raised her gaze to the dark glass thirty-story building. She knew it well. Will had moved into it shortly after buying their condo. After Bennett Architecture had taken off, Will had decided he needed a lavish office in the heart of the city's Central Business District to impress clients. To Lexie, it was excessive.

She chastised herself for not making Will come with her. He would want to know what Kalila had left her. But part of her, the black part, was glad he hadn't come. The darkness urged her to spend less time with her husband, in case the truth slipped out. But hiding her problem from her best friend had become torture.

I can't keep this up much longer.

In a sleek lobby, she anxiously scanned the crowd, searching for familiar faces and then berated her paranoia. She wasn't doing anything wrong.

Thin sheets of gold-painted metal arranged on the walls around her were meant to represent waves on the water. In the center, a gold sphere suspended above a pond captured beams of light coming through the glass ceiling. The warm light filling the lobby eased her jittery nerves.

Then something black in the shape of a man floated across the gold sphere and stopped. Lexie tensed as her gaze darted amid the crowd, eager to see if others spotted the shadow spirit.

No one seemed to notice. Then the apparition faded away.

"I've got to get rid of those bastards," she muttered, strolling across the white marble floor.

Ahead, a hallway of gold elevator doors sat right behind a round security desk made of dark wood.

A security officer, dressed in a gray uniform, greeted her.

"Hello, Mrs. Bennett. You meeting your husband for lunch again?"

Lexie gripped her purse, glancing at the guard's nametag. "Ah thanks, Randall, but no. I'm going to the fifteenth floor."

"That's right above your husband's floor." Randall lowered his gaze to her cane. "Wasn't aware we had anyone up there yet. Must be a new tenant."

The black tightened her chest with insistence. The uncomfortable sensation urged her to move. She gave the guard a quick nod and darted for the elevators.

"Stop stalling," he said inside her head.

The sound of him sent a chill through her. It was as if he grew stronger with every passing day.

The floors ticked by, and she held her breath as the car passed the fourteenth floor. Once she reached fifteen, the elevator opened, and she stepped into a darkly lit corridor.

She peeked around the hallway, wondering why the lights were so weak. She took a few steps and stumbled into an etched glass entrance that hid the office behind it. Above, a sign with black lettering announced the law firm of Kinder, Archer, and Lance. They even had a cool logo—a circle with three lines cutting through the center.

She pushed the glass doors open. The first thing she noticed was the aroma of leather furniture and cedar air freshener. It was rather strong, and Lexie wrinkled her nose in protest.

The gray reception area had no paintings, decorative rugs, or even magazines set out on their coffee table. There were no panoramic windows with views of the French Quarter or the river, and no knickknacks hinting at the local flavor, like her husband's office. This place had an almost oppressive atmosphere.

How can anyone tolerate working in such a dismal office?

"Can I help you?" a dowdy receptionist asked from behind a walnut desk with roaring carved lions in front.

The furniture reminded her of the Baroque period but she could tell it was a cheap imitation of an original piece.

"Um, yes. Lexie Bennett to see Mr. David Hutchins."

"Of course." The dark-eyed woman with black hair motioned to a door in the walnut paneling. "Go on through."

Lexie nervously patted down the front of her white dress and walked toward the door. She was thankful she'd left her turban at the shop.

But before she could reach for the handle, a slight breeze caressed her arm, making her hair stand up. Then the door popped open.

After spending the last several months firmly entrenched in the spirit world, her first instinct was to suspect something supernatural.

"Is there a problem?" the receptionist asked.

Lexie glanced back at her, forcing a smile. "Ah, the door just—"

"They're automatic locks. They pop open like that."

She moved through to the inner offices.

Something is weird about this place.

On the other side, the dreary interior didn't get much better. Drab dark blue wallpaper and gray carpeting decorated a dimly lit hall with flickering fluorescent lights. There was no one around, and the offices attached to the narrow corridor were eerily silent.

Before she had even shut the door behind her, a man came out of nowhere.

"Mrs. Bennett?"

With a radiant smile and a thick head of brown hair, the stranger held out his hand. "I'm David Hutchins. So glad you could come by."

She took his hand, and the first thing she felt was cold. It was an uncanny sensation that seeped into her. Waves of darkness rose in her center and crested like a turbulent ocean stirred by the wrath of a hurricane. She withdrew her hand.

Never had she encountered a human who made her feel that way, only spirits. But from his prominent Adam's apple to his heavy use of cologne, he was utterly human.

Maybe he, too, is touched by darkness.

David politely escorted her down the hallway, and the sounds of a busy office rose around her—typing on keyboards, printers humming and murmured conversations, all the things she expected, but she never saw anyone else.

They arrived at an open office door. To her relief, the room was bright, had a breathtaking view of the French Quarter, leafy green plants, and walls filled with diplomas and certificates of merit.

Her rigid posture relaxed. *Thank goodness. Something normal.*

David Hutchins pulled out a red leather chair in front of his desk and motioned for her to sit.

"I'm glad you could come by so soon. We've been trying to close on Miss La Fay's estate, and you were the last piece of the puzzle we needed."

Lexie rested her purse in her lap and her cane on her chair. "I'm not sure I understand why Kalila left anything to me."

David sat in his black desk chair and opened a manila folder. "She made it quite clear in her will. You were the heir to the bulk of her estate. She had some personal effects distributed to distant relatives, but according to this …" He tapped the open folder in front of him. "She left you her house and property. Close to thirty acres, mostly swamp, but there is some land in there."

Lexie sat, stunned into silence.

"Her house? Me? But I barely knew the woman. We met once right before she died."

David leaned over the folder and picked up a single piece of paper. "She says here, 'I leave my home and the surrounding property to Lexie Arden.' She never gave us your married name, and I had to do some digging to find you. That's the reason it took so long to contact you."

She squeezed the leather purse in her lap, overwhelmed by the windfall. "I still don't understand why she left her home to me."

"I've seen stranger things, Mrs. Bennett. I once had a client leave his entire estate of two million dollars to a clerk in a grocery store. They never spoke to each other, but he stated in his will, her smile always made him happy." He retrieved something from his desk drawer. "And then there's the time a widow left her house and sizable bank account to her cat. That was a legal nightmare from the start." He tossed a set of keys on the desk.

The silver and brass keys suddenly made everything happening to her seem very real. It wasn't a hoax; her name hadn't been confused with someone else. She had inherited Kalila's property. But still, she had a difficult time believing the experienced priestess had picked her.

"Those are the keys to the house and car. According to the property review, it includes the house, a work shed, two docks along the rear, two boats, and Ms. La Fay's 2018 Cadillac ATS coupe." He rested his folded hands on the desk. "Any questions?"

Lexie tentatively picked up the keys and turned them over, trying to recall the one meeting she'd had with Kalila.

"Did she give any reason for naming me?"

"Nope. She just named you in her will." David removed another slip of paper from his file. "I need you to sign this. It states you accept the property. The taxes for this year have been paid, and an annuity goes with the estate to cover taxes, repairs, and household expenses. It's quite sizable. You'll never have to spend a penny on the place."

The mention of money made Lexie crush the keys in her hand. This didn't feel right. Surely the poor woman had someone else besides her.

"You said she has family. Shouldn't they get her house, her car, her money?"

David sat back in his chair, a pensive frown on his lips. "That's not what Ms. La Fay wanted. My job is to make sure her final requests are carried out. And for whatever reason, she wanted you to have her property." He sat forward, sighing. "Who knows why people do what they do? I advise you take what she has given you and enjoy it. Sell it if you don't want it, but she felt you were the right person to take care of what she treasured."

Magnus came to life in the leather chair next to hers, his fingers impatiently tapping his cane.

"Are you sure about this, dear girl? Something doesn't feel right."

She had to agree with him. The entire situation felt rushed and decidedly nonlegal. Attorneys were exacting people who checked and double-checked facts. She should know—her stepfather, Kevin, had studied law before entering politics and had taught her how to understand it. She decided to play along.

The ribbon connecting her to Magnus hummed. She sent him a surge of reassurance and hoped he picked up on her lead.

Lexie read the form on the desk in front of her, biting her lower lip, and hoping she came across as naïve. "Should I ask my husband to read these papers before I sign anything?"

"For once, I agree with you," Magnus said. "Will needs to know about this."

"That's your prerogative, Mrs. Bennett," David told her. "But since there are no taxes to pay, and no debt to incur from the estate, I'm sure your husband will be eager to settle the accounts and accept the inheritance." David pushed the paper needing her signature closer. "If you do not wish to take the estate, you have seven days after signing to refuse it."

Lexie relaxed. Seven days gave her plenty of time.

"What happens if I refuse?"

"The state seizes control. It's what happens when heirs refuse their inheritance." David picked up a pen and held it out to her. "Are you sure you want to deny Ms. La Fay her last wishes?"

Lexie pictured the dark woman who had tricked her into drinking rum laced with gunpowder. She'd been coerced into the introduction by Kalfu, and Lexie questioned if the conniving spirit had manipulated Kalila's will as well.

"Are you sure these are Kalila's last wishes, Mr. Hutchins?"

"Of course. Why do you ask?" David pushed the pen toward her.

Magnus tilted closer. "Lexie, think about what you are doing?"

"I'm going to sign." Lexie took the pen.

Magnus shook his head. "Will won't like it."

Lexie ignored him and scribbled her name.

David chuckled, sounding pleased. "Excellent. The property is yours. I will file all the paperwork with the state transferring the deed over to you."

While he stacked the papers and placed them back in the file, Lexie attempted to decipher what other documents made up Kalila's estate. There had to be more than one paper for her to sign.

But before Lexie could raise her questions, David was out of his chair, snapping up the set of keys on the desk.

"I'm so glad we could conclude this matter." He put the keys into her hand, took her elbow, and helped her from her chair. "If you have any questions about the transaction, please get in touch. Your paperwork should arrive in two to three weeks."

Once in the hallway, Lexie barely had time to put the keys in her purse before David set his hand in the small of her back and ushered her to the reception area.

His brusque manner added to her suspicions. Something had been off from the moment she'd entered the office.

David said nothing to the receptionist as he guided Lexie to the etched glass doors.

She took a good look at the waiting area. No one else was there.

"Wonderful meeting you, Mrs. Bennett."

He shook her hand once more and then let the glass doors close in Lexie's face.

Magnus frowned at his reflection in the glass. "That was rude."

Lexie turned away, anxious to see what Kalila had left her. "Let's go."

Magnus floated alongside her. "Where are we going?"

At the golden elevator doors, she hit the call button. "To find out why Kalfu made Kalila leave me everything."

"You know why," Magnus insisted. "She belonged to him and now so do you."

The down arrow above the elevator lit up. Lexie tapped her foot.

"Perhaps, but I doubt Kalfu has studied the inheritance laws of Louisiana. Kalila's family does have rights to her property and can contest her will. David never mentioned that. My bet is they don't know she's dead."

"Or Kalfu doesn't want them to know," Magnus added.

The doors opened, and Lexie was thankful they had the car to themselves.

She stepped inside, and Magnus followed.

"Which is why I signed the papers. There's something at that house he wants me to see."

The doors closed and Lexie's mind hummed with possibilities. She hoped she could find something to help her with Kalfu. After all her years of dealing with him, Kalila must have left behind some helpful advice.

He arched an eyebrow, a condescending sneer on his lips. "What will you tell your husband?"

She was about to tell him not to worry about Will when the elevator stopped on the floor below. The doors quickly opened. She glanced at the person waiting to get on, and her heart rose in her throat.

"Lexie?" Will squinted at her. "I was just coming to find you."

She fought to come up with something to say, but her mind went blank and her stomach shrunk into a tight ball.

The long silence between them was only broken by the

elevator alarm buzzer screeching as the doors tried to close, but Will blocked them with his thick arm.

"Tell me you didn't sign anything," he grumbled.

Lexie stuck out her chin, attempting to sound upbeat. "Kalila left me a house."

"What?" Will got into the elevator, an irritated gleam in his eye. "You should have called me from their offices before you signed anything. I was only one floor down, for God's sake. I could have met you there."

"I told you he would get mad." Magnus stood behind her husband, peering over his shoulder.

Will punched the number fifteen on the console key several times.

"What are you doing?" She pulled his hand from the console. "You have to calm down. You can't go marching into those offices demanding to see the paperwork."

Will's cheeks turned a deep shade of red. "Lexie, for once, will you let me handle things?"

Magnus adjusted his Ascot tie. "Tell him I didn't want you to sign those papers."

She faced Magnus. "You know damn well why I did it."

Will slapped the wall right next to Magnus. "Is he in here?"

"Yes, he's here." Her exasperated voice raced around the car. "He didn't want me to sign those papers, either."

"Thank God, one of you has some sense." Will tossed up his hand as the car came to a stop.

"What is that supposed to mean?" She stormed up to her husband. "I have sense!"

The elevator doors opened.

Will's dark eyes tore into her. "Lexie, no one accepts an estate from a stranger without checking a few facts. Like back taxes and liens."

"He has a point." Magnus floated out of the car.

"I know that. David Hutchins was lying to me," Lexie argued. "I signed those papers to find out why."

"Who is David Hutchins?" Will stuck out his arm, holding the elevator door open, and blocking her way out. "And why was he lying to you?"

She pushed his arm away. "He's the attorney for Kinder, Archer, and Lance Law Firm." Lexie walked past him. "But they don't exist."

She stopped right outside the elevator in front of a wall of unfinished sheetrock and a plain wooden door with a *For Lease* sign stapled to it.

Magnus floated up to her, examining the wall. "You were right, dear girl. Someone is toying with you."

Will walked up to the wall and touched it. "There hasn't been anyone on this floor in months. I checked with the front desk. That's why I was coming up to find you. I had to make sure you told me the right suite number last night."

She went up to him, grinning. "And I thought you weren't paying attention."

Will didn't return her smile. His somber expression caused a funny pinprick to travel across her forearms.

"You know who did this, don't you?" he demanded.

A wall of black rose around her heart, blocking her desire to tell her husband the truth. Never had she come so close to letting him know everything about her new life. Like a knife driven into her gut, Kalfu's evil sucked away her breath and reduced her will to confide in her husband to an ugly, stabbing pain.

She clenched her fists, determined to ignore it.

"Don't push me."

His menacing, vile voice frightened her into submission.

"I have to go."

"Go?" Will shouted. "You tell me you've been left some dead woman's house by a law firm that doesn't exist. You're not going to give me any explanation?" He shook his head, his shoulders sagging. "Sometimes I don't recognize you anymore."

Wasn't living a lie better than losing him forever?

Instead of assuring him, she went to the elevator and hit the call button.

Will came from behind and held her.

His embrace tore a hole in her heart the size of the moon. She wanted nothing more than to share the hell she'd endured, but she couldn't. His battered face that night at the plantation still haunted her. She had to keep Will out of her battle with Kalfu. It was the only way she knew to protect him.

"I'm terrified I'm losing you, baby."

The black prodded her to push him away. The heaviness pressing down on her chest made her wiggle out of his arms.

"You're not losing me. I have some things to figure out."

He backed away, his wide-eyed shock cutting her to the bone. "Like what? Us?"

The elevator doors opened, and she dashed inside, before her blackness made her say something she didn't mean. She slapped the button for the lobby and kept her head lowered, unable to look her husband in the eye.

The doors closed and she fought back her urge to cry. She had to stay strong for both of them.

"That was harsh, dear girl."

She stroked the snout of the dragon on her cane. "It was necessary. If I get angry, Kalfu's power rises and ... I have to keep Will safe."

"You need to tell him. Secrets don't help a marriage; they hurt it. Will loves you, not your power. He loved you before you became what you are, and he will love you still when it has gone away. Don't shut him out."

From a ghost who had been at odds with her husband from day one, the comment was unexpected. "Never thought you would be on his side."

"I'm on your side. I've always been." He lowered his voice, avoiding her gaze. "Will is a part of you, so I will advocate for anything that keeps him with you. You are stronger with him than without him."

Before she could argue further, Magnus faded.

Frustrated, she stomped her foot. *Damn, the infernal ghost.*

But Magnus was right. If she didn't do something soon to get rid of Kalfu, she would lose the only man she'd ever loved.

Chapter Eight

Once outside on the sidewalk, she breathed in the spring air. Despite the bustle of people on the street, she wanted to scream at the top of her lungs that something evil had made its home in her, and she was desperate to free herself.

"He's here," Magnus said, his image fading. "He will send me away to talk to you, so be careful what you say."

Car fumes from the busy street tainted the air, but then the hint of fresh-cut grass slipped in, teasing her nose.

Kalfu arrived amid a flurry of people walking along the sidewalk and chatting amongst themselves. They never detected the handsome man in the sleek black business suit among them.

The slight breeze lifted his blond hair as his sparkling eyes swept over her.

Without acknowledging Magnus, he snapped his fingers, and her ghost departed.

"You're angry with me." He brushed something from his sleeve. "I know it was silly, but if I made it official, I assumed you would not question my gift."

She narrowed her gaze, her stomach churning. "Giving me a dead woman's house—a house that should have gone to her family—is not a gift. It's theft."

He took her arm, encouraging her along the sidewalk. His touch made the black in her soul purr like a nursing kitten.

"As my priestess, I wanted to make sure you were cared for. What better way than a house of your own?"

Lexie wanted to shout at the detestable man but kept her voice low to avoid any unwanted stares.

"You've never cared for me. I'm an object to you. Nothing more."

Kalfu glanced up at the building.

"On the contrary, you are very important to me. Your power, your growing fame as a mambo, and your husband's recent success are all due to me. Granted, Will is a talented architect, but I gave him a boost by making sure several projects in the city went his way. All to keep you happy and economically comfortable."

Revulsion cascaded through her, sending up waves of nausea. To banish his blackness from her being would impact Will.

"I never asked you to do anything for Will. You should have told me."

He guided her along the sidewalk, taking her arm. "Just another means of keeping you loyal."

She wanted to slap the smile from his face, lash out, something to show him how she felt, but she didn't. His black in her would rip her apart from the inside out.

Lexie became distracted by the people crowding the walkway. Instead of getting in front of them, or blocking their path, everyone magically went around them. Their eyes stayed ahead, or on their cell phones, but no one noticed them. The way he manipulated the rest of the world disgusted her.

"I know you, Lexie Arden. You would have turned me down. You're mine and are entitled to all the things I can provide for you. Take the house and car. You and Will can use the cottage as a weekend home. And if he has a problem with it, I can change his mind."

She came to a halt, her baton juju banging the sidewalk.

How dare he threaten Will?

"You're never to touch him, do you hear?" she growled. "You're never to manipulate Will, to coax his thoughts, or even enter his head. If I find out you betrayed me, I will rid myself of you forever, and then I will show the world what you are."

The mocking glimmer in his steadfast gaze sent a ripple of contempt all the way to her toes.

"Haven't you already been searching for a way to break free of me? Isn't that what you were asking during your little tête-à-tête with Madame Henri?" His mouth stretched into a tense smile. "And you shouldn't listen to Maman Brigitte, either. That silly bitch is only good for minding the dead. She's worthless to the living, no matter what she promised. Only I can grant your deepest wish—a child."

Blind fury swept through her. It was one thing to take her fertility away—it was quite another to use it as a means of keeping her compliant.

"I'm not a fool. You're a death spirit and can never grant life."

His *tsk-tsk* rose in the air. "Spare me your simplistic ideology, Lexie Arden. The spirits of voodoo are more than what you read in your books. Any of our kind with power can create life and take it away. I am capable of both." He angled closer to her ear. "My power will be passed from you to the child."

He walked ahead, the people clearing out of the way as if pushed aside by invisible hands.

She almost crumbled at the thought of any child she had belonging to the twisted creature. But then the white ribbon in her center blanketed her heart with a warm reassurance.

"What about Damballah? The child would inherit his power, too."

He stopped a few feet away. His back arched. She'd struck a nerve.

"As long as you remain his, any child you have could end up belonging to us both. I'm hoping you give him up before I give you a child."

She caught up to him in two anxious steps. "What if I give you up?"

He faced her, a sneer on his lips. "I control your life. What you do, say, and hear is approved by me. There is not one thought you have that I haven't already guessed, one dream that I haven't already seen. What you are is what I determine. So unless you want me to flay the skin from your bones and send what is left to spend eternity in my darkest dungeon, I would suggest you start going along with my design and stop testing me at every turn."

He walked on, but her feet remained glued to the sidewalk. The threat terrified her. She knew he was capable of unspeakable torture. She'd seen his thoughts once, gotten a glimpse of the broken souls he kept in agony in his hellish world. It kept her compliant, but she was confident he wouldn't kill her—not yet anyway. He had to keep her around to get what he wanted.

She fell in step next to him, taking in the sunlight peeking between the buildings. It amazed her how the shadows somehow hovered over them as they walked.

"What do you want from me? You wouldn't go to all the trouble of giving me a house without a reason."

Kalfu glanced over at her, one eyebrow arched. "Perhaps I like to reward loyalty."

"Bullshit. You know how I feel about this relationship. You've known since the moment I agreed to be yours. You want me to do something for you, and you're bribing me."

Kalfu stepped to the curb and rested his hip on a black Cadillac ATS coupe.

"Do you like your car? I can change the color if you like?"

Lexie ignored the car and went up to him. "You once asked me if I ever played chess. The night I went to confront Emily Mann you said, 'You sometimes have to blind an opponent by doing one thing when you mean to do another.' That's what you are doing now—blinding me."

"I keep forgetting how clever you are. Kalila was never clever. It's one of the reasons she's dead."

"Cut the crap. What's going on?"

He folded his thick arms, and a wrinkle creased his brow. "Now and then the spirts in my realm like to challenge each other. Fight for territory. Damballah and I have always clashed, but he rules the realm of light and me, the darkness, so such rivalry is accepted. But recently one of my own, a spirit of death, has been gathering soldiers to pit against me. Maman Brigitte's collecting power from your world and hoping to use it to displace me."

The concept seemed absurd. Who would challenge him? Weren't there defined realms the spirits of voodoo controlled?

"I don't get it. Why is she trying to overthrow you?"

"Not overthrow, but cut into my power and use it to raise her position in our world. She's unhappy being a minor god." He stood, folding his hands in front of him while all around traffic sped through the street, and pedestrians hastened by. "She's trying to use you to get it. She's not interested in helping you; she wants to hurt me."

She inched closer to the car. "You're not interested in helping me, either, Kal."

He placed his hand over his heart and pouted. "That hurts, Lexie."

She ignored his act. "What has your battle with her got to do with me?"

He slinked up to her, his hands in his trouser pockets. "You're the prize, but if she can't have you, she will find another to eliminate you. You need to watch your back."

The cane kicked in her hand, sensing her distress. The marbled wood surged to life, comforting her.

"I have your power and Damballah's. She can't hurt me."

"But she can try." Kalfu placed his hand on the hood of the car. The engine turned over. "Go visit your new home. There's something there you could use."

He snapped his fingers, and Magnus reappeared.

Her ghost stood next to the car, his lips pressed together, conveying his displeasure.

Kalfu motioned to Magnus. "Take your Mr. Blackwell with you. You will both find it interesting."

The congested traffic and large malls of the Jefferson Parish melted behind towering cypress trees rising from the swamps. The bright morning sun filtered through the windows of the Cadillac, warming Lexie's face and hands while the tangy aroma of stagnant water permeated the car.

Magnus sat next to her in the black leather seat and warily perused the busy dashboard, his curiosity lightening her mood. The way he inspected every gadget brought a smile to Lexie's face.

"I like Will's car better. There are too many buttons in here."

She steered the car along the narrow road. "Will's is German. This is American. Two different takes on cars."

"Why did you accept the car and house from him?" He sank lower in his seat. "If you want to be free of him, you have a strange way of showing it."

"Kalila dealt with Kalfu for years. I'm hoping there's something at the house that can help me learn more about him. And maybe some way to rid myself of him."

She glimpsed the dense green brush, hiding her apprehension. If she couldn't uncover some clue about dealing with Kalfu at the house, she didn't know where else to turn.

"I fear the house will only bind you to him more, dear girl."

"Maybe I can use it to my advantage. He told me a conflict is brewing between him and Maman Brigitte."

Magnus's eyes radiated his concern. "Careful. You might find yourself caught in a dangerous game."

Ahead, the road curved and a tin roof twinkled in the sun. Cypress trees sagging with green, leafy branches hugged a single-story, dingy gray Acadian cottage. A rickety screened-in porch circled the structure while two slanted stone chimneys peeked out from behind the low-hanging branches. There was a circular driveway composed of broken white shells nestled next to wooden steps that climbed to a sagging porch.

"Not as creepy as the last time we were here," she muttered as she pulled the car up to the house.

Magnus inspected the home through the windshield. "Are you sure you want this place?"

Lexie switched off the engine and grabbed her dragon cane from the passenger seat. "I want to see what's here before I decide to get rid of it."

She shoved open the door and climbed from the car. The pungent aroma of the stagnant swamp rose around her. It took getting used to. She wished she'd brought Will with her to share in the adventure. He would have loved the old home.

Dried cypress needles blanketed the ground around the car. They covered parts of the tin roof and accumulated atop the steps leading to the porch.

Magnus glided from the car, floating through the cypress knees and prickly, long-leafed plants dotting the front yard. He went to the edge of the algae-covered swamp and stood, gazing out at the water.

The downturn of his lower lip, and his far-off look, concerned her.

Lexie walked up to him, making sure not to trip over the few cypress knees jutting up through the leaves.

"Is everything okay?"

"They're gone." He pointed his cane at the water. "The dead. They're not here anymore."

Lexie searched the swamp, opening up her center, but nothing came to her.

"There were hundreds of spirits here before," Magnus told her. "Spirits bound to Kalila."

"Maybe they were freed when she died."

He turned to her, sadness teeming in his gaze. "And will I be free of you when you die?"

The question floored her. She'd not considered an afterlife without Magnus. Lexie believed he would always be with her, but perhaps it was selfish to think that way.

"Without me holding you back, you could go to your family and Katherine."

"You haven't held me back—my sins have kept me here." He glanced up at the cottage, hiding his face from her. "He's waiting for you."

She moved toward the house, but he didn't join her and remained at the water's edge.

"Aren't you coming with me?"

Magnus shook his head. "His force flows from the house, warning me to stay away. The dead are not welcome in the home."

Lexie turned to the structure, searching the wrap-around porch and sending the ribbon of light in her center through the nooks and crannies of the building. She detected nothing unusual. Neither the white or black light in her changed. All was calm.

What had he sensed? They had always been so in tune with each other. Now, he felt a world away.

"Are you sure?"

He urged her on with a wave. "You're alive, dear girl. You can't feel this energy, even with all your power."

Magnus had sworn to remain by her side, but it seemed the strange circumstances taking over her life worked to pull them apart. She'd grown so accustomed to him, that without his presence, she felt naked and vulnerable.

Lexie gave him a slight smile and headed for the steps, eager to see what she could find. This was one adventure she would have to tackle on her own.

His heart heavy, Magnus longed to go with her, to protect her, but the black force keeping him from the home was too strong. It pushed against his being like a curtain of lead, unrelenting and cold. Magnus waited by the edge of the swamp as she retrieved the keys and struggled with the front door lock.

"Fuck!"

Classic Lexie.

He grinned, glad some parts of her hadn't changed.

She shoved the front door open and marched into the unknown without him. He hated not being with her.

He remained apprehensive about their return to Kalila's home. The memory of the dead he'd seen in her swamp persisted. But he couldn't save them—that was something only Lexie could do.

Once Lexie slipped inside the home, he glanced back out over the stagnant water, reaching out with the power Damballah had entrusted him with, searching for any hint of those poor souls he had encountered.

A strange breeze came off the water. The branches next to the house swayed, sending brown leaves plunging to the ground. Then, the dark light within him stirred.

"Where have you been?"

The childlike voice sounded as if it came through a long tunnel.

A light flashed out of the corner of his eye. The chirping birds, rustling leaves, and buzzing bugs went silent. A mist slithered up next to him. It bent and swayed and then a mass formed in its center. Before he could touch it, the fog retreated, and a translucent figure took its place.

A boy, not much older than six, stood next to him. He appeared resplendent in a blue-velvet jacket and a matching pair of short pants. His cherubic face, blond curls, and red cheeks sent a cascade of disbelief through Magnus.

Mesmerized, Magnus waited to see if the ghost would disappear, but the little one's energy seemed to strengthen. He went from being cloudy to almost as solid as any living creature. His face sharpened like a picture on television. His brown eyes and long lashes became instantly recognizable.

"Edward?"

The unmistakable likeness was of his younger brother—the one Magnus had lost many lifetimes ago.

The young boy drifted closer, his black lace shoes floating above the ground. "I've been searching for you, Gus."

Gus. It was the nickname Edward had given him because Magnus had been too hard to pronounce.

The heart-wrenching grief Magnus had locked away after the death of his mother and only sibling came crashing back.

"Edward, is it really you?"

The boy smiled just as his brother had, with the gentle goodness of their mother and none of his father's ruthlessness.

"Why aren't you in the river with us? We're all there waiting—Mother, Father, and a nice lady named Frances. She wants to visit with you, Gus. She wants to forgive you."

Magnus ached to believe it was his brother, but since joining Lexie, he'd come to recognize the lands of the living and the dead were filled with more fiction than fact.

"Who sent you?" He knelt to get a closer look at the boy. "Who told you to come here?"

Edward tipped his head and never lost his smile. "Come home, Gus. I miss you."

Then the only person Magnus ever truly cared for in life faded before his eyes.

The stab of pain was as debilitating as the time he'd seen his brother's small body lowered into his pine coffin by their father. Edward had been his only happiness. And when death had taken him, all Magnus had left was Reynolds. His father's contempt molded him into the emotionless creature he'd become. After Edward's death, he'd vowed never to care for another, and he'd kept that promise until Frances.

Overwhelmed, Magnus yearned for the comfort of the woman who had saved his soul. With his hand on his cane, Magnus bowed his head and fought to connect with Lexie.

A storm of emotion swirled inside him—colors of white and black entwined in a jumble of knotted ribbons. He sensed the forces pulling them apart were growing more insistent, but he attempted to broach the chaos and called to her, asking her to hurry outside and join him. He didn't want to be apart from her strength any longer. They were a team, and he was nothing without her.

Chapter Nine

A strong scent of pine wafted through the living room. The gentle hum of the refrigerator came from the adjoining kitchen. The sounds and smells helped her ease her tight grip on her dragon cane. There was nothing sinister in the red-velvet mahogany furniture that tastefully covered the polished hardwood floor. All was quiet.

Above the stone hearth's mantel was a recreation of St. Louis Cathedral at dawn, done in pastel tones of pink, orange, and red. The inviting light from the piece seemed at odds with the lifestyle of the woman who had lived in the home. Directly below the painting were two silver goblets.

Lexie winced at the memory of sipping from one of the goblets. The taste of rum laced with gunpowder still burned in her mouth. The strange concoction had changed her life. It had led to her first meeting with Kalfu and set her on a course few could understand.

She stopped at the cypress coffee table and admired the shine on the wood. Intrigued, she swept her hand along the smooth surface.

Not a speck of dust in sight.

Her curiosity piqued, she set her purse and cane aside and moved deeper into the room. She caressed the decorative swirls carved into the sofa's armrest, giddy at the knowledge the antique Georgian Chippendale pieces were hers. She'd always wanted a home filled with such luxury, and now she had it.

Or did she?

On the walls were old oil paintings of green plantation fields. Some looked expensive. It felt wrong to claim them, like receiving an unwanted gift.

An inkling of unease twitched her fingers as she headed to the kitchen. It was as if the cozy charm of the home hid a threatening force beneath it. She opened the old refrigerator, checked the dishwasher and even perused the dishes and glasses crowding the cabinets.

It was an ordinary kitchen. There were no secrets hidden there.

She ventured into the hall from the living room. The dark cypress wood added a creepy vibe to her search of the dead woman's home.

Lexie held her breath as she closed in on the first of three cypress doors in the hallway. Her dread ran through her veins like ice water. She grasped the brass knob and held her breath, half expecting someone to jump out at her.

Behind the door was a cozy bedroom done in pale shades of yellow with a mahogany four-poster rice bed and a long dresser.

Not what she'd expected of Kalila. It seemed too frilly for a priestess of the dark realm.

Atop the dresser, a mounted mirror caught her eye, and she gasped at the face she saw there. Pale skin and blonde hair showed up almost translucent in the weak light from the hall. She chuckled when she realized it was her and not some ghost in the mirror. Lexie made a mental note to wear more blush. She looked like one of the spirits with which she communed.

She eased down the hall, entranced by the charcoal drawings of landmarks in New Orleans on the walls. But it was the lack of pictures, photos of friends and family, or personal mementos strewn about the home that gave her pause. Had someone already removed Kalila's things?

After passing a small bathroom, she approached the last door, and her expectations for finding anything worthwhile floundered.

With a lack of enthusiasm, she pushed the last door open. Pitch black greeted her, and she froze. Tentatively, she reached inside and patted the wall to find the switch.

When the recessed lights came on, she stumbled backward.

Bookcases, dozens of them, lined the walls. Shelves crammed with a wide variety of covers, from leather-bound tomes to paperbacks, gave off a musty smell.

"Now, this is more like it."

Book after book, title after title, was about magic, witchcraft, and voodoo. Lexie estimated there had to be a few hundred books in the room. Many were rare editions that collectors would kill to get their hands on—including Lexie.

She selected a leather book from the shelf titled, *The Loa of the Voodoo Religion: Myths, Facts, and Mysteries*. She sneezed as the dust rose into the air.

Dust. There had been none in the home, but the books and the bookshelves had a thick layer.

Why is it only in here?

She flipped through the pages, intrigued by a chapter on infighting among the spirits of voodoo. Disputes between the guardians of voodoo were pretty common.

"I've heard 'bout you." The voice was coarse, craggy. "The spirits speak of you. The mambo who serves two masters."

Lexie almost dropped the book. Like a soft caress, a chilly breeze brushed her cheek. She stepped back from the shelf, searching the room for the intruder, but no one was there.

"I can't see you."

"But you can feel me. Your blackness knows me."

The voice was female.

She was about to question the spirit when a reading lamp on top of a pedestal turned on. Lexie tried to reach out with her power, but nothing came to her.

"Who are you?"

A shadow emerged from behind the pedestal. Black, cold, and fading in and out, it made the light flicker as it got closer.

Lexie held the book against her chest. The shadowy figure blocked her only escape from the room. The aroma of sweet pipe tobacco tickled her nose as the umbra moved away from the pedestal.

"You're in my home. Where I used to live when I walked among the livin'."

Lexie's fear fizzled as her inquisitive nature took over. "Your home? This was Kalila La Fay's home. She was—"

"And before her, it belonged to another servant of your master, and another, and another." A gravelly cackle rocked the air. "There have been so many, but only Kalfu knows all their names."

For the first time since entering the home, the black in Lexie spurred to life. It felt safe here, but the rest of her didn't.

"This house belongs to the priestess who serves Kalfu, doesn't it?"

She wanted to kick herself for being so stupid, but why hadn't her inner working warned her?

The spirit made of shadows moved closer. "Which is you now."

Lexie's bounding heart sounded like thunder in her ears. "How do you know that?"

The shadow rocked back and forth, and with every movement, specks of color showed against the blackness. Red appeared on the lower portion of the figure. The swaying motion soon became a rustling and a long skirt, one that reached the floor, materialized. A black shawl, woven in a pattern of squares, and a plain white top came into view. Her neck, the loose flesh around her jawline, and the dark color of her skin surfaced next. Her face came into focus, but what Lexie noticed first were the scars—ugly ones on her cheeks and across her forehead. A corncob pipe protruded from her lips, billowing black smoke crept upward in a lazy spiral. The last bit of her wardrobe to manifest—the red turban on her head.

"I can feel him on you. You're his new prize. That's why you're here. To learn more about him."

Her weathered skin and ungodly black eyes were quite intimidating. The spirit stepped closer, and Lexie noticed her limp. The afterlife had not given her freedom from infirmity like the other apparitions she'd seen. The disfigured face and sad appearance had only one explanation—a curse. Lexie had seen it before, with Magnus and others. When the atrocities of life remained like scars on the soul, the spirit had been doomed from the moment of death to suffer for its sins.

"You were a priestess, like me."

"I ain't nothin' like you. You practice city magic. My skills came from the swamps. Lotta power there people know nothin' about."

Whatever power she may have had, it didn't explain her haunting the library.

"How did you end up here?"

"I drowned in this house when the storm of 1915 hit. The water came up so fast, I never had a chance. Been here ever since."

Lexie remembered the storm and the priestess who had predicted it. "You're Julie Brown. You belonged to Maman Brigitte."

The old woman glided up to her, motioning to the book in her hand. "You don't belong to one master. Neither did I." Julie Brown swept past her, heading to a corner bookcase. "We can choose who we allow to guide us, and who we wish to banish from our soul. But you gotta be real careful 'bout not lettin' one spirit get stronger than another. That was my mistake. I let Kalfu take over. Maman Brigitte wasn't happy about it."

Lexie's legs wobbled, and she fought to regain her balance. Julie Brown had been like her—one priestess bound to two masters. Suddenly, the woman's life became important.

Julie pointed to a thick black-leather book on a corner of the shelf. "What you're lookin' for is in there."

Not sure what she meant, Lexie pulled the book from the shelf and read the faded title on the spine.

Journal of Julie Brown

Lexie patted the book, overcome with hope. Perhaps the answers she needed were in this book. But she'd been here before.

Gifts were not handed out readily by those in voodoo. There was always a catch.

"Why are you showing me this?"

"Because you're one of us. This is the library of all the priestesses who have lived in this house, goin' back almost three hundred years." Julie scanned the shelves, her loving regard eclipsing the ugly scars on her face. "All the knowledge each of us learned we put in these books to help the next one of our kind. But it ain't for no one else to see."

Lexie browsed the books in the room, not sure how she felt about belonging to such an elite club. The off-putting Julie Brown didn't exactly stir confidence.

Julie pointed at the door. "The books can't leave this room. As long as they stay in here, they're protected from fire, flood, and destruction. If you try and take them out, they turn to ash."

"Why are these being kept from the world?"

Julie's ragged, cold snicker careened around the small room, setting Lexie's teeth on edge.

"Because there are secrets in here that shouldn't get out. You'll learn all about him, too—his past, his women, and his power. He can't come in this library. A long time ago one of the women who lived here hexed the room to keep him out. It's nice not havin' to see his ugly ass lookin' over your shoulder as you read."

The remark struck her. "Ugly? You see Kalfu as ugly?"

Julie shuffled to the open door and peeked into the hall, fear in her eyes.

"He used to come to me as my late husband, Lester. Ugliest man I knew, but he had a good heart. It was his heart I loved, not his face. I was devastated when he died, so Kalfu used it to win me over. Stupid me."

Lexie crept closer to the ghost. "Why are you still here?"

A scowl deepened the scars on her face, taking away the last hint of kindness.

"I have to stay away from him. I did somethin' before the storm, somethin' he ain't forgotten. So, I keep to this room to make sure he never gets me."

Her quavering voice, the wringing of her scarred hands, and her fretful, wide-eyed stare, told Lexie the spirit was petrified.

She understood the depths of Kalfu's evil, had felt it teeming from his being, and knew not to cross him. But what if she did? Would her fate be the same as Julie Brown's?

"Perhaps there's a way to free you in these books. I could study them and try to find—"

"Ain't no help for me." Julie hobbled back toward the pedestal. "You got bigger troubles." Julie slowly eased into the corner. "Use what's in here to save yourself. Bad times are comin'."

Lexie chased after her, wanting more information, but the ghost morphed into a shadow. Her shade rocked and weaved as it grew smaller and before Lexie reached the corner, Julie Brown became a thin line of darkness that dropped to the hardwood floor.

Lexie stood next to the lamp, reaching out with her center to find any trace of the woman, but to no avail. She glimpsed the books in her arms and those on the shelves. There were so many.

I've got a lot of reading to do.

She waited by the car for Magnus, the rays from the midday sun failing to chase away the chill settling over her. Julie Brown's words revolved in her mind—a merry-go-round of doom and gloom.

"Are you all right?" Magnus showed up in front of her. A frown marred his handsome features. "You're worried. I can feel it."

His concern touched her. He was a far cry from the uppity ghost she'd first met at Altmover Manor.

"I found a library in the house. It's where all the priestesses of Kalfu left their books and journals for others coming behind them to use. The house belongs to Kalfu, or to the women Kalfu owns."

"He doesn't own you," Magnus angrily asserted. "He never will. You will decide your fate, not him."

Since the moment she'd agreed to Kalfu's terms to save her husband, she'd felt like a puppet on a string—half in her world, and half in the darkness. But Magnus had a point. Her will was still hers, and she could decide the course of her life, no matter what Kalfu said.

"And what if I don't like your choices?"

The smooth man's voice came alive in her head.

She frowned. *"Not everything in my life is about you."*

The slight trembling of the black inside her was unexpected. She didn't know what to think of it but at least it wasn't pain. He liked to punish her with pain.

The driver's side door of the sleek car opened. Magnus waved her inside.

She gripped her cane, feeling better than she had in several weeks. "We need to head back to the city. I've got a business to run."

Chapter Ten

Cool breezes laden with hints of red pepper, paprika, and the distant thump of an upbeat jazz tune wafted through the open door of Mambo Manor. An array of tourists dressed in anything from shorts to jeans scoured the displays, pointing out oddities, and whispering about the strange voodoo traditions. The mumblings amused Lexie as she strolled amidst the strangers, but she yearned to dispel the rumors of bloody sacrifice and devil worship. She wanted the rest of the world to see the same sense of peace and optimism voodoo gave her. Well, had given her before Kalfu.

With her long baton juju gently tapping the brick floor, she debated her future with the crafty spirit of the underworld. Then something caught her eye. At first, she thought it a play of light from the open shop door, but as it moved along the wall, slithering like a black snake, she knew it was something more sinister—a shadow spirit.

"You're going to tear a hole in the floor if you keep pacing like that."

Nina blocked Lexie's path. The sunlight coming inside highlighted the beauty of her light mahogany skin and doe-like brown eyes. She wore a white dress matching Lexie's but had passed on wearing a red turban, leaving her long black hair in a ponytail.

"Do you want to clue me in on what's bothering you?"

"It's nothing. Just mulling over a case I have with Detective Glapion."

"Sounds like you're making headway. You always wanted to work with the police as a psychic."

Lexie traced the outline of a brick on the floor with the tip of her cane. "I'm not making a lot of headway. Harold Forneaux is pressuring the department not to use me. Unless I pick up something significant soon, Emile won't be able to keep me on."

Nina gave her forearm a reassuring pat. "It will come. You didn't think you would waltz in there and solve crimes from day one, did you? And forget about Harold. He's all hot air. Everyone in town knows it."

Lexie wished she could believe her, but threats had been coming from both the living and the dead lately. Between the shadow spirits, Harold, Kalfu, and Maman Brigitte, Lexie felt her time was running out.

"Nina!"

A handsome man with striking, rugged features, well-gelled, sun-kissed brown hair and broad shoulders came barreling across the shop toward them. In a pinstripe gray suit, which accentuated his ample chest and arms, he waved a bear-like hand and offered a boyish grin. He reminded Lexie of a bouncer rather than a businessman.

The excited expression on her store manager's face gave Lexie an inkling as to who the attractive young man was.

"Mike!" Nina rushed up to him.

Lexie took in the way the couple only had eyes for each other. She'd heard Nina mention Mike many times as she kept her updated on their evenings together. Nina's excitement when she spoke about her boyfriend reminded her of how she had felt about Will in the beginning.

"Oh, Mike Le Breaux." Nina smiled at Lexie, her cheeks flushed. "This is my boss, and the mambo of the city, Lexie Bennett."

Mike held out his hand. When Lexie took it, his strength astounded her. She figured Mike spent most of his time at the gym, rather than his office.

"It's a pleasure, ma'am," he said, sounding like he'd grown up in the South. "Nina has told me an awful lot about you."

Lexie eyed the eager way he took Nina's hand.

"What are you doing here?" Nina asked, beaming up at him.

Mike cleared his throat. "Ah, I was on my way down the street to do a final inspection of a building for my boss. Since he's gonna use it as rental property that I'll manage, he sends me."

Lexie tilted her head, interested in any news on real estate sales in the French Quarter. She, like many other shop owners, wanted to adhere to the charm of the old city and keep big retail names from setting up shop.

"What property?"

"The place used to be called the Shop of Divination. The owner died a while back." Mike leveled his gray eyes on her. "My real estate office is handling the sale, and when it came up, I told my boss about it."

Lexie recoiled, blood draining from her face. "Shop of Divination on Royal?"

Mike perked up. "You heard of it?"

She reined in her shock. "Yeah, I knew the owner."

Nina went to her and clasped her hand. "I didn't know about Renee's building, Lexie."

She gave her a gentle squeeze. "It's all right."

Mike scratched his head. "I'm sorry. I didn't realize you knew the woman who died. I keep forgetting what a small place The Quarter is."

Lexie regained her composure. "Property is hard to come by down here. I'm sure your boss is interested in the ideal location of the shop. He could rent it to any number of businesses."

"Oh, he's not interested in the locale, just the building."

"The building?" Lexie's voice cracked. "What's so important about the building?"

Mike raised his gaze to the beams in her ceiling, inspecting the structure.

"These old places have a lot of history to them. My boss is interested in that. He wants to get a jump on picking up properties with a notorious past of murder, heartache, or betrayal. Like that Shop of Divination. He thinks the vibes it gives off are going to be worth a lot of money."

Lexie rubbed her forehead, trying to understand. "How can you make money off such a thing?"

Mike wrapped an arm around Nina's waist. "With all the talk by local politicians about making the French Quarter a theme park, there's potential to turn these houses into spiritual attractions. Sort of like a haunted Disney World."

"The whole Quarter is haunted. People see spirits all the time here, especially those creepy shadow ones." Nina scrunched her face.

Lexie eyed the girl with trepidation. She wasn't the only one who had seen them in their building.

Nina nudged Mike with her shoulder. "What's so special about the place you're going to inspect?"

"It has a history of murder and suicide going back almost two hundred years. The owner before the last one shot himself in the courtyard. Then the one before that was found with his throat cut in the kitchen. My boss feels all that could be turned into something lucrative."

Lexie was astonished anyone would want to make money off the tragedy of another's past. Those who didn't speak to the dead wouldn't comprehend the pain they inflicted on the spirits who still inhabited their old residences.

"Who is your boss?" Lexie demanded.

"H. Cory. He's some rich banker from the Northeast." Mike gave a nonchalant toss of his head. "I've never met him, but I've spoken to him on the phone several times."

For Lexie, something was going on here that didn't feel right.

"Why would a banker from outside of Louisiana be interested in these buildings?"

Mike gave an exaggerated shrug with his broad shoulders. "Got me. I don't care who he is as long as I get paid. With all the old haunted places down here, I expect Mr. Cory will be hunting for more spots to buy, which is fine by me. I sell them to him, and then he pays me to manage them for him. It's a sweet deal for me."

Lexie knew little of the man, but now having met him,

something seemed off about his story. Perhaps she had dealt with too many unconscionable spirits lately and needed to stop questioning everyone's motives.

Mike turned to Nina. "I have to get going. I just wanted to stop by." Mike took one last gander at the shop. "You've got an interesting place here, Mambo. Love the apartment upstairs. It's got a real cool vibe."

Nina escorted the young man to the door, giggling as she went. Nina was smitten, but the young man's interest didn't seem as intense. Lexie sensed apprehension from him about the relationship. Her center picked up on it, but little else. It was as if he had a wall around him, protecting him from the likes of her.

That's odd.

"Isn't he great?" Nina all but floated as she came back to Lexie.

"He seems nice." Lexie ran her thumb over the handle of her baton juju, debating how much to say. "Do you spend a lot of time together?"

"When we're not working, yeah." Nina scanned the few customers still in the shop. "We go out to dinner or spend most of our evenings either at his place or mine. But Mike prefers my place. He's been doing a lot of research on all the Creole townhomes and cottages in The Quarter for his boss, and he dug up some interesting facts on this building."

A flutter swept through Lexie's stomach. "What facts?"

Nina kept her eyes on a couple riffling through the T-shirt rack. "Just stuff on a former owner. He kept his mistresses here. And they all died under mysterious circumstances. Cool, huh?" She hesitated as the customers started pulling T-shirts off the rack and trying them on. "I better see to this."

"I've never encountered any dead mistresses," Magnus said,

appearing next to her. "Nina's new suitor is taking advantage of her. I've seen that young man leaving your old apartment at all hours of the night. Their unseemly behavior could reflect badly on you."

Lexie's jazzy ringtone carried across the store.

"Unseemly behavior? Coming from you, that's rich."

She went behind the long glass display counter to the cash register and retrieved her phone.

The second she saw Emile's name, she forgot all about Mike Le Breaux.

"Hey, Emile. What's up?"

"Where are you?" he asked, the bustle of traffic in the background.

"At the store. Why?"

"Rebecca Soter, the anthropologist I work with at Tulane University, has finished reviewing the pictures from the crime scene of Otis Landry. My supervisor wants you with me on this. Maybe you can ask her questions I can't think of about the spell used."

Her nervousness turned to excitement. "That would be … great."

"Meet me outside your shop. See you in a few minutes."

Lexie gripped her phone, smiling. This is what she had hoped for, to be able to use her ability to help others, not just her customers. Becoming an integral part of an investigation would hopefully build new relationships for her within law enforcement.

Magnus rested his elbow on the glass display counter. "A few months ago, they wouldn't speak to you; now, you're helping to investigate cases. Harold's hold on the NOPD must be slipping."

"Let's hope he's losing control of more than the police." She gathered her large black bag from under the register. "Watch out for Nina while I'm gone."

He squinted at her. "I should go with you."

"I'll be with Emile. Nina could use your help more than me."

He arched an eyebrow. "Perhaps I should use my power of suggestion to get her to stop seeing Mike."

"It's the twenty-first century, Magnus." She eased out from behind the counter. "Women can take care of themselves.

His snide snicker rose around her. "So you keep telling me. But I have yet to see a woman from this time not need a man's advice, help, or brawn. Including you."

She stopped and glowered at him. "Sometimes you really are an ass."

Chapter Eleven

Tremendous oaks with heavy limbs resting on manicured green lawns gave a hint of Southern charm to the parklike setting of Tulane University. Students were everywhere, strolling the walkways, soaking up sun on the benches, playing touch football on Gibson Quad.

Reminds me of the good times I had in school, before taxes, insurance, and ghosts.

Lexie climbed the gray steps to an Elizabethan-style structure while reveling in the youthful energy around her. Made of Alabama limestone, brick, and concrete, Dinwiddie Hall sat at the entrance to the university campus on St. Charles Avenue.

"It's beautiful."

Emile held the heavy wooden door for her. "It is. I've been to a few of the buildings on campus, but spend most of my time at the hospital. A physician there gave me Rebecca's name a few years ago when carved bodies started showing up in the swamps."

Lexie inspected the polished stone floors and wooden beams in the ceiling. She was about to follow Emile when she caught a glimpse of a child's shadow. It had no face or discernable characteristics as it ran across the white wall.

They're everywhere.

"Where did you go to college?" Emile asked, motioning to a set of straight stairs.

Lexie directed her attention back to him. "Suffolk in Boston. I studied interior design." She started up the steps, making sure to maneuver around a few students.

"Is that where you met Will?" Emile asked, keeping up with her.

"No. We met on a job." She stopped on a second-floor landing, inundated with a rush of emotion.

Flashes of their courtship stoked her regret over what they had become—two married people, still very much in love, but kept apart by the evil inhabiting her soul. She recounted the path that had brought them to New Orleans—Altmover Manor, the baton juju, Magnus, and the lure of voodoo. Perhaps if they had stayed in Boston, they would have been happier, but Lexie doubted she would have been content.

She eyed the doors in the long corridor with the names of the professors teaching in the building painted on the frosted glass.

Emile pointed to the right. "Rebecca's up here."

Lexie passed several students, concentrating on their laptops or iPads. Her mind drifted back to the books locked away in Kalfu's library. She wondered if the spell keeping the books bound there could be circumvented by technology. A book might not be able to leave the library for fear of becoming ash, but could a picture be smuggled out?

At the fourth door on the right, Emile stopped and beckoned to Lexie. She read the nameplate.

Rebecca L. Soter, Ph.D. - Professor Anthropology.

Her exuberance fizzled at the idea of meeting with an expert in her field. Never had she felt more like a fledgling in the nest of voodoo. Other priests and priestesses she could handle, but put Ph.D. behind someone's name, and Lexie was sure she would come across as a babbling idiot.

The cramped office had no secretary or sitting area and the sunlight coming from a side window tracked across the linoleum floor to Lexie's feet. The rays soothed her until she spotted the collection of diplomas and certifications on the wall. On the opposite side of the room were an array of wooden shelves cluttered with a variety of bones, skulls, plaster impressions of bones, and some partial skeletons. The macabre objects brought on an unexpected rolling in her stomach, but when she saw the collection of small animal-skin drums in the corner of the shelves, her trepidation turned to delight.

The objects called to Lexie. A hypnotic beat played in her head. Some no bigger than her closed fist, the drums had strange symbols carved into them.

Lexie caressed the closest drum, letting her fingertips absorb the vibe from the skin. Images flashed, a brilliant kaleidoscope of color blended with soulful sounds.

She came out of her trance and found she was no longer in the office, but standing at the edge of a body of water—a bayou, perhaps, or a small lake. Flickering torches circled her, and a stiff breeze made the firelight dance. The pounding of a drum, at first far away, steadily grew louder. People dressed in white appeared caught up in a feverish dance. Seduced by the drums, they swayed, bent, and gyrated to the beat, undulating like pliant dolls in the hands of a master puppeteer.

Her insides tickled. It was a light sensation at first, but then it became more insistent. A woman emerged from amid the dancers, floating above the grassy ground, her long dress caught up in the wind. She had lovely high cheekbones and a delicately curved jaw. Her round black eyes stared at Lexie, her face a mixture of surprise and joy. She dipped her head, the white turban she wore accentuated her bow, and then she motioned for Lexie to join her. Her movements were mesmerizing. Lexie's feet moved, without her commanding them, and she floated toward the woman, carried on a thick cloud of mist.

Black smoke from the torches burned her eyes as she got propelled forward. She wanted to shout for someone to help her, to explain what was going on and as she opened her mouth to call out—

"Lexie?"

She was instantly back in the office. There was no bayou, no powerful priestess compelling her to the shore, no dancers, nothing. Emile was next to her, touching her forearm, the lines on his forehead knitted together.

Her knees buckled, and she clasped his hand, needing to hold onto something in case she tumbled to the floor. She attempted to orient herself, but the lure of the woman who had bewitched her remained.

"You okay?" Emile asked.

"My drum collection often fascinates my students when they come into my office," an airy voice asserted.

A woman stuck her head around Emile's shoulder and smiled.

104

She had creamy, light brown skin, short-cropped black hair, and the prettiest blue eyes Lexie had ever seen. Her high cheekbones and straight nose eluded to her Creole heritage.

"I'm Rebecca Soter." She came out from behind Emile. "I've heard a lot about you, Mambo."

Lexie let go of Emile's hand and straightened. *Get it together.*

"It's a pleasure, Dr. Soter. And please, call me Lexie."

Tall, with the lean figure like a dancer, the professor's movements imitated the woman she'd seen in her vision.

"That's a magnificent piece." Rebecca crept closer. "An authentic baton juju." She clasped her hands together and rested them against her chest. "You're what I've spent years studying. The lore and legends of voodoo."

Emile went to the desk, momentarily distracted by the different papers piled there. "Rebecca is one of the few authorities on voodoo in the country. She's well-known in academic circles for her expertise."

Lexie watched as the woman examined her cane. "Why voodoo?"

Rebecca closed in on the dragon's eyes. "I grew up outside of the city and heard all the stories of Marie Laveau and voodoo practitioners as a child. When I got older, I wanted to find out what was fact and what was fiction about the religion. It's become an obsession."

Emile stepped forward, an impatient furrow across his brow. "Lexie is working with me on the Landry investigation."

Rebecca's gaze swept up and down Lexie's white dress. "The NOPD is lucky to have you. My area of expertise is the religion of voodoo from an anthropological perspective, but I can't explain what you can."

"Which is what?" Lexie asked with a twinge of self-doubt.

Rebecca gave her an indulgent smile. "You can feel the power behind the spells, envision the magic. Only the chosen can do that."

She went to the drum on the shelf Lexie had caressed and picked it up.

"What did you see when you touched this?"

Lexie weighed her sincerity, and then the white light in her sent out a calming pulse, letting her know the professor's interest was genuine.

"A ceremony next to a body of water. Torches, men, and women under the influence of drums, and a woman of great power."

"This drum was said to be used by Marie Laveau during her St. John's Eve celebration on Bayou St. John." Rebecca took the drum to her desk. "You were right, Emile. She has the gift."

"Titu believed in Lexie. So do I." He folded his arms and making the muscles beneath his brown jacket bulge. "Have you found out any more from the pics of the symbols on our latest victim?"

She went behind the desk and hit the space bar on her computer. Pictures of Otis Landry's body came on the screen.

Lexie wished she could close her eyes, but she had a job to do.

"It's the same devouring spell as on the other victims. The carvings look identical." Rebecca motioned to the monitor. "I'm not a trained physician, but even the way the symbols were carved, the depth of the wounds looks the same."

"They are." Emile raised his head to Lexie. "The pathologist thinks the same knife was used on all three victims—a smooth-bladed knife with almost the same efficiency as a surgical scalpel."

Rebecca tapped her finger on her lips, appearing lost in thought. "There's a knife used by pagan religions for slaughtering ritual animals. It's called an athame. It's a black-handled knife with a flat blade, sharpened like a razor. The term comes from Latin for quill knife, which was used to sharpen the pens of scribes. They sell them on Amazon by the hundreds."

Emile let out an exasperated sigh. "Which makes them practically impossible to trace through a vendor."

"What else can you tell us about this devouring spell?" Lexie asked. "Emile said it's used for revenge, but that wasn't the motive here."

Rebecca moved out from behind the desk. "It wasn't created as a revenge spell initially, but as a means to drain an enemy of their power. The spell goes back at least a hundred years and was more common in the swamps than the city."

Lexie faced Emile. "Your last victim was found in the swamps."

He rubbed his chin, nodding. "And he wasn't found far from the spot where our first victim, Gus Favaro was killed."

"But Renee died in the jail," Lexie countered. "Nowhere near either man."

"But she had the swamp with her in her cell," Rebecca added. "Lot of power in the swamps."

The comment sent an uncomfortable jolt through Lexie. Julie Brown's words about the power of the swamp came back to her.

With a spring in her step, Rebecca returned to her desk chair.

Lexie went to the desk and waited as Rebecca opened a file on her computer. Unexpectedly, pictures of Renee, naked and on the floor of her cell at Central Lock-Up, appeared on the screen.

Lexie covered her mouth, shocked at the sight of the woman's bloody body. The last time Lexie had seen Renee alive, she had been terrified and begging for help. Lexie had done nothing to stem her fate. Knowing she had left Renee to the hands of the animal who had cut her into ribbons deepened her grief. She should have done more.

"See that?" Rebecca pointed to a corner on her screen. "Around her feet. There's mud there."

Rebecca enlarged the photo, closing in on Renee's muddy feet.

Emile squinted at the monitor. "My men chalked it up to the guards coming in and out of her cell. It was raining that night, had been raining for days. Everyone had mud on them."

"My guess is that's swamp mud. As long as something of the swamp where those two other men were found is placed on the body of another victim, then he or she symbolically dies in the same place." Rebecca waved at Lexie. "There must be some significance to the swamp. The spell originated there, and perhaps is performed to increase its power."

Lexie gripped her cane, doubting Rebecca's theory. "I can see why they used the revenge spell on Renee. Absorbing her power makes sense. But why use it on those men? They had no power."

"No power that you know of," Rebecca corrected. "Power isn't just about magic. Power can come from money, political connections, property, family ties, anything."

Emile paced in front of the desk. "All the men and Renee Baptiste had in common was they all worked in the French Quarter."

"Which is a powerful place," Rebecca affirmed. "The buildings down there have such a long history. Three hundred years of death, bloodshed, and heartache leaves its mark."

The comment struck Lexie. "What kind of mark?"

Rebecca folded her arms. "In theory, the trauma of the past can imprint on a building, just like a person, and leave a type of energy behind. Ghost hunters claim that accounts for a large percentage of hauntings—residual energy."

Lexie rubbed her thumb back and forth over the handle of her cane, an uncomfortable idea forming. "So, the more trauma happening in a building, the more energy it could have stored up."

"What are you getting at?" Emile demanded.

"There's a man searching The Quarter for properties with traumatic histories. He's a banker out of the northeast, H. Cory. He's getting ready to buy Renee Batiste's old building."

Emile retrieved his phone. "I'll have someone check the other properties belonging to Gus Favaro and Otis Landry. See if any are up for sale or being picked up by this H. Cory."

Rebecca came forward. "But buying up property in the French Quarter from these murder victims isn't a crime. Nothing stays for sale there long. Everyone wants to live there."

Emile frowned at her. "But it's the only lead I have right now to tie the murders together."

"You have the swamps," Lexie insisted. "Whoever did it wanted the murders tied to the swamps. I have a feeling their energy flows through there or is associated with it."

"There's one other thing—voodoo," Rebecca proposed. "The devouring spell used was powerful; it has to be to take the power of its intended victim. It's not something an inexperienced priest or priestess could do. The way the victims were carved, the skill used to kill them reeks of someone very familiar with the black arts. And there aren't a whole lot of people in this region who can do it."

Emile typed something into his phone. "We'll get to work

checking into all the priests and priestesses in the area. Maybe we can find a break."

"There's only one problem with that, Detective." Rebecca went back around her desk. "The person who did this got in and out of a secured prison cell without anyone hearing a thing."

Emile put his phone back in his pocket. "What's your point?"

Rebecca took her chair, staring at the two of them with a grim line across her lips. "What you're looking for isn't a living voodoo practitioner; it's a dead one."

Chapter Twelve

A cool breeze wafted through her living room from the open windows. Settled at her pricey Swedish dining room chair, she examined her husband over the rim of her glass of Chianti. They had decided to make a night of it, with Will offering to cook since they had both arrived home at a reasonable hour with no plans for the evening.

Will scooped up a plate of grilled steaks and carried them to the table. She admired the rope-like muscles of his forearms peeking out beneath his rolled-up sleeves. The ugly images of Renee's cut-up body faded as her love for her husband wrapped around her like a warm blanket. Not only did he put up with her strange ability, supernatural job, and her pesky ghost, but he supported her when things got rough.

"I'm sorry about running out on you like that this morning." She peered into her wineglass. "There's nothing to figure out with us. I love you, and I want you with me always. I was just a little frazzled after meeting with the attorney. Forgive me."

Will set the still sizzling sirloins onto the center of the table.

"There's nothing to forgive. But I'm glad you told me that." Will pulled out his chrome and oak chair. "You had me worried."

"But he cannot give you what I can."

His smoky voice floating through her head chased away the warmth of the wine.

"Go away."

The guilt of her secrets weighed her down. She sipped more wine, anxious for the numbing effects to help her forget about the dark spirit that owned her soul.

"What did Emile say?" Will asked, taking his seat.

"He blew a fuse," she told her husband. "He started tearing into the poor woman telling her there was no way a ghost could have killed Renee. Then he dragged me out of the office before I could ask Rebecca any more questions."

"But why? He knows about Magnus, met him, spoke with him. Why is he so against believing a voodoo priest or priestess could come back from the dead? Emily Mann did."

She put her linen napkin in her lap. "Because he fears the voodoo priestess coming back could be his aunt."

Will paused, his hand halfway across the table to the open bottle of Chianti. "Titu?" He crinkled his eyes. "No way."

Lexie waited as he refilled her glass.

"In the car, he kept asking me over and over if I had seen her or felt her around. He was terrified she might be the one coming back."

"Why terrified?" Will poured his glass of wine. "Wouldn't he want that?"

"No. He believes if she came back, she would suffer, or her immortal soul would suffer. Emile is a devout Catholic. Thinking of his aunt not resting in peace upset him."

Will set the bottle down. "So, you guys any closer to figuring out who did it?"

"No. Nothing adds up. There's nothing to tie the two dead men to Renee, except for the French Quarter. They all had businesses there."

Will lifted the serving tongs. "I bet you're going to have a lot of people waiting to snap up those businesses. Property in the French Quarter is like gold, I hear. I've got several local clients waiting years to get a prime spot there." He nudged a piece of meat onto her plate.

"How can a guy from out of state snap up real estate on Royal Street when you have local clients waiting to buy property?"

He selected a steak. "What are you talking about?"

The aroma from the plate drifted past her nose, and her stomach rumbled. "Nina has a new boyfriend. He's a real estate agent and has been working with some banker from the northeast buying property in The Quarter. He's interested in certain types of homes—ones with a macabre history."

Will eagerly sawed the tip off his steak. "You mean haunted properties?"

She picked up her fork. "I guess. He wants ones where a lot of bad things happened."

"This is the only city where you see Haunted signs hanging below For Sale or For Lease signs. Haunted homes go for bigger prices in The Quarter. You've got a lot of people into ghosts nowadays. Imagine if word got out about you and what's his name? You'd probably get a reality TV show." He popped the piece of steak in his mouth.

"Stop calling Magnus that."

"Yes, tell him to stop." Magnus sat at their table. "I find it rude."

Lexie set her fork aside and cast a wary gaze at Will.

Magnus held up his hands as if expecting a harsh chastisement. "I know, but something has come up."

"What is it?"

Will glanced up from his plate. "What's what?"

She nodded to the side of the table where Magnus waited, knowing Will would not be happy about his visit.

"We have company."

Will set his knife and fork aside, frowning. "He promised to stay away."

She put her hand over his, begging her husband's indulgence. "Magnus only comes if something is wrong. Let's hear him out."

Will stood and put his napkin to the side of his plate. "You hear him out while I open another bottle of wine. I have a feeling we're gonna need it."

He walked into the kitchen.

Lexie sighed, sensing Will wasn't happy. She sat back and reached for her wine.

"Why are you here?"

Magnus arched his back, a dissatisfied glint in his eyes. "You must do something about Nina and her young man."

Lexie sagged in her chair. "Are you kidding me? You interrupted my dinner because of Nina and her boyfriend?"

"No, I interrupted your dinner because of what Nina's boyfriend is doing in your shop right now."

She wasn't interested in what Magnus had to say. It would be more of his nineteenth-century values offended by twenty-first-century realities.

"Magnus, I don't care if he and Nina are—"

"He's robbing you."

Lexie banged her wineglass on the table, stunned. "What?"

"He and two other men are in your shop right now. He sent Nina upstairs to her apartment to get ready for the date while he stayed in the store. When she was gone, he opened the door and let two others in. They started going through the place. I came right away to get you."

She stood, and Will came rushing up to her.

"What's wrong?"

She found her purse and dug out the keys to the Cadillac. "Something is going on at the store. Magnus said we're being robbed."

Will's expression fell. He snapped up his wallet and phone. "I'll drive. You call Emile."

Blue lights bounced off the surrounding buildings in the narrow French Quarter street when Will parked his BMW outside of her shop. Two police cars sat at odd angles and had attracted a crowd of tourists eager to see a seedier side of the city.

Lexie glanced up at the Creole townhouse with its second-floor balcony wrapped in romantic wrought iron. Lights in the apartment above her shop were ablaze and she could hear people shouting inside.

Her ribbon undulated, the black and white in a turmoil. She

reached out, but a disturbing picture presented itself. It wasn't a robbery. Something else was going on.

Will came around the side of the car and put a protective arm around her. He guided her to the entrance where a police officer in his dress blues stopped them.

"You have to stay out here."

Lexie broke free from Will while trying to peek inside. "This is my shop. I own it. Is Detective Emile Glapion here? We called him before we came."

The officer with bulging biceps shook his head. "No, ma'am."

Another policeman, wearing a wrinkled black jacket with a badge hooked on his belt, came to the door. In his hand was an iPad. When he saw Lexie and Will, he wrinkled his brow.

"Are you Lexie Arden?"

"Lexie Bennett," Will corrected. "My wife."

The officer ignored Will. "You're mambo, right?"

She held her head up proudly. "Yes, I am."

The officer waved her inside. She climbed the step into her store and immediately searched the floor for any destroyed merchandise. But nothing was out of place. The shelves of voodoo items, books, and racks of T-shirts were all as she had left them earlier that evening.

"Lexie, why did you call the cops?" Nina rushed up to her wearing a pretty blue sundress, her hair pinned atop her head and red gloss brightening her lips.

"We were being robbed? I ..." She felt the eyes of the other policemen gathered in her shop. "I got a signal from ... my alarm company."

Nina raised her eyebrows, about to say something, then stopped and gave Lexie a knowing gaze.

"Did your *alarm* tell you Mike was down here getting my purse." She looked behind Lexie. "Or did he miss that part?"

Magnus popped up next to Nina. "I know what I saw. Mike let two others into the store. I'm dead, not senile."

Lexie shook her head, not sure who to believe. The situation seemed incomprehensible.

"I came down from the apartment." Mike came up and wrapped his arm around Nina's waist. "Maybe I forgot to turn off the alarm."

Lexie's gaze shot to Nina. The store didn't have an alarm.

"Okay." The detective stepped forward. "We'll have to write this up as a false report. If we get called out again for another alarm trip, you'll be fined. Have a good evening, Ms. Arden."

"Mrs. Bennett," Will grumbled behind her.

Shit! How was she going to talk her way out of this with her husband, Mike, or even Nina?

Her black ribbon rippled, oozing with smug satisfaction. Kalfu enjoyed watching her discomfort. Every situation that filled her with dread, he delighted. Anger, disgust, and fear strengthened his hold on her. Without Will to hold her back from the brink, she feared what she might become under Kalfu's masterful hand.

Lexie went to the shop door and secured the lock after the last officer left. She rested her head against the glass, summoning the courage to endure the backlash sure to come. She was so tired of juggling everyone's emotions and concerns while ignoring her own.

When the flashing blue lights coming through the windows stopped, she counted to ten before she faced the others.

"Mike let the intruders in. He's up to no good." Magnus hovered to the side, resting an elbow on a rack of T-shirts. "You have to believe me."

Nina took a step closer, her hands on her hips. "Did *he* tell you Mike was a robber?"

Lexie slowly trudged back to the center of her store.

"Did who tell her?" Mike asked.

"Magnus," Nina and Will said in unison.

"Magnus? The ghost you told me about?" Mike snickered, his broad shoulders shaking. "I thought you were kidding about that."

Nina opened her mouth to speak, but Lexie cut her off. "This conversation ends here. Mike, I do have a ghost named Magnus Blackwell. He's my spirit guide. Yes, Nina, he told me we were being robbed. He mistook Mike for an intruder."

A blast of cold air passed on her left, and then Magnus stood before her with a menacing scowl.

"Don't doubt me, Lexie. I've never doubted you."

Will grabbed her hand, forcing her to turn away. "Enough of this. We're going home."

She wanted to reassure Magnus she wasn't angry, and just as suspicious as he was, but Will's furious grip told her not to do anything. She had to deal with her husband first.

"He should apologize," Nina said when she stopped before the french doors to Royal Street.

Will undid the deadbolt. "Don't hold your breath. He's not the kind to apologize for his mistakes."

Before Will shut the door, Lexie locked eyes with her ghost. The sense of betrayal she felt in him tore at her.

"Our first quiet evening together in weeks wasted," Will muttered under his breath.

He held the car door open as she climbed inside.

"You need to talk to him."

"I will, don't worry." Her anger came through in the low

growl of her voice. "But no matter how many times he does things like this, you must remember, we're in this together."

Will knelt, his mouth pulled tight like a drum. "I'm trying damn hard to make room for your ghost in our lives, but when we have children, when we have family and friends over for the holidays, when my clients visit, how will we explain him?"

The lump in her throat silenced her. The mention of children added to the guilt festering in her soul.

Will's furrowed brow softened, and he patted her hand. "I'm sure we can come up with something." He got up and gently closed her door.

Lexie focused on the street, fighting like hell not to cry. Will could never see her black tears. No one could.

Thick drifts of mist swirled around Magnus's feet as he stood at the doorway to his world of shadows. Lexie's pale face in the window of Will's car erased his determination to go after her and press his argument. He didn't have the heart. The blonde with the smashing figure and radiant blue eyes had become his world. Any suffering he caused her desolated him.

The white ribbon connecting them felt heavy. Her pain was his. Magnus vowed to do everything he could to bring some joy to her world. In life, he'd strived to make people miserable. In death, he wanted to help Lexie experience happiness. How the tables had turned.

"You care deeply for her, don't you?"

The seductive voice cascaded through his being, creating a

ripple of angst.

The mist thickened to his left, taking on a shape. Colors swirled, vibrant hues of green, red, and sea blue.

A smiling Maman Brigitte stepped from a column of fog, radiating an ethereal light. The heavy mist around her retreated to reveal a deep green cape and matching velvet gown.

Magnus gripped his cane, angered by her question. A man who never readily revealed his emotions to anyone, he wasn't about to start, especially not with some upstart spirit of death.

"This is a surprise."

"She doesn't appreciate you, Mr. Blackwell. You survived years of torment to be by her side. I could give you so much more."

He grinned. *Ah, there it is—the lure.*

"What would you give me? Eternity at your beck and call? A spirit bound to do your bidding? I belong to Lexie; that's enough for me."

"But what if I could free you of her? You could join your family, your Frances, your Katherine. You could return to a time where you reigned as a king. You would feel at home again, and not stuck in the digital age where everything either has a damned whistle or bell or horn coming out of some small black box. It's bullshit." She wrinkled her brow as she frowned.

"Are you the one sending my family to tempt me back to the land of the dead?"

Her coquettish smile reminded him of the women from his time. The pretty ones like his Katie who had used the subtle gesture to captivate men.

"Alas, Mr. Blackwell, I'm not the asshole here. Your family has been freed from the River of Shadows, and though I may have guided them your way, I didn't release them. You already know the smug shit who did."

He rocked his head back, his frustration growing. "Yes. I know what Kalfu did."

A smile still painted on her pretty pink lips, she drifted closer to him. "But the time is coming when your family and the others in the city must return to the River of Shadows. The longer they stay, the greater the danger to humans. The living and the dead aren't meant to exist on the same plane."

"But they do coexist," he argued. "Have for a long time. But I, for one, would not like to float into my family in this world. Death is hard enough without the constant reminder of the losses one has endured."

"But your family will return to the river, and you can go with them. I can arrange it. And you will find joy, not unhappiness in your reunion. The way it was meant to be."

What he knew of death wasn't pleasant, and he doubted it ever would be.

"My duty is to Lexie."

"Your duty is to a woman who doubts you, who ignores your advice, who puts other humans before you? You have so much to offer, and she refuses to acknowledge it. It seems your skills are wasted here. I could use a ghost with your balls. Join the others in the river. I can elevate you above the rest to work with me."

Magnus had spent enough time among the living to know when someone was conning him. He found her blatant attempt amusing.

"Thank you, dear lady, but I will remain where I am."

Maman Brigitte snickered and wrapped her green cape around her. "The offer will remain open, Mr. Blackwell. One day, you will want to accept it. Of that, I have no doubt."

The hem of her cape changed into green smoke, climbing upward like a spiraling staircase and obliterating every last trace of her clothes. When the mist covered her face, Maman Brigitte grinned and then faded. A cold breeze blew away the last traces of eerie green fog.

Magnus let his murky world envelop him, eager to shut himself up so he could think.

The games these spirits play. Makes me miss the living.

Chapter Thirteen

The flash of light blinded Lexie as Will hit the switch just inside the door to their condo. The lingering smell of charbroiled steaks hung in the air. She mourned the loss of her dinner. Having not eaten all day added to the fatigue coursing through her limbs.

"What the hell got into Magnus?"

She flinched when Will slammed his car keys on the table by the door.

"After the day you had, you didn't need any more stress. Neither of us did." He went to the dining table. "If he wasn't already dead, I could kill him for upsetting you like that."

Lexie slipped her big black purse from her shoulder. "I believe he saw something. Magnus may be a lot of things, but he's a sharp man."

"I knew you would take his side on this." Will tossed up his hands. "Sometimes I think you have a better relationship with your ghost than you do with me."

He headed to the corner of the kitchen counter and snapped up the bottle of scotch.

"I'm not married to Magnus. He was chosen for me. You're the one I chose to be with." She pointed to the bottle. "Put that down and let's talk about this."

"Now you want to talk? Since we moved here, you've been avoiding talking about what's bothering you." He cracked the seal on the bottle and then went in search of a glass. "If we're going to talk, you go first. You owe me that."

She massaged her throbbing temples, the black in her rippling with annoyance. She concentrated on keeping her darkness quiet. The last thing she needed was letting the black in her take control.

"I don't want to argue. Can we talk tomorrow when we are both clearheaded?"

He poured a drink, a glint of fury in his eyes. "No, Lexie. We can't wait anymore. I'm tired of tiptoeing around you, afraid of upsetting you. You've been miserable lately. I want to know why. I've done everything I can think of to make you happy. I even spent a fortune on this place because I thought you wanted to have a home."

Like the snap of a dry twig, the black in her shifted and careened throughout her body, filling her veins with icy anger. Her headache forgotten, Lexie stormed up to Will.

"You're the one who wanted to move here. I wanted to stay in our apartment over the shop. There we were happy. Here—" She froze, realizing the blackness had taken over.

Will's cheeks reddened. He banged the bottle on the counter. "Here, we're what? Say it!"

A battle ensued inside her body—the ribbons of black and

white entangled. Part of her wanted to hold back, appease her husband and keep the status quo, but another part, fueled by Kalfu's need for chaos, wished to speak out.

"We're miserable!" she shouted as she tossed her handbag onto the breakfast bar. "I thought I used to know you. But then you went on those spending sprees in antique shops and expensive furniture stores, claiming we had to fill our home with the best. You've changed."

He rested his hip against the counter and combed his hand through his thick brown hair. "We used to want the same things, have the same goals—to have a great home and a family together. Then you found that baton juju and everything changed. He came into our lives and I thought we could work around the voodoo and the spirits floating in and out of our house. I've put up with a hell of a lot, Lexie. How much more do you expect me to take before I can't do this anymore?"

It had always been there between them—his unspoken misgivings about her world. The ghosts, the voodoo, the store, and Magnus had intruded on their marriage, but she had never realized how much it had bothered Will until then.

When they had set out on this journey, uprooted their lives in Boston and moved to New Orleans, she'd thought it was because Will supported her. Having his support yanked from her shook her.

"See? Your life with him has been a lie."

Kalfu's voice compounded her anger. Her gut burned with betrayal.

Suddenly, it all became too much. Kalfu, Will, her life … She needed to get away.

Will's anger melted from his eyes and the deep lines in his face smoothed. He moved toward her, brushing his hand over her hair and cupping the back of her neck.

"I'm sorry. I didn't mean it, baby. I'm hungry and tired. You know how grouchy I get when I don't eat."

He tempered the tension between them with a smile, but it did nothing to ease her fear. Perhaps Kalfu had been right. Will had been playing along, appeasing her, maybe with the hope she might one day grow bored with her shop and her ghost and return to him, ready to start anew.

"I think you did mean it." She backed away, her insides a black cloud, smothering her reason. "We both know things have gotten worse between us."

"Lexie." His deep voice rattled around the kitchen. "It's just a rough patch. All marriages have them. You're stressed. My business is busy as hell. We're both just tired and hungry, that's all."

He went to put his arms around her, and she wanted nothing more than to curl into his chest and tell him how much she loved him, but something stopped her. If she stayed, if she opened up to him, he would learn the truth. She couldn't let that happen.

It tore her apart to pull away from him, but she did. The cold enveloped as she stepped back, avoiding his eyes.

"I think it would be best if I were alone for a little while."

He tensed and wiped his face. "What? You want me to go to a hotel? Sleep in my office? What do you want?"

She bit her lower lip, fighting back the tears.

I should leave before things get worse.

She grabbed her purse. "I'll see you in the morning."

Lexie took off for the front door, desperate to get away before she fell apart completely.

"Where are you going?" he called, running after her. "Lexie, stop."

She fumbled with the lock, hurrying to open the front door before he reached her. "I'll be fine. You don't have to worry about me."

She slammed the door in his face, her heart racing.

Tears blurred her eyes. Barely able to see, she hurried down the dimly lit hall to the elevator, numb with heartache.

She needed some place quiet to figure out what to do and regroup so she could face Will again and not fall apart. It was getting harder to keep her secret from him, but she had to, no matter how painful.

She frantically pushed the call button for the elevator, and then the creak of a front door opening sent her heart climbing into her throat.

The idea of confronting Will one more time weakened her knees. Thankfully, the elevator door opened and she slipped inside.

Just as the doors closed, Kalfu's face floated in front of her.

She should have known he would appear at her worst moment. He fed off her misery. Like a tick, he sucked whatever strength she had and took advantage of her weakened state.

But there was one thing he could not penetrate—her resolve. She had to stay sharp, no matter how physically drained she became.

"I'll see you at the cottage," he said. "We have work to do."

Chapter Fourteen

The moon spread tendrils of silver light over the dark water next to the Acadian cottage as Lexie maneuvered her car along the shell-covered drive. She released her death grip on the steering wheel, flexing life back into her stiff fingers. Her mind consumed with the argument with Will, she hadn't paid attention to where she was going, but somehow had arrived at Kalila's old home.

The beams of her headlights shone on the dark swamp water as she wondered what to do. Did she go back to the city and make up with her husband? Or did she stay here for the night?

"You can't stay here."

Magnus bloomed next to her, a dim light growing in wattage as his red waistcoat and shiny black coat came into view.

"Alone in the middle of the swamps? You turn around and head back to the city."

"Magnus, I can't go back. I'm too damned tired and upset to

drive anymore. I'm amazed I even got here."

"Why did you leave?"

She traced the outline of the stitching in the leather steering wheel. "I was afraid Will would find out about me. All I could think to do was run away." A black tear snuck down her cheek. "If he finds out, he'll leave me or worse—hate me."

"He will never leave you, especially when he finds out what you did to save him."

"But will he be able to live with me?" She wiped her nose on her sleeve. "Knowing what I am. What's inside me." She gazed up at the moonlight-bathed cottage. "I have to figure out what to do. I was hoping I could come here and think … alone."

He haughtily snorted. "Why you were determined to come out here is beyond me."

She collected her purse and reached for the door. "It's all I could think of."

The crisp night air and gentle breeze tossing around the tops of the trees re-energized her. It felt good to be out of the car. The scratching of the branches on the tin roof frightened her until she realized what it was. Frogs, crickets, and an assortment of light bugs serenaded her as she made her way across a blanket of brown cypress leaves to the porch steps.

She climbed one step at a time while hunting in her purse for the house keys. She was sure she'd left them in there, but there was no light for her to see what she was doing. The boards of the porch moaned as she inched closer to the door.

"Where are those damn keys?"

The porch lights came on.

Magnus frowned. "He's been expecting you."

The lock clicked, and the front door creaked open.

Magnus put his hand across the doorway. "I will be out here if you need me."

His concern was hers for a moment. The heaviness in him added to her guilt.

"I'll be fine. He won't hurt me."

"No, he won't. He'll play with you for a while until he grows bored."

"That's why I have to find a way—"

A shimmering light appeared in the open doorway. It spread like a radiant star about to explode. Then the brilliance got sucked into the center of a figure standing inside the house.

In casual jeans and a snug T-shirt, Kalfu had the stunning looks of a Greek god. His malevolent blue eyes ran up and down Lexie's white dress. He gave her a perfect smile.

She cringed. All her nightmares began with that smile.

"It is your Mr. Blackwell with the long history of hurting women. I worship them."

Magnus puffed out his chest. "We both know better."

Kalfu flicked his wrist and sent Magnus hurtling backward into the railing.

"Run along, ghost. I will care for my charge."

"Stop it." Lexie gave Kalfu a wary glare and strutted inside.

Kalfu shut the door without laying a finger on it. "Where is your cane?"

She hadn't realized she didn't have it until he asked.

"I left it at home."

"Never venture into the swamps without it. Your cane reminds people who you are."

She set her purse on a square dining table, her mind a jumbled mess. "Tonight, I want no reminders of who I am. I just want a little peace."

Kalfu laughed and strolled across the floor, his bare feet not making a sound.

"There is no peace for you." His voice took on a hard edge. "You're something the rest of the world longs to be—powerful. You cannot let silly little fights with your husband interfere with your duty to me."

His arrogance infuriated her. "Will is more important to me than you will ever be."

"But he can never give you what I can. He will try and control you and keep you under his thumb. I will never do that to you." Kalfu crept closer. "Swear your sole allegiance to me. Cast off Damballah and his fake promises."

She should have guessed. He would never want to share her with Damballah. Owning her would hurt the balance of power, and shift the forces of the universe in his favor.

She boldly snickered. "Fake promises? That's your department."

"Do not test me." His voice dropped, quivering with anger. "I took your ovaries, but I can do far worse. Others have displeased me and their suffering continues in my realm. Be smarter than they were."

"Yes, I've seen what you can do. The Chez twins bear the marks of your disapproval."

The darkness in his face lifted. He sat on the dining room table, clapping his hands together.

"What are you talking about? I never touched Madeline Chez's daughters. She was a whore with a penchant for hard liquor. I don't waste my powers on such trash."

Lexie frowned. "I was told you blinded them."

His laughter echoed throughout the house. "And you think I'm the one telling you lies. Think again. The Chez twins are great deceivers, just like the bitch who rules them. Maman Brigitte is well-known for her deceptions. Tread carefully around her girls. They're as vile as their master."

Lexie was sick of the games, sick of second-guessing the intentions of every spirit she met.

"You can trust me, Lexie Arden." Kalfu got off the table and took a step toward her. "I can give you everything you want."

Disgust rolled in her stomach. She put her hand over her belly, holding back her desire to explode with a litany of curse words.

"I want a family and my husband. I love Will and wish I was with him now, but I bet something as cold and dead as yourself could never understand what we share."

Kalfu snapped his fingers. A dinner service of gold plates and gold stemware became visible on the table. The crystal goblets, filled with red wine, glistened in the light.

"You're overwrought and not making a bit of sense. You need food."

She backed away, anxious to get out from under his gaze. "I don't want anything from you."

"You are stubborn." Kalfu studied her face. "What will it take for you to cast off Damballah and serve only me?"

Lexie remembered the library down the hall and Kalfu's inability to enter the room. Perhaps she could find some way to free herself of the insufferable spirit. The sooner she did, the better for her sanity and her marriage.

She took another step back, determined to get to the library. "I will never give up Damballah. He's the goodness and white energy within me. You're the one who needs to go."

Kalfu didn't react, didn't move a muscle in response. He kept staring down at her, devouring her with his eyes. His caustic gaze reached into her soul like a slithering snake, gauging her sincerity. A tightness rose in her chest. This was how it began—his punishment.

Maman Brigitte's words came back to her. She pictured a child in her arms. Her child, warm and beautiful, and filled with the love she and Will would give it.

The wall of white light rose from her center. The black retreated, the tightness faded.

Kalfu cocked an eyebrow, his face as impassive as stone. "What is done is done, and once bound to me, you can never be unbound. All your predecessors tried to be free of me and failed. So will you."

Lexie swallowed her revulsion. She would spend her entire life, if necessary, searching for a means to free her soul.

He walked up to her, the sly smile back on his lips. "Enough of this fantasy of leaving my control. It's time to get to work, Lexie Arden."

She opened her mouth to protest, but a black shroud slammed down in front of her, blocking Kalfu's evil grin. A cold breeze swirled around her.

Lexie wrapped her arms around herself. She needed to be alone. Her gaze went to the hallway entrance. The library. There she could think without interruption.

She took off and ran toward the library.

In the hallway, the candle-shaped sconces on the wall flickered on, one by one, lighting her way.

His constant presence, the way he watched her every move, added to her fright and desperation.

"Leave me alone."

She reached the thick cypress door to the library and wrestled with the doorknob. When the lock gave way, she stumbled into the room.

Instantly, she knew he wasn't there. The blackness in her retreated and peace permeated her being.

Sanctuary.

It was the only place she'd been free of his constant, suffocating presence since the moment she'd thrust her hand into the pile of herbs that fateful day she'd committed herself to him. The burden of what she'd endured lifted from her shoulders. Here she was free to think, speak, and plot how to break from his control.

At the first bookcase, Lexie ran her fingers along the dusty spines, reading the titles. She took her time, getting an impression of the books housed there. Several titles surprised her.

How to Become a Voodoo Priestess in 30 Days. What Voodoo Means to You. The Voodoo Diet. Having Fun with Voodoo

Some titles seemed too hokey, but they were there.

The older, leather-bound books—faded and cracked by time—interested her the most. Any spell to help her banish Kalfu had to be in one of those.

She went through the shelves, searching for the oldest of the books. It took her a while, and soon a thin layer of dust stained her dress. She set the books she collected on the floor in the middle of the room.

Her fingertips tingled when she opened the first book—*A Compendium of Rituals and Spells Used in Voodoo.*

She scanned the table of contents but found nothing on spells to unbind a spirit from a mortal. She put it aside and picked up another book.

A craggy voice across the room said, "That's not the one you want."

Lexie peered into the shadows gathered in the same corner where she'd last seen Julie Brown. She waited, eager to make out the older woman's shape. Then a twinkling ball of faint light manifested a few feet above the ground.

It stretched into a thin beam, shooting up to the ceiling. The shadow of a hunched over woman shone inside the light. Her figure was small at first but steadily grew as her outline took on depth and color. When she reached full height, the red in her long skirt and turban stood out. Her black shawl came into focus. Then her scarred face and desolate eyes turned to Lexie. She moved from the light, shuffling as she went. She approached Lexie, her gaze downcast, a defeated soul trapped in her self-imposed purgatory.

"The unbindin' spell you need ain't in those old books." She removed the pipe clenched between her teeth and pointed it at a shelf. "It's there in the journal of another once bound to Kalfu. It tells you how to get rid of him."

Lexie got up from the floor. "How did you know?"

"It's what every priestess tied to him looks for when they first come here."

Lexie went to the bookcase. "And what happened? Did any free themselves?"

"One did," Julie replied in a cold, harsh voice. "But the rest gave up."

Lexie was about to question why the others had given up when she spotted a notebook. The binding was warped and cracked, and its pages had crinkled and yellowed with age. She gently worked it out from between a few other books. After wiping the dust away, she strained to read the name printed on the cover. She finally made out the letters and her breath caught in her throat.

Madame Cecily Henri

"This is Madame Henri's notebook."

Julie inhaled a deep breath from her pipe. "Yes, Cecily crafted the spell to free her of his power." Wafts of pipe smoke drifted around her head. "She was devoted to him at first, but then she grew to hate him, almost as much as you."

Lexie gripped the notebook, her mind reeling.

"She never mentioned this spell to me."

Julie puffed on her pipe. "She still fears what else Kalfu will do to her if she tells, but that doesn't mean she can't compel you."

Lexie lost Julie's face behind a veil of smoke, unable to read her features.

"Cecily wanted me to find this?"

"If you can free yourself of him, you will be a mambo like no other. To bend the gods to your will is somethin' mortals don't have the power to do."

Lexie tipped her head, deliberating her comment. "What about ghosts? Can mortals control them? Make them do what we want, go where we want, or even disappear?"

Julie emerged from behind the smoke of her pipe. "What you have in mind?"

Chapter Fifteen

The ugly burn of uncertainty consumed Magnus as he paced the porch of the cottage. Not a word from Lexie in hours. He could not reach her, could not feel her inside the home. The vile Kalfu had cut him off, sending only waves of blackness to block Magnus's connection to her. Unable to go inside or call for help, he waited, paced, and prayed.

Damn you, Kalfu.

The ribbon of black and white in his being pulsated, letting him know something was amiss. He felt the change anytime Lexie's world went through a shift or when trouble was nearby. He had to investigate the disturbance, but that would mean leaving Lexie. The vibration continued, becoming more insistent. Without resisting, he let the disruptive energy pull him away from the cottage.

He passed through a layer of mist and arrived in Lexie's shop.

The streetlights outside streamed in through the glass in the french doors, creating enough light to show Magnus why he'd been called to the store.

The streetlamps allowed Magnus to inspect the displays of votive candles, gris-gris pouches, and amulet charms. His intuition itched. All was not what it seemed.

The murmur of conversation drifted from a corner of the shop, next to a shelf stuffed with children's toys. His alarm rising, he floated closer. It was the middle of the night.

No one should be in here.

Three figures stood shrouded in shadows. Then the taller of the three moved into a ray of light coming through the windows. Magnus instantly recognized his face—Mike Le Breaux.

Mike's cohorts, both of whom wore black hoodies, examined the wall, patting the textured plaster with their hands.

Magnus wanted to wrap his cane across the backs of their heads, but instead of lashing out and showing himself to scare them away, he crept closer. He needed to know why they were in Lexie's shop.

"They're here," a high-pitched woman's voice said from under one of the hoodies. "Lexie Arden's ability has turned her shop into a beacon of light for the dead. It's just as powerful as Renee's shop."

A passing car on Royal Street sent a bright beam into the store. It was enough to reveal the faces hidden beneath the hoodies.

Two women with flaming red hair and piercing blue eyes stared right at Magnus.

The Chez sisters? He'd recognize the detestable disciples of Maman Brigitte anywhere.

"We must get possession of this place," one of the sisters said. "We can attract them to this building and hold them here."

SEIZE

They weren't speaking in riddles or acting like the insane priestesses whose antics he had witnessed in the past. And their eyes were normal. But why were they with Mike?

They must have been the ones with him earlier.

Magnus wanted to rush back to Lexie and report what was happening, but until he had something substantial to give her, he had to remain and learn all he could.

"And the girl? You positive she's out?"

Magnus wasn't sure if it was Corinne or Helen speaking. The women looked alike to him.

Mike stepped away from the wall, shoving his hands in the pockets of his jeans. "I gave her all of your potion. She'll sleep until morning." He surveyed the shop. "What about the mambo's ghost? What if he shows up again?"

A muffled cackle erupted from both women.

"Once the mambo is out of the way, he will return to the land of the dead," the other quickly added.

Out of the way?

His fury ignited. They could threaten him, but they'd better not touch Lexie.

Mike went to a small table covered with rosary beads decorated with voodoo symbols. He picked up one of the trinkets, eyeing the details in a beam of streetlight.

"I want more money this time. This building will cost double the others."

The tension in the air thickened. Magnus swore he heard one of the twins growl.

A black hoodie darted up to Mike, going around a display of miniature coffins filled with candy skeletons.

The way she maneuvered the tight aisles made Magnus

139

question if she was blind. He couldn't wait to tell Lexie.

"You agreed to a price for each building you closed when Harold set up this deal. You must stick to the arrangement," she argued in a raised tone.

Magnus shook with anger. They had all lied to Lexie. Mike's intentions for Nina were nothing more than a ploy to get access to the shop. Lexie's rival, Harold Forneaux, was determined to put her out of business.

The other sister flew to her sibling's side, her wild red hair bouncing on her shoulders as she skillfully dodged a pile of decoratively painted skull candle holders.

Mike staggered backward, his eyes wide with fear. "Wrangling the sale of the other buildings didn't require me to sleep with the tenants. And I'm not going to let you hurt that girl upstairs."

"Silly boy." One of the women got right under his chin. "We won't hurt her. It's the mambo we want. If she's gone, then we can control the city."

The black in Magnus ignited. He had to warn Lexie.

Magnus summoned his energy, ready to depart when the air changed. Something cold and evil reached out to him. It circled one of the sisters and then slithered deeper into the aisle. A black tentacle weaved and bobbed as it traveled toward him.

"Someone's here," one of the sisters whispered feet from where he stood. "A ghost of a man."

"Is it her ghost?" Mike asked, balling his fists.

Time to go.

Magnus pictured the cottage in the swamp and willed himself to Lexie's side.

He materialized in the same spot he'd left. The light in the window next to him was out, and the only whisperings he detected

140

were those of the insects and animals in the swamps.

Magnus directed his center to the house, attempting to reach inside, but a barrier of black smoke barred his entry. Frustrated, he banged his cane on the porch boards. He would have to wait for Lexie to come to him. He peered into the night, an uncomfortable sensation gathering in his center. He was not alone.

The eerie howl of a dog cut through the swamp. Coyote or wolf, he wasn't sure. He'd been raised on a barren island in Maine and amid the social set of Boston. What did he know of wildlife in Louisiana?

A second howl followed but sounded closer than before. He swore there was something off about the low, long call. It seemed less animal-like, and more human, almost like a man in pain.

Silence returned, but this time there was no buzzing of insects or hoots of owls to remind him where he was. A dead calm carried through the still night.

A rush of footfalls came from the shelled road. He floated toward the front of the cottage, attentive to the rumble of someone or something charging toward the house.

On the porch, he took on a defensive stance, ready to confront the intruder. A low, guttural growl came from the front yard. He frantically searched for anything that could have made such a noise. It was difficult to see, but when a cloud passed in front of the moon, the entire swamp turned pitch black.

Magnus used all his senses to discover what drew closer to the cottage. His insides rippled, and a pressure weighed on his center—an individual was there. Alive or dead, he wasn't sure. Something was off. It was as if the being couldn't make up its mind what it was.

I've never encountered this before.

The cloud passed, and the moonlight returned, sweeping over the grass. Magnus scoured the land, inspecting every knotted pine tree and shrub. A rustling came from behind some bushes at the edge of the driveway. Unable to detect anything with his eyes or his ability, Magnus brandished his cane, ready to face whatever approached. He could not harm any living thing, but his old human instincts died hard.

He thought he saw movement in the shadows of a nearby cypress. Then something darted from one side of the yard to another. It did not move like a man but an animal.

He didn't like this. Animals were unpredictable and could attack and kill without provocation. He needed to keep Lexie inside the cabin.

A creature, crouched on four legs, crept toward the porch. All black, it moved like a hungry predator.

A growl rose from the grassy land. The wind swept past, rustling the branches of the nearby trees.

It stepped into the light and fear knotted in Magnus's center. It was big and had a broad snout.

Magnus edged closer to the railing to get a better look, and the animal's glowing yellow eyes tracked him. The large dog couldn't have seen him. Convinced the beast had spotted something else, Magnus waited at the porch steps.

But the frightening eyes stayed locked on him, sending a wave of shock through Magnus's system.

Another passing cloud sent the entire front yard into darkness. Magnus lost the canine. He trotted down the steps, examining the yard, eager to find it again. Seconds ticked by. There wasn't a breath or sound. When the cloud moved away and a line of moonlight crossed the yard, there was no trace of the creature.

A large black shadow leaped in front of him, sending him tumbling backward on the steps. When Magnus looked up, a massive paw came down next to him, shaking the boards beneath.

He raised his gaze and came face-to-face with a huge black snout. A wet nose came right up to his chin and sniffed. He inspected the thick, matted coat. There were traces of fresh mud. The lips on the dog's round snout curled back, revealing a set of sharp white fangs.

Magnus stared with fascination at the hulking brute.

"You can see me, can't you?"

With a powerful thrust from its hind legs, the dog jumped on the porch, sniffing the cane and keeping a wary gaze on him.

Magnus reached out, not expecting to make contact with the animal's coat, but to see if he picked up any other strange impressions.

The moment he got close, the black in him trembled. This was no ordinary swamp wolf. His essence would only register such a tremulous reaction if magic protected the animal—black magic.

Magnus stared into the beast's fiery eyes, attempting to use his ability to find out where it had come from. But the creature was as impervious as the house next to him. He knew the swamps contained many mysteries—Lexie's books included lots of legends—but this animal was real, and someone with evil intentions had created it.

Another howl came from a swath of trees not far from the house. Magnus stared across the terrain, eager to see if there was another wolf.

The dog's ears pricked. He sniffed the wind, then crouched and growled.

Apprehension raced through Magnus. Whoever was out there,

the dog didn't like them.

He reached for his cane, feeling safer with it in his hands. The dog leaped from the porch and took off across the yard.

Its speed was incredible. Magnus soon lost it in the night. He'd encountered many entities since becoming a ghost, and none of them had unsettled him as much as the dog. It was as if the powers of the living and the dead resided in the beast, and such an abomination required a great deal of depravity to create.

He remained on the porch steps, cane in hand, to see if the impressive animal returned. But when the early traces of sunlight broached the horizon, he gave up.

Soon, Lexie would come outside. He needed to warn her about the Chez twins and what Harold Forneaux had planned. She was in danger, and until he was sure Lexie was safe, Magnus wouldn't leave her side.

Chapter Sixteen

Lexie opened the front door, letting the early morning sunlight stream into the cottage. She stepped onto the creaky boards of the porch. Her heart still heavy from the argument with Will, she wanted to breathe in the fresh air to clear her head from the musty library before calling her husband.

"Where have you been?"

Magnus stood next to her at the railing, his nostrils flaring.

She rarely saw her ghost agitated. Usually, he was the calm one.

"I've been reading. I lost track of time."

He glimpsed the open door, an anxious wrinkle in his brow. "Something happened last night at the shop." He arched closer. "Mike let two women in—the Chez twins. He's working for them. They want your building."

Apprehension slinked through her. "Go on."

"Harold Forneaux is involved. I believe he and the twins plan on doing something to you. They want you out of the way so they can control the city."

She tapped one finger on the railing, putting the pieces together. "Harold has already made it very clear that he wants me to step down as mambo. I'd hoped he'd given up on taking away my baton juju."

"The Chez sisters are liars. Corinne and Helen can talk and aren't blind. They mean to get rid of you."

"Kalfu warned me about them. Their mother never sacrificed their sight to him. Everything they do, Maman Brigitte puts them up to." Lexie sucked in the humid air, her outrage escalating. "But why do they want my building?"

Magnus rested against the railing. "The sisters put their hands on the walls as if they were testing the place. They spoke about how the energy in your shop can hold many spirits. Mike is to make the arrangements to purchase your building. It's the reason he seduced Nina."

Her shop assistant was in danger. The guilt she'd experienced after Will's abduction came back in a heated rush. She could not go through that again. She needed to protect Nina.

It all made sense. Harold, along with the Chez sisters, had eliminated property owners in The Quarter to snap up their buildings.

"If Altmover Manor held you because it was your home and the place where you died, then a building in the French Quarter could do the same thing—hold the spirits trapped there, either by death or a past association."

Magnus studied the baton juju in his hand. "But since Altmover burned to the ground, I've been bound to you."

"But we know spirits can attach to people and places. Be drawn to them and held by them." She paused, trying to recall something. "What did Mike say about searching for buildings with a tragic history? Death, heartache, and murder all leave behind a mark on a person or structure."

"A mark composed of energy." Magnus's eyes widened. "They must want to use your shop as a place to bind spirits. To hold them prisoner."

Lexie's heart sank as she rested her hands on the railing. "Not just my building—the others belonging to Otis Landry, Renee, and Gus Favaro."

"But what spirits?" Magnus asked. "New Orleans already has so many."

The vast number of spirits she'd encountered since taking the reins as mambo were tied to people or buildings, making their unbinding an almost Herculean task for any voodoo priest or priestess. But one group of spirits were not bound to any place in the city—the spirits stolen from the River of Shadows.

"The shadow spirits," she muttered. "They could be bound to my building and any other with relative ease."

"And by keeping the spirits out of the river, they could return the city to chaos like before."

"Harold could step in and eradicate the problem, making him the most sought-after priest in the city." Exasperated, Lexie tossed up her hand. "That has to be what they're up to."

Magnus tapped his cane on the porch. "Then Harold would get all the support he needs to get you kicked off the voodoo council and take away your baton juju."

Despair settled in the pit of her stomach. Her fight to remain mambo was far from over. She hoped she had the fortitude to see this through. Her determination to keep her baton juju had stalled under the burden of her troubles.

Lexie rubbed her temples, ashamed she'd not discovered what was happening before now. "We have to tell Emile. We have to implore him to pick up Harold and the Chez twins for questioning."

Magnus's snicker circled in the air. "Lexie, I may have been dead for over a hundred years, but even I know a ghost can't testify against Harold or the Chez sisters. You need a living person for that. All you have now is hearsay."

"Well, what the hell else do we do? We need something to give Emile other than—"

Something ahead on the shelled road caught her eye.

She squinted and swore she saw a large black dog sitting in the middle of the drive.

"What's that?" She pointed to the road.

Magnus peered ahead. "I believe that's the beast I encountered last night. It came right up to the porch and stared at me."

"It could see you?"

Intrigued, she went to the porch steps.

He followed. "Yes. I found the entire encounter rather disturbing. To have such a big, ugly creature sizing me up like a steak almost made me feel human."

Lexie climbed down the steps, wanting to get an up-close look at the dog. She wouldn't put it past Harold or the Chez twins to send another one of the voodoo spirits after her.

"But they don't know you're here. I'm protecting you."

Would his voice ever leave her alone?

"Where are you going?" Magnus called behind her.

More curious than afraid, she eased down the road, her white tennis shoes crunching on the shells. The size of the dog did intimidate her the closer she got. Its enormous muzzle would have sent anyone running, but not Lexie. There was something more about the animal than could be seen with the eye. The nudge of tightness in her chest let her know other forces were at work—magical forces.

She stopped and got down on the dog's level. His thick fur was jet black, matted, and filled with patches of wet mud. He had a muzzle like a St. Bernard and huge paws. But it was the eyes that fascinated her. Bright yellow, they mesmerized.

She stretched out her hand.

"Hey there, baby." She spoke in a high tone of voice, hoping it would put the beast at ease. "You're beautiful. Are you from around here?"

The dog stood and immediately came up to her. He put his cold nose against her hand. She gently rubbed his head, and as she grew more comfortable, scratched his neck and chest.

"You're just a big teddy bear."

"He's obviously a pet." Magnus stopped a few feet away, eyeing the dog.

The creature left her side and walked right up to Magnus. It sat down in front of him.

"He can see you."

Magnus didn't look comfortable. "I've gathered that. Can you sense if he's one of the voodoo spirits?"

Lexie opened her center, but the blackness in her became constricted. However, her white side of power reached out. The animal was friendly, but wary of most people, and then …

Flashes of running through the swamps under the full moon. The thrill of the hunt, the chase through the water and brush. The stray felt alive but it also wasn't a dog anymore but a—

"Lexie? Did you get anything?"

The white ribbon siphoned back into her chest. The tie was broken and the images faded. She wasn't sure what to make of it.

She patted the mutt's head. "He needs a home. A place to sleep and food. He's been on his own for a while."

She was drawn to the creature but had no explanation as to why. He made her feel safe and his presence tamed the black within her. She never wanted to be parted from the dog.

"You're going to keep him?" The shock in Magnus's voice surprised her.

"Yep. With all the shit going in my life, I could use a good watchdog. Maybe this big boy will make Harold and the Chez twins think twice."

"You'll need more than that to protect you. But I would prefer another to keep you safe when I can't." Magnus glanced back at the house. "Who knows what else Kalfu may do to keep me from you?"

A battle was on the way, one for mastery over her cane, and her soul. No matter the outcome, things would change in her life, she sensed it. Lexie hoped all the people she loved would still be beside her when the dust clouds settled. Perhaps then, she could finally become the mambo she felt certain she could be.

Magnus rolled his eyes. "Somehow, I don't see Will being as excited as you."

The mention of her husband brought back the tightness in her chest, but this time it wasn't her power dictating her feelings, it was her heart.

"We'll see."

Chapter Seventeen

The morning sun shone down on her gray warehouse building, sending streams of light across the dull surface. Lexie eased her Cadillac up to the gate entrance of the parking garage beneath the structure. She punched in her code and waited for the gate to rise, tapping her steering wheel as her trepidation squeezed her chest like a vise.

This is gonna suck.

"I did not think it possible a living creature on this Earth could breathe as loudly as that dog. He has not stopped panting since we left the swamps."

Magnus sat next to her, drumming his fingers on his cane.

She turned to the back seat where the animal lay, utterly content.

"Louis can breathe as loud as he wants."

Magnus hiked his upper lip in a condescending sneer. "You

can't be serious about that name."

"I like it." She reached into her purse and turned on her phone.

Almost instantly, a jazzy tune rang out.

She sighed, knowing she could not put off speaking to her husband anymore. She ached to feel his strength and hear his voice.

"Where have you been?" Emile's bellowing deep voice blasted through the speaker. "Will just called me. He's frantic, Lexie!"

A shred of disappointment meandered through her. It wasn't Will. But she did need to update Emile on all that had happened. If he knew who was conspiring against her, he might understand the reasons she'd left.

The yellow lights of the garage shimmered on her car hood as she drove up the ramp to her level. "I have something you need to check out. The two people Mike let into my shop were—"

"Yeah, I got the report from the robbery detective on the scene," he cut in. "He said you claimed it was a false alarm."

She spotted her parking place next to Will's car. "Mike La Breaux went back to the shop later last night, and Magnus saw them. The Chez twins were with him. They mentioned Harold Forneaux is working with them. He's got to be the one behind the killings. He wants to get his hands on the properties in the French Quarter. The devouring spell is proof Harold and the Chez sisters are involved. Who else could do it? They're taking the power of their victims to own all they possess."

Emile remained silent. When he came back, he sounded calmer. "Do you hear what you're saying? I can't go to my department head and ask to bring Harold Forneaux or the Chez sisters in on suspicion of murder because of something your ghost overheard."

She parked the car and turned off the engine. "There has got to be something you can do. We know what they are up to. We have to be able to set them up. Can't you have them followed or watched, or something?"

His heavy breathing kept her from offering any more suggestions.

"Where are you?"

She glimpsed the elevator to her condo a few feet from her car. "In the city. Almost home."

His voice ticked higher. "Until I figure out what's going on, stay in your home. You're not safe alone."

He hung up.

She climbed from the car and pushed her seat forward for Louis to get out.

Magnus popped up next to her. "Do you think the detective will help us?"

She grasped the rope she'd found to use as a leash. "If I know Emile, he'll do some digging."

Magnus walked with her and the dog to the elevator. His attempts to stay out of the lumbering creature's way kept her mind off the inevitable confrontation with Will.

She punched the call button several times, hard.

"You can't go up there angry," Magnus told her. "I remember enough about being a man to know if you attack him, he will get defensive."

"And what if he attacks me?"

Magnus grinned as his black coat and Ascot tie slowly faded. "You can sic Louis on him."

She smashed her lips together, wishing he had hung around. Will might not have wanted her ghost in their condo, but today, she sure did.

The elevator came to a stop on her floor. The doors opened, and she peeked into the hall, expecting to see Will.

On the drive back from the cottage, she'd sent him a text telling him she would be home soon and turned off her phone. What she wanted to say would sound better face-to-face.

She'd practiced her speech in her head while driving, hoping she would sound convincing by the time she gazed into her husband's eyes.

At the polished oak door to her condo, she gripped Louis's rope, hesitating.

Before she had touched her key to the lock, the door flew open.

Already dressed for the day in a gray pinstripe suit, Will stood before her, his hair still damp, and his brown eyes bloodshot.

A flood of emotions tore through her—regret being the biggest. Running away had been a mistake, she knew that, and the misery it had caused both of them would take a while to repair. But part of her acknowledged that the night in Kalfu's cottage had opened her eyes to her future as mambo. She had discovered her way out from his dark embrace, and if she could pull it off, she and Will could have the life they'd planned.

Louis growled.

Will's tense expression changed to wide-eyed disbelief. He scratched his head, staring at the creature and seeming at a loss for words.

"Where did you go?"

The black in her barreled upward, ready to unleash on Will. It set off a chain reaction in her, urging her to reply with a sarcastic quip or equally provocative remark, but instead, she reached for

Louis, seeking the stillness the large dog brought her.

"I know you're pissed. I should have called, responded to your texts, and I'm sorry I didn't. But last night something happened in the swamps, and I might have—"

"You were in the swamps?"

She rubbed Louis's head. "At Kalila's house."

He rested his hand on his hip, his shoulders relaxing. "I'd hoped you would go to Nina's or a hotel. Not out there, alone."

A torturous silence rose between them. Lexie struggled to find the words for the feelings floating in her heart. But instead of saying something she feared would make the tense situation worse, she said nothing.

"You got a dog."

He didn't sound angry or surprised, but gentle and encouraging.

"I found him in the swamps."

Will raised his eyebrows. "And he smells like it, too."

Relieved to be talking—even if it was only about the dog— Lexie smiled. "Nothing a good bath can't fix."

Louis growled again.

She knelt and got in the dog's line of sight.

"This is your new home, and this is my husband, Will. You must protect him, too."

Will moved away from the door. "A dog for protection might be a good idea."

She kept her smile hidden as she strolled through the door and set her purse down on the table.

Louis sniffed the air, and she let go of his leash. He trotted into the living room and buried his nose in the sofa.

She sucked in a fortifying breath and faced Will.

He came up to her, his hands in his trouser pockets, a glum expression sagging his features. "I shouldn't have blown up at you like that. I'm sorry."

Louis proceeded to climb on the expensive sofa and make himself at home.

Will pressed his lips together, his cheeks growing red.

Lexie took his hand. "It's just a sofa."

"I'll do whatever you want, Lexie, just don't leave like that again."

She moved closer, desperate to feel his warmth.

His thumb caressed the top of her hand, moving back and forth. "I kept remembering what happened with Renee that night at the plantation and I became terrified. I never realized how afraid I was of losing you until I spent the entire night pacing the floors, going nuts because I couldn't talk to you. I called Emile a dozen times to find you. He even tried to hunt down Kalila's house, but according to the state, Google Maps, and St. John Parish tax website, it doesn't exist."

She came up under his nose and nestled against him, not sure how to tell him about the strange house. "That may be hard to explain."

Will's arms closed around her. "Please, try. I've been up all night terrified about where you are and—" He rested his forehead against hers. "I promised myself I wouldn't get angry when you came back."

She kissed his lips. "I need you to trust me, Will. What I'm doing is for both of us."

He cupped her face and raised her eyes to his. "What more do you want me to do? I'm trying to accept what voodoo takes away from us. I've been as supportive as I can, but still, I feel you slipping away. I don't know what to do to make things better. I want to stop feeling so angry all the time. Tell me how to do that?"

The misery she saw in his face was her doing, and it nearly destroyed her. Her duty to Kalfu had not just influenced her life; it had changed Will's as well.

The time had come to tell her husband the truth about what she was. Perhaps if he knew, they might be able to fight the darkness together.

"Will, I need to tell you something. It will explain why Kalila's house doesn't show up on a database and a lot of other things happening to us lately."

He sucked in a deep breath, expanding his broad chest. "Okay. I'm listening."

She stood before her husband, knowing she would never feel braver than she did at that moment.

"Will, I didn't have enough power to save you when Renee kidnapped you. I had to go to someone to get it. He's a spirit of the underworld in voodoo. I pledged myself to him, and he gave me his vital force. It's a dark power that makes me angry at times, and I think it may be why things have been so difficult between us. Kalfu's—"

His eyes crinkled around the edges. "Kalfu?"

"He's the voodoo god of darkness, sort of like the devil."

"The devil?" His voice cracked, and he paused, rubbing his chin.

She waited for his reaction—yelling, screaming, laughter—anything to tell her how he felt. It was the quiet Will she feared most; the one who kept what was in his heart from her.

"Why didn't you tell me this before?"

Her shoulders sagged. "I was afraid if I told you I gave myself to a black spirit, you wouldn't love me anymore." The words tumbled from her laden with so much emotion, her voice almost faltered.

Will tossed his arms around her, pinning her against him. His warmth rallied her courage. She had done the right thing.

"Lexie, I could never stop loving you. No matter what spirits are around you." He tucked her head under his chin. "So how bad is this one? Can't be worse than Magnus."

"No. He's much worse." She looked up at Will, unsure of how to describe her dark master. "Kalfu's ruthless, manipulative, and cruel. He wants control and doesn't care who he destroys to get it. But he is very powerful and feared by many. Since I pledged my loyalty to him, I get to share in his power and protection."

Will shook his head, the despair on his face weighed on her heart. "I don't understand. Why would you align yourself to something so sinister?"

"To save you." She traced the outline of his lips. "I needed his power to confront Emily Mann and rescue you. It was the only thing I could think of."

His expression softened, and his lips parted, but his eyes took on an incredulous gleam. "You did this for me? But dark spirits, power, pledging loyalty to this Kalfu … It doesn't make any sense. You're already powerful. You didn't need him."

Will had always been a concrete thinker, probably the reason her world seemed so foreign to him. She took his hand, ready to give him a demonstration.

"Let me show you what he can do."

Lexie placed his hand against her chest, right over her center. She summoned the black and white ribbon. It rose on command. She willed it to wrap around Will's hand, sending it up his arm, hoping to make him understand.

His lips twitched as the ribbon climbed higher. When it reached his neck, his mouth slipped open. He stared at her with a mixture of horror and awe.

"What is that?"

"Power." She let go of his hand, and the connection broke. "The black is Kalfu; the white is Damballah. They coexist in me, but sometimes Kalfu's influence overpowers me, and the darkness takes over. It's why I've been moody and difficult lately."

"I know you've grown since we came to New Orleans. You're a spiritual leader and all, but this ..." He lifted her head to him. "I never realized you could do such amazing things."

The pride in his smile meant everything to her. All the emotional turmoil she'd suffered keeping it all inside faded away. All that mattered was Will understood and would remain by her side through whatever lay ahead.

She exhaled, letting go of her misgivings, and renewing her dedication to her husband. "None of this means anything without you. I can't go on being mambo and having this power unless I know you're with me."

Will dipped his chin and warily searched the room. "What about Magnus? How does he feel about this newfound power?"

The question took her by surprise. That Will would concern himself with her ghost meant that perhaps the two might have learned to tolerate each other.

She could almost hear Magnus's snide remark. "He's still getting used to it."

Will took her hand. "Whatever spirits come into your life, good or bad, I want to hear about them. Share everything with me, baby. I never want to have another night like the last one. Together we can conquer anything."

He kissed her, a long and passionate kiss that harkened back to their first few dates. It was sensual, all-consuming, and sent a fiery glow all the way to her toes, shutting out Kalfu's chill.

Will led her down the hall, nibbling her ear, and Lexie's heart soared. She had told him the truth, and he hadn't blown up or asked for a divorce. Hope permeated every crevice of her being. They had a chance.

You didn't tell him everything.

This time it wasn't his voice, but hers.

Lexie's girlish giggle drifted into Magnus's murky world and enlivened his spirit. He watched through the foggy doorway to Lexie's condo as the happy couple retreated to their bedroom. Will was a better man than he'd surmised. In his shoes, Magnus didn't know if he would have been so accepting. But he had never loved as profoundly as Will and Lexie.

A muffled, low-pitched noise carried in the smoky essence around him. He glanced at the source of the racket—the black dog reclining on the sofa. The beast was not what it seemed. From the moment the giant had come up to him at Kalila's home, Magnus knew it was not all animal, but part human. That Lexie had not sensed what he did baffled him, but he intended to find out why the creature had wormed his way into her life.

With a determined stride, he stepped from his foggy domain and entered the living room. The mongrel, out like a light, never stirred.

He approached the fancy leather sofa and stood over the formidable canine.

"When are you going to tell her what you are?"

A draft ruffled the fur on the sleeping stray. But this was not a breeze brought on by air-conditioning or an open window; this wind was ethereal—the kind Magnus had seen used by many spirits to announce their arrival.

One yellow eye opened and the dog glanced up, then the air circling him turned into a brisk gust, swirling its long black fur and lifting its short black ears. Roused by the brisk wind, the brute climbed from the sofa and stood, intently studying Magnus.

Magnus took a cautious step back when strange, twinkling pinpoints of light exploded all over the dog's black coat. The dazzling display rose and created a thick cloud. It turned into an impenetrable fog while the illuminated specks continued to hypnotize Magnus. The mist rose upward as the lights danced inside, reaching almost to the height of a man.

Magnus could see nothing behind the veil—no definition, and no more yellow eyes. Then, as if washed away by a strong wind, the mist retreated, falling to the ground and vanishing beneath the hardwood floor.

When the last of the mystical elements had drained beneath Magnus's black boots, a man stood in the same spot where the dog had previously been. Naked as the day he was born, the dark-skinned individual grabbed the closest pillow.

Magnus grinned as the young man covered himself. "Finally. Now, who are you?"

He was handsome and no more than twenty. His gentle, coal black eyes, perfectly symmetrical bone structure, and smooth jawline reminded Magnus of the men he'd seen employed by

Madame Simeon Glapion in old Storyville. Men she'd used to keep customers like his friend, Oscar Wilde, happy.

"My name is Antoine La Salle." He spun around, taking in the room. "I've never seen such wonders in a home. It's been forever since I was inside." He touched the remote control on the coffee table and then spotted the kitchen. "What are all these wonderful things?"

He took off for the kitchen.

Magnus walked up to the breakfast bar as Antoine opened the refrigerator.

"Appliances for keeping food and preparing it."

Still clutching the pillow, Antoine shut the fridge door and opened it again, fascinated by the light. "I've never spoken to a ghost who converses so readily with the living. How do you do that?"

Magnus went around the breakfast bar. "I am bound to the mambo, Lexie Arden. The woman who rescued you."

Antoine shut the fridge door. "I sensed her immense power the moment I saw her. The spirits protect her."

"Is that why you are protecting her?" he asked with a skeptical smirk. "Because of her power?"

"What do you know of the swamps?" Antoine scooted closer to the counter, running his finger along the silver veins in the black marble. "The legends, the myths."

"I know nothing about them. My home was in Maine when I died. I came to New Orleans for Lexie."

"My home was in New Orleans when the evil one turned me. I was sent to the swamps to deliver a letter to the priestess Julie Brown. The witch wasn't happy with whatever news my mistress sent. She took her wrath out on me and changed me—what the people in the swamps call a *rougarou*." He pressed the buttons on the coffeemaker. "I begged her to change me back, and she promised she would, but then she died in the storm, and I was trapped."

"What else can you do?" Magnus sat on one of the stools at the bar. "Are you only a dog or is there more?"

"At night, when I hunt, I become like a wolf. During the day, I appear like a dog. And at times, when I have the energy, I can turn back into my old self. But not for long."

"So why did you not run away when Lexie approached you?"

He turned his sad brown eyes to Magnus. "Because I knew she could save me. She could reverse old Julie Brown's spell."

A woman's giggle carried into the room from the hallway.

Magnus guessed she and Will had made up.

He was about to question Antoine further when the funny light he'd seen before returned. It crowded the man, dancing in swirls around his head. It stretched into streams and covered his body. Tufts of black fur cropped up here and there on his dark skin.

"I must go back," he said to Magnus. "I will tell you more when I can return."

The black tufts spread like leprosy, devouring him. He flopped over to the floor and crouched on all fours. His nose jutted out, and a horrid bone-crunching sound filled the air until his snout and black nose manifested. His head flattened, scrunching down his forehead and spreading apart his eyes. Magnus cringed as he took in the metamorphosis, reading the pain of changing back in Antoine's grimacing face. He glanced up at Magnus and blinked. His brown orbs turned an unearthly shade of yellow. The last part of him to develop was the long tail. It extended off his back and his spine undulated beneath the black fur until it reached its full length.

Within seconds, the wooly black dog was back, but when Magnus peered into its eyes, he saw the gentle gaze of Antoine.

Magnus stood up. "Your identity is safe with me. But I might suggest telling Lexie when you can. She doesn't like secrets in those who are loyal to her."

A louder giggle floated by. Magnus decided it was time to return to his world.

He let the mist crowd around him, drawing him back to the place where there was no light and no dark—just gray. He melted into the cloud, becoming one with it. He could rest and recharge until Lexie called him to return to her side.

Chapter Eighteen

The mid-morning sun streaked across the sheets on their king-sized bed as a contented Lexie lay wrapped in her husband's thick arms. She drank in the woodsy smell of him, his taut muscles, and the tickle of his hairy chest against her skin. It had been ages since they'd spent so much time together, but she vowed from now on to make her life with Will a priority.

"The office will be wondering where you are."

He kissed her forehead. "I'm the boss so they can wonder a little while longer."

She traced the muscle in his forearm. "I should get to the store."

He hugged her tighter. "Just five more minutes. Besides, you have Nina to take care of things for you."

The reminder brought on a beleaguered sigh. There was another conversation she dreaded. How could she talk the young woman out of seeing Mike?

Will sat up, taking her with him. "That didn't sound good. Is there something else you need to tell me?"

She gazed into his eyes, aching to tell him everything, but their morning together had been perfect. She didn't want to ruin it.

Will's mouth turned downward. "Lexie, I want no more secrets between us. You're my wife, and I don't care if it's about voodoo spirits or maxing out your credit card, I want you to come clean. We're in this together."

The truth about what she'd sacrificed to Kalfu was on the tip of her tongue, but she couldn't make it come out. It was still too raw for her, and knowing what it would do to Will—it could keep a while longer.

"I promise I will tell you everything, from now on."

He kissed her, one of those long, luscious kisses they used to share before Kalfu.

Before she was ready, he pulled away.

"That's all I wanted to hear." He settled back against his pillow, a crease across his brow. "You really want to keep the dog?"

She picked up her pillow and batted it against his chest. "Yes, that's non-negotiable."

He took the pillow away and tossed it to the foot of the bed. Will pulled her to him. She nestled against his chest, more content than she'd been in a long time.

"A dog and a ghost. You're amassing quite the collection of pets."

She chuckled. "Don't you let Magnus hear you say such a thing. And you forget, I have a cat. He lives in the shop, remember?"

"Ah, yes, the big gray one." He brushed his hand through her hair. "With the creepy green eyes. I ran into him in the courtyard quite a lot. Next, you'll be wanting a snake."

"No snakes. I don't like them."

Will swept the sheets aside. "Thank goodness for that. We've had our five minutes. We'd better get ready to face the real world again, Mrs. Bennett. We've played hooky long enough."

He climbed from the bed and headed to the bathroom.

She admired his firm backside, sorry their morning in bed had ended.

He stopped at the doorway and glanced over his shoulder at her. "I love you, Lexie. Never forget that. No spirits or dogs or whatever craziness your voodoo brings into our lives will ever change that."

He dashed into the bathroom and left the door ajar.

Lexie settled back on the bed, glowing with happiness. They had found their way back to each other, and the torment of the night before had only strengthened their relationship. Teeming with plans for spending more time together, she turned her head and admired the sunlight coming through the bedroom windows. Its warm embrace reminding her of Will and how he made her feel—alive.

A single cloud breezed in from the horizon. Dark and out of place in the clear blue sky, it drifted in front of the sun. The rays streaming into her room stopped, and she sat up, uncomfortable with the chill enveloping her. The cloud grew in size, getting bigger and blacker until all the sunlight disappeared.

The cloud then moved, coming down out of the sky and easing closer to her window. The black in her chest quivered. Soon, her entire bedroom was engulfed in darkness.

Clap, clap, clap, came from the corner of the room.

"Quite a performance, my dear." Kalfu suddenly stood next to her bed. "But you can't keep the truth from him for long."

She rushed to cover herself with her sheet. "Get out of here."

He sat down on the edge of the bed, gazing up and down her figure. "You need to know a man never stays after their woman commits to me. Kalila's lover left her. So did Cecily's. So did Julie Brown's. All women who swear an oath to me end up belonging only to me."

Her blood boiled. "Not me."

He walked across the room to the window, his purposeful stride exuding confidence.

Kalfu stopped and admired the black cloud blocking her window, a slight smirk on his lips. "Being truthful with the one you love has its benefits, but there is a point where a man will be a man and demand you leave me. And I always win those ultimatums. No one leaves me."

"Cecily did," she blurted before she could stop herself.

His composure cracked and his smile wilted. He slipped his hands into the pockets of his casual black slacks and lowered his gaze. He stood, appearing to debate his next words.

The giant ball of darkness outside her window pressed against the glass, adding an oppressive atmosphere to her bedroom.

Reason told her to curb her outburst with the spirit, but her passion wanted to let him know no one would master her.

"I take it that bitch in the library has been filling your head with her stories."

"And whose lies are worse? Yours or hers?"

His eyebrows went up as if impressed.

"Julie Brown would do or say anything to be free of that room. I have no such agenda with you. If you don't believe me, ask your dog about her. Antoine has quite a story to tell."

"Antoine?" She wrapped the sheet around her, and sat up on the side of the bed. "Are you saying my dog—?"

Kalfu touched his finger to his lips and pointed to the ajar bathroom door. "He's waiting for you to join him in the shower." He stepped back and tipped his head toward the bathroom. "Go. Enjoy your time with him. But if you ever try to leave me, I will take Will away from you. I can make him fall in love with another woman, or worse." He grinned, rubbing his hands together. "What would be more painful? His loving another or being sent to my world? Think about it."

A flash of brilliant light blinded her. She covered her eyes. After the light died, she looked again; he was gone.

The black cloud dissolved and the sunshine once again beamed into her room, but the warmth she'd enjoyed before did not return. His warning about taking Will from her repeated in her head. The tension coursing through her set her on edge as she sat back on the bed.

I have to end his hold over me.

More determined than ever, she had to find a way to leave Kalfu. It wasn't just her happiness at stake—it was Will's, too.

Chapter Nineteen

Lexie glanced at the clock on her dashboard as she took a sharp right turn into the parking lot. Her heart pounded when she peered up at the rundown two-story brown clapboard building. With bars on the windows and a flashing neon sign that said, *Joe's*, the hovel represented part of the backbone of the New Orleans economy—alcohol.

Located across from the ruins of Dixie Brewery on Tulane Avenue, the shady establishment had been selected by Harold for the emergency meeting of the voodoo council. The one for which she was already thirty minutes late.

Her morning in bed with Will had sent all thought about the critical meeting from her head. It wasn't until she picked up her phone and saw the three text messages from Nina that she'd remembered and rushed out of her condo with Louis in tow.

"I don't think this is seemly for a married woman." Magnus

turned to Louis, sprawled in the back seat. "Our slobbering friend, however, will fit right in."

She grabbed her baton juju and rope she used for Louis's leash. "Harold hopes to intimidate me."

Lexie coaxed Louis from the car.

"Do you think it wise to bring the slobberer with us?" Magnus asked.

"I'm not leaving him in the car," Lexie balked. "Maybe Louis can intimidate Harold."

Magnus eyed the establishment. "Only if he takes a chunk out of Mr. Forneaux's sizable ass."

"You're impossible."

With her cane, her dog, and her ghost, Lexie marched across the cracked blacktop of the parking lot to the front door. Bright neon signs of local beer companies lit up the three small windows across the front of the first floor and second floor. The windows had a layer of grime, muting the brightness of the neon lights while weedy vines crept up the clapboard along the entrance.

The hinges squeaked with protest as she yanked the thick wood door open.

"Careful you don't catch something, my dear."

She ignored Magnus and strolled inside.

Beer, musty air-conditioning, and bleach greeted her as she stepped into a wall of blackness. A moment of trepidation gripped her while her eyes adjusted to the dim lighting. She wouldn't put it past Harold to set up a trap or worse, considering what she knew about his plans. The thread of animosity she picked up from the building set her black side to quivering. It seemed her darkness loved a good fight.

But as the room inside came into view, she realized the red

171

ALEXANDREA WEIS WITH LUCAS ASTOR

and white neon Dixie Beer sign above the bar and the few rickety tables and mismatched chairs were far from threatening. An old jukebox and dark-paneled walls filled with beer posters added a sad, dated ambiance to the establishment.

Two men with sagging pants and oversized T-shirts sat at the long oak bar, beer bottles perched in front of them. A bald, ebony-skinned bartender with biceps the size of cantaloupes nodded at her.

"Upstairs, Mambo." His gruff voice didn't offer a warm welcome. "They're waitin' for you." He then noticed the dog. "He can't come in here."

She was about to tell the rude man her dog went wherever she went when a low, deep growl came from Louis.

The two men at the bar leaned back on their stools adding to the unfriendly feeling in the room.

"Better get control of that thing," one of the customers called out.

Lexie loosened her grip on Louis's leash, and he lunged forward, taking advantage of the slack.

"Careful, who knows what he will do if I let him go. The gods of voodoo gave my beast great power and very sharp teeth." She raised her head, staring the men down. "Are you sure you want to anger him ... and me?"

Magnus chuckled next to her. "There are moments you do surprise me, dear girl."

With a grunt, the bartender waved her to the door with Private etched on a brass plate at the top.

On the other side was a partially obscured staircase.

Clucking to Louis, Lexie gripped her cane. The power it sent surging through her—black and white tendrils of light—snaked up her arm and spread throughout her being.

I'm ready for you, Harold.

Each step she took, her defiance rose. She had earned her baton juju through hard-won battles. Lexie was damned if she would let a murdering bastard like Harold rule over New Orleans. The city had endured his kind under the yoke of Bloody Mary and others of her ilk. Never again.

Heated voices carried to the staircase. A deep, gravelly cry for *Order* rose above the murmurings. She recognized Harold's voice and grinned. He didn't have control of the council.

Her baton juju planted firmly on the linoleum floor, she stepped into a dimly lit storeroom. Packed metal shelves along the walls overflowed with bar supplies, glasses, and bottles of alcohol. In the center, and caught beneath the dingy fluorescent lights, six people sat around a rectangular tabletop set on a few beer kegs.

"We still have to put it to a vote in order ..." Harold's voice dwindled when he spotted Lexie.

Silence descended.

Lexie reached out with her ability. The blend of respect and revile she detected amused her. Harold had not turned everyone against her after all.

She tapped the tip of her baton juju on the floor as she approached, the dull thud resonated about the room. All eyes went to her cane.

That was good. She needed to remind them whose cane she possessed.

Lexie browsed the cramped quarters, attempting to hide her smug grin. "This is a step down from Jacques Krieger's office in One Shell Square."

Madame Henri stood from the table, her black shawl slipping

from around her shoulders. "Glad you finally arrived, child. I was getting worried." She pointed a craggy finger at Harold. "This cretin was about to call for a vote to oust you as mambo."

Lexie kept her eyes on Harold as she eased closer to the table.

Louis came out from behind her and the shocked gasps from the table tweaked the left side of her mouth into a half-grin.

They know who the real mambo is.

"What is that?" Claude Melancon, a banker from Mid-City and the newest member of the council, gawked at Louis.

"My guard dog." Lexie leveled her gaze on Harold. "One can never be too careful. New Orleans is a dangerous city, especially for those who have something others want."

Lexie waited for his reaction. His icy stare told her the message had hit home.

Several around the table fidgeted as Louis sat by Lexie's side, his yellow eyes taking in the council members.

The Chez twins jumped to their feet, moving as one. They raised their faces to the ceiling and held their arms open as if receiving a divine message.

"A beast of flame, a force of fire, the one you call a dog is a liar," they said in perfect unison.

They turned to Lexie; their milky white eyes locked on her.

Before Magnus's revelations, she might have been intimidated by their words and glare. Now, she knew the conniving women behind the façade and the spirit who backed their power.

Your days are numbered.

Lexie took the last few steps to the table, ready to get to the meeting's objective.

"There are many liars in this room, Helen and Corinne. How can you tell them apart?"

The twins' openmouthed, shocked expression pleased Lexie immensely.

"Surely you don't mean your council, Mambo."

The sickeningly sweet voice was new, as was the face. The woman in the burgundy dress with her honey-colored skin and bright red lips stood. Her presence created a stinging wave that traveled through Lexie's center like a razor blade.

Called the Mistress of Magazine Street, Lily Farber started as a hairdresser to the wealthy living in the Garden District. Word around town was she catered to every wealthy person she met, and married men were her biggest vice. Lily had fashioned her life after her icon, Marie Laveau, and had climbed high in the ranks of priestesses in the city to attain a coveted seat on the council. But despite Cecily Henri's adamant assertion that Lily devoted herself to the white side of voodoo, Lexie had her doubts.

"Not you, of course, Lily." Lexie clasped her hands over the handle of her dragon cane. "Why did you call this meeting, Harold?"

In a shiny black robe secured with a white belt of rope, Harold attempted to stare Lexie down.

"Perhaps you should put your baton juju on the table and call Damballah to join us so we can begin the meeting? It's been months since the council has met to discuss business. And our new members must be introduced to the god."

Lexie dropped her gaze to her cane. With one onyx eye and the other pearl, she debated who would come if she placed her cane on the table.

"You had no right to call this meeting." She peered around the room. "And in such an unseemly location."

"I have every right." He banged his fist on the table. "The

shadow people are still here. Complaints are trickling in from my followers. They come to me asking for help, but I have none to give." He pointed at her. "You are mambo. You must send them back to the River of Shadows."

Louis came up alongside her and growled.

"I suggest you mind your tone when you address me." She patted the dog's head. "Or you will upset Louis."

"Mambo." Claude stood. "I have also had trouble with these spirits. People are coming to me asking for help. There must be something you can do."

Lexie cocked an eyebrow at Cecily as if to say, "And you wanted him on the council?"

"We must have faith in our mambo." Lily gracefully wrapped her cream scarf around her neck. "She will find a way to help us."

"This coming from a woman who cheats her clients out of thousands of dollars by giving them fake gris-gris and false hopes." Harold edged closer to the table, sneering at Lily. "No wonder the false mambo selected you for the council. It takes one fraud to recognize another."

Lexie raced to Harold's chair, the black in her slithering, enticed by her anger. She leaned over him, relishing the dot of sweat on his brow. Her fury bloomed, fanning her desire to show Harold what she could do when pushed too far.

"I know what you're up to with Renee's old building and mine, Harold." She stood back, delighting in his thunderstruck expression. "Should I let the council know about that?"

"Mambo," Cecily called. "Think about what you're saying. This is not the time or place for accusations."

"Yes, you should be careful who you accuse." Harold took a step backward as Louis challenged him, his teeth bared. "You're not our mambo. Everyone in the city feels it. It's why chaos reigns and people are scared of the darkness returning. If you don't send back the shadow spirits, it will prove you're not the chosen one."

The Chez sisters lifted their hands, entreating the spirits. Their frizzy red hair whipped around their shoulders, and their milky eyes raised to the ceiling.

"A false priestess rules our land, but the time of reckoning is at hand," they said in unison.

Those underhanded bitches!

The others gathered at the table murmured amongst themselves. Their suspicious gazes directed at Lexie heightened the tension in the storeroom.

Her hands throbbed with power. Her black swelled, nudging her to act and destroy her enemies. She hoisted her mighty baton juju in the air, overcome with rage. The thrill of Kalfu's power pulsating in her muscles compelled her. With all the strength she had, Lexie brought the magical staff down hard on the table.

The *whack* resonated and rose, changing to a low rumble like thunder as it echoed across the room. A blast of cold air overtook the table. All the council members shivered, their accusing stares turned to goggle-eyed gaping.

Louis cowered on the ground and slinked away from Lexie's side, his tail between his legs.

The tabletop shook, vibrating on the metal kegs beneath. A *crack* rang out. An ugly black stain, like old dried blood, etched across the wooden tabletop. It made a zigzag pattern right down the center.

A few of the council members, the newer ones, jumped from their chairs, alarmed. Harold and the Chez twins didn't budge. Cecily's steadfast glare warned her to temper her rage. But Lexie didn't care what the older woman thought. She had a point to prove.

The rumbling intensified, and the room became like ice. A momentous *clap* boomed. The bloodline burned into the wood blackened and then the tabletop spilt in two. Each half slid off the kegs and fell to the floor.

Harold motioned to the broken table at his feet. "What have you done?"

Lexie squeezed the handle of her cane. "I've reminded everyone who is mambo around here."

Magnus slid in next to her. "That could have gone better."

Her anger cooled as a few frightened council members backed away from the table's remains.

She had never experienced such a rush. To command such power was intoxicating, but it also concerned her. This wasn't how she meant to lead. Threats and intimidation would not instill loyalty.

"But now they know what you can do. What we can do."

Kalfu sounded pleased, but Lexie wasn't.

"I think our meeting has come to an end," Cecily announced, her calm voice bringing a sense of order.

Most of the council members negotiated their way around the debris and scurried for the stairs. Harold and the Chez twins remained.

Lexie could guess why they hadn't followed the others. With the lines drawn, the battle could begin.

Cecily came up to her and snatched the baton juju from her.

The power surging through her ended. Lexie's racing heart calmed, and beads of sweat broke out on her brow. She had lost control and given into the darkness. Kalfu was right—now everyone would know what she was.

"He's getting stronger," she whispered. "You need to act soon." She handed Lexie back the cane. "Before he controls you completely."

She wrapped her hands around the staff, willing the white of Damballah to chase away Kalfu's negative energy. She set the cane's tip on the floor, the shaking in her muscles easing, and his black grasp over her soul lessened.

Cecily headed toward the stairs, not looking back at Lexie.

She appreciated the woman's advice but questioned if it was already too late. She had never envisioned such an outburst before. And that she could not keep it from happening, left her defeated.

Harold came up and haughtily raised his head.

"We both know who rules your soul."

Lexie pushed the blackness back into the pit of her being. She would not let Kalfu's energy get the better of her twice in one evening. She pictured the white in her center, and the warmth returned to the room.

She met his caustic stare with her own.

"Do not threaten me, Harold. Ever. You know what I can do."

Harold clapped his hands, a distasteful grin on his lips. "You may have a lot of power, but so do I. You have no idea the mistake you are making."

Lexie inched closer to the imposing man, the darkness in her begging to rip him apart. "I know what you've done—all of it. Maman Brigitte can't protect you anymore. I suggest you carefully consider your next move. It may be your last."

Harold had resisted her appointment as mambo from their first encounter. Soon, she would have to eliminate him. If she didn't, he would get rid of her.

She left him at the smoking remains of the table, anxious to get away before she did something she would regret.

On the steps, Magnus stuck close to her side. "Are you sure that was the best tactic? Inviting trouble eventually lands you in it."

She scratched Louis's neck, seeking his soothing effect on her, as they came to the bottom of the staircase. "Since when have either of us shied away from trouble?"

Magnus paused on the step below her, his mouth drawn into a flat line. "How can I keep you safe against a man like Harold Forneaux?"

She walked through him, stepping onto the dirty stone floor of the bar.

"I can take care of myself, Magnus. I always have, and I always will."

A burning pain shot through him. Something Magnus rarely experienced, except when around Lexie. She had become so much a part of him that even the slightest offhanded comment caused distress.

He remained on the step, watching as she and the furry black beast headed out of the bar. The bright sunlight beaming into the establishment was another reminder of the differences in their two worlds—he was the darkness, and she was the light.

Well, not all of her is light.

He hated what Kalfu had done to her. The carefree woman he'd first encountered on the steps of Altmover Manor was not the

Lexie Arden he had come to know. But there were moments when he saw glimpses of her old self in a smile or her giggle. During his lifetime, and all the people he had known, none had endeared themselves to him more than her. She'd turned into more than his spiritual anchor; she'd become his family.

"Careful, Mr. Blackwell."

The sinister woman's voice behind him awakened a bitter stirring of revulsion.

He glanced back up the steps. She was there, Maman Brigitte, fitted in a red gown dotted with white skulls, the baton juju resembling a black rooster in her hand.

She glided down the steps, her devilish smile the only unattractive feature on her perfectly carved face.

"She will hurt you in the end."

He dipped his head to the spirit. "It is a pain I would happily suffer."

She alighted on the step above him, resting her hands on her black cane.

"I could give you peace, and your heart's desire."

Magnus suspected the visit had a purpose—one that would benefit Maman Brigitte and not him.

"My heart's desire is to remain with Lexie. As for peace, what soul ever knows it? My father and brother are not at peace. Was their disturbed slumber your doing?"

She quirked her lips into a funny smile. "I was not the one who woke them. Your mistress's appointment as mambo set off a chain of events which has disturbed the balance of the universe. When the powers of good and evil are at odds, the dead do not sleep. But you could change all that."

She waved her hand at the wall. The ruddy brown color came

to life as shadows moved across it. The play of light and dark gave the wall the feel of an impressionist painting, the kind he had admired before his death. Then the shadows died away, and unidentifiable shapes formed. They rose, stretching the paint taut, and then receded like a wave back into the muddy landscape. The bulging forms became more distinct. Faces, masked by a veil of brown, jutted from the wall. Their features pressed against the surface, the heads floated as their mouths opened in silent screams. The ghostlike images swarmed, rising and sinking in an orchestrated frenzy.

It wasn't peace Magnus saw in the contorted faces of the dead, but pain. He thought of his brother in the wall, part of the ballet of the grotesque Maman Brigitte had staged for his entertainment. His suffering cut him in two.

"Magnus?"

It wasn't Maman Brigitte's voice. It was another woman. He recognized the dulcet tones instantly.

"Frannie?"

A woman's face came through the thick covering. He noted the color on the cheeks and the highlights in her honey-colored hair.

Her smile was the same earth-shattering one he remembered from their life together. That she was a part of the repugnant display dimmed his strength. Of all the souls he never wanted to see again, hers was the one he dreaded the most. His guilt over her demise came back like a thousand arrows tearing into his chest at once. The love, jealousy, betrayal, and regret he felt from their time together seemed even more poignant.

Her sweet lips were inches from him. He longed to touch her once more, but he knew he could not give in to Maman Brigitte's torture.

"You need to come home, Magnus. Come and rest with us. I miss you."

The face might belong to Frances, but as he studied the depth of her brown eyes, something was missing—her fire. The woman he knew would never have come across as so lifeless. His strength returned, and so did his contempt.

"That's not Frances McGee."

Maman Brigitte tapped the end of her rooster cane against the wall. "Frances O'Connor, you mean."

Frances's face dissolved into the brown paint. The rolling motion stopped instantly, and the wall became what it was—a lifeless piece of sheetrock.

Incensed, he glanced back at Maman Brigitte. "You created her to tempt me away from Lexie. Just like you created my father and brother. She's not real. None of them are."

"I didn't create the spirits, Mr. Blackwell. They exist in my world and are waiting for you to join them. Think of it. The peace you could experience. No more worry, no more heartache. Just existing with those you love for eternity. The trials of life gone, forever."

Magnus hardened his soul, the sorrow of seeing Frances forgotten. "The memory of life never leaves the dead, Mistress. It's the iron which forges their spirit. And all the dead have left to cling to. Had you ever lived, you would know that."

Maman Brigitte's smile fell away. "She will cast you aside soon." Her voice grew colder. "Kalfu wants you gone. He is her advisor, her guide now. You're just a pest waiting to be squashed."

No one could replace him in Lexie's life. He would never leave his charge in the hands of such a diabolical spirit. Kalfu's hate and villainy would snuff out all the sweetness and caring that made Lexie so special. No matter what fate awaited him, what hell lay ahead, he would give up eternity to make sure Lexie remained safe. It was his duty as her spirit guide and his desire as her friend.

"Lexie and I are bound to each other. I can never leave her. You can parade every dead family member before me time and again, and I will still refuse to join them. Give up this masquerade before she finds out. Do you want the Mambo of New Orleans as an enemy or an ally?"

The bitter scowl spreading across her face tainted her beauty. Maman Brigitte collected her black cane and angrily swept the thick folds of her gown behind her.

"We will meet again, Mr. Blackwell. This isn't over."

A cloud of mist rose around her, covering her being. It shifted and billowed turning a dark gray. Flashes of light dotted its canvas and then subsided. The fog thinned and faded into the steps before disappearing completely.

Magnus started across the floor of the bar toward the entrance, fretting over the conversation.

He headed into the sunlight, still debating whether to tell Lexie of the encounter. She had so much on her mind he didn't want to bother her. Still, another part of him longed to find out if she would care.

But I was hers first. And I can never let anyone push me aside.

Chapter Twenty

Lexie stood at the open door to her shop. The last dregs of sunlight cast an eerie red glow across the stone floor gathering around her feet. The color reminded her of Kalfu's anger threading through her. Lexie feared what would become of her and those she loved if she didn't free herself of his hate.

"Okay, I've locked the storage room and turned off the coffee maker." Nina came alongside her while rummaging through her purse. "I fed that dog of yours. He's sleeping in the kitchen. Before you leave, feed Damballah. He won't eat with the dog around."

The laughter of tourists walking on the street distracted Lexie. Why wasn't she enjoying the city? Her entire life seemed fraught with danger, intrigue, and anxiety. Sometimes she longed to be as she had been—a woman more worried about her boyfriend, hairstyle, and the money in her bank account.

Nina nudged her. "Hey? Are you listening to me?"

The green-eyed cat arrived at her feet, brushing up against the hem of her long white dress. She gazed down at the creature and chuckled to herself.

Her life had changed so much that even a cat wasn't just a cat anymore.

Lexie picked up Damballah and held him against her chest, comforted by his warmth.

"I'm listening. Just have a lot on my mind. You go on. I'll close up."

Nina gripped her keys and tugged her purse over her shoulder. "I can stay. I don't have to meet Mike for dinner."

Lexie turned to her shop assistant, sensing an opportunity. "Do you like him?"

Nina shrugged, her face scrunched. "He treats me well and we have fun together. I'm not sure how I feel yet. He takes some getting used to."

Lexie needed to convince Nina to stay away from the man, but she feared any advice would only drive her to him. Her mother had tried the same thing with her and Will. Good thing Lexie never listened.

"Sometimes people aren't what they appear to be."

Nina's stance turned aggressive as she shifted her hips. "What's that supposed to mean?"

"I've heard things around town about him. He's been seen with a lot of women. I don't tell you this to hurt you. I care about you."

Nina's posture sagged. "Yeah, my friends don't like him, either. They've heard the rumors about him, too." She raised her head, her brown eyes brimming with sadness. "There are times I think he likes me. And then, I get this funny feeling that he's using me for something."

Lexie put the cat down and went to the young woman. She clasped her forearm, hoping to gentle her advice with a gesture.

"You need to trust that."

The energy flowing from Nina assured Lexie the young woman's doubts had gnawed at her for a while. She had enough experience with dating to know Mike would not last long.

Nina broke free of her grip and turned to the door. "I'll see you tomorrow morning."

She took in the way the young woman walked, with her head down and a lack of energy in her step. She hated seeing it but it was necessary. Mike had to go.

Encouraged, Lexie shut the door to her store. The cat next to her meowed.

She turned to the fluffy, gray Maine coon. "What?"

The white part of her ribbon tingled, sending the sensation all the way to her toes. It comforted her, something Kalfu's blackness never did. It reminded her of how Louis made her feel whenever she caressed his thick coat.

Smoke puffed up from between the brick in her floor, covering the cat. It climbed higher, rising above Lexie's head. A year ago, such an occurrence would have sent her shrieking out the door. Even the magical display of the gods had become routine.

Damballah developed in the smoke, his white suit shining in the remnants of sunlight. A gentle chilly breeze blew across the store, taking the mist around Damballah with it.

"You are upset, Lexie Arden." His deep, baritone voice matched his formidable height and broad chest.

She eyed the graceful man. "Is that an impression, or are you reading my thoughts like Kalfu."

ALEXANDREA WEIS WITH LUCAS ASTOR

Damballah tossed up his thick hand. "I am not Kalfu. He looks for the unhappiness in a person and thrives on it. He would not appear to you offering a shoulder to lean on."

She gazed into his fascinating green eyes and found reassurance, not judgment. "Why does Kalfu feel so much stronger than you? I never hear your voice in my head, or feel your influence pressing against me. You never come to me, to talk me out of being his."

Damballah came alongside her, a hint of a worry line on his ample brow. "His kind must press their case, turn another to their way of thinking. I do not have to because what I am is what feels right to many." The worry waned from his features, and his smile returned. "I prefer to let a person decide what they want. Coercion makes for false believers. You have a good heart, Lexie Arden. He knows that and will try to change it."

She moved toward the counter, the burden of her responsibilities weighing her down. "I never figured it would be this hard."

He browsed the empty store. "What did you expect? A mambo is a beacon to her people and to the gods she serves. It's not a role many would embrace."

She twisted her hands together. "I'd hoped my role would be to help people. To tend to the sick and downtrodden like the queen, but all I seem to do is fight for my position. I keep having to prove myself, thinking I will win over the doubters. In the end, I only create more conflict."

"Being a leader is never easy." He lifted a stuffed voodoo doll from a display nearby and squinted at it with wonder. "And part of leading others is continually showing them you are the person meant to guide and nurture them. All people need convincing that

188

someone is better suited to a task than they are. It's one of the many quirks of your species—you hate to be led, and prefer to lead. But not everyone can lead, can they?"

She crossed her arms, the chill soaking through her dress. "Are you ever going to tell me how to fix this mess?"

"No." He returned the doll to the pile with the others. "But you already knew that. If I told you what to do, I would be no better than Kalfu. But I am around if you need me. I hear all who speak to me."

She hugged herself, the warmth of his visit fading. "I hate feeling so alone."

His raucous chuckle bounced off the walls of the store. The shelves of merchandise vibrated.

"You're never alone." He raised his thick arms and gazed around the shop. "You are alive. And where there is life, there you will find me."

White smoke oozed from the floor, covering his feet. It slowly crept upward, snaking up his white trousers. His jacket was soon engulfed, along with his shoulders and neck. Before it covered him completely, Lexie saw a young couple peering in the windows of her shop door.

She glanced back at Damballah, but the spirit's white smoke was gone. At her feet, the green-eyed cat stood, gazing up at her.

"I guess you're always around."

She went to the door. The first thing that struck her about the couple was their black T-shirts touting pentagrams with horns. An unsettling tickle awakened in her center.

They had painted their faces, making their features indistinguishable. Dark circles covered the skin around their eyes and lips. A dark gray paint concealed their foreheads and cheeks.

She found the display unusual considering Mardi Grad had just passed, but this was the French Quarter—festivals, costume parties, and wearing masks had become a way of life.

The young man jiggled the handle on the door and pushed it open. Lanky with a lumbering gait, he strolled into the shop, leaving his short girlfriend behind him on the street. The ungentlemanly gesture aroused Lexie's ire.

This guy is bad news.

The cat stuck close to her, rubbing up against her legs.

"Hey, cool place." He scanned the merchandise on her walls.

His girlfriend strutted in the door, her army boots clanging on the floor.

The hair on the back of Lexie's neck stood up. Something wasn't right. Hundreds of customers had come through her doors, but these were the first two who made her uncomfortable.

The cat meowed at her feet. Lexie sensed warning in the animal's tone.

"Cute cat." The girl leaned down to pet Damballah.

Before her hand reached him, Damballah hissed and backed away.

The young woman popped up; anger radiated from her venomous little eyes.

Lexie wanted them out of her store, but couldn't afford to provoke them. She had to play it cool and use her wits.

"Are you looking for anything in particular?" She sized up his skinny figure and baggy clothes, trying to get a read on his intentions.

"You got anything we could use to cleanse our apartment?"

He wasn't there to chase away a ghost. She picked that up immediately. Money was what he was after, but not hers. The impressions confused her.

"Yes, I do." Lexie waved him to a wall on her left. "Our herb packet and smudge sticks are over here."

She kept an eager eye on the petite blonde, who remained by the open door as she moved across the store.

Lexie showed him to a wall of glass shelves decorated with sage sticks. Her insides prickled as the man drew nearer.

"Sage is the best for cleansing a new home or apartment."

The *click* of a lock made Lexie turn around.

The young woman had shut her front door and set the deadbolt.

"Remember what I told you about chess?" His voice came alive inside her.

Lexie carefully weighed her options.

The blonde walked to where she'd left the baton juju resting next to the counter.

"What we got here?"

The young woman picked up the cane and caressed the dragon's head. "I thought a mambo was never to leave her baton juju unattended."

Lexie called to the power in her center, readying it to strike. But before she could approach the woman, the boyfriend grabbed her from behind.

"You pissed off the wrong man, Mambo."

His fingers slipped around her neck and squeezed.

A disorienting panic rose from her depths as the air got cut off from her lungs. She lashed out but the scrawny man was too strong. He batted away her attempts to break free. The abject fear in her screamed for help, and she reached out to the only person she knew who could hear her.

Magnus!

He presented himself, inches from her, his face riddled with distress.

"Lexie, hold on. I'll get help."

Her attacker's grip tightened. Lexie clawed at his hands, begging Magnus with her eyes to help her. The young man was deceptively strong for one so skinny. Through the haze of spots closing in around her vision, she saw the young woman, carrying the cane across the store to her.

Magnus vanished. Her panic skyrocketed.

Don't leave me.

The black and white eyes of the dragon cane made her remember her power. Light, black and white, coursed through her muscles, filling her with strength.

She dug her nails into the man's hands and kicked behind her. A warm trickle eased down her neck.

"Bitch, stop hurting me!"

His grip became impossibly strong. The air cut off completely. Lexie felt her fight quickly fading.

The woman stood in front of her grinning. "So much for the new mambo."

A *crash* resonated around the room. Almost as soon as she heard the sound, the man released his grip. She clutched her throat gasping, and dropped to her knees.

A woman's piercing scream sent a shell-shocked Lexie diving for the floor. When she turned her head, the shadow of something next to her made her look up.

The woman stood over her, the baton juju in both her hands, raised like a bat ready to strike.

Strains of a struggle brought Lexie out of her stupor. She

pulled herself to her knees and peered behind her.

The black dog had her attacker pinned to the floor, his muzzle gripping his throat. The young man lay perfectly still with wide, terror-stricken eyes and his arms outstretched in surrender.

Lexie wanted to shout for joy.

"Let him go, you shit!"

The female assailant charged the dog, brandishing the cane and ready to bring it down on Louis's head. Lexie screamed for her to stop. Then something black lunged in front of the young woman. The baton juju flew from her hand and crashed into glass shelves stacked with herbs. Shards of glass tinkled on the ground. She heard a *thunk* as the girl's head connected with the brick floor. Something materialized next to the woman's lifeless body— Magnus straightened out the sleeve of his black coat.

Lexie got to her feet, still woozy.

"Are you all right?" her ghost asked.

She didn't answer but ran for her purse behind the counter.

Still shaking, Lexie got her phone out and dialed 911.

"I'm at 901 Royal Street," she shrieked. "Please hurry. Someone just attacked me in my shop and they're still here."

While the 911 operator took her information, Lexie checked on the couple. The woman lay sprawled on the floor, unconscious. Her partner had not moved a muscle as Louis's fangs remained pressed precariously against his carotid artery.

Checkmate.

Chapter Twenty-One

Blue lights shone through the windows of the shop, adding to the somber mood of everyone gathered inside. Lexie, wrapped in a blanket, waited at the door as paramedics loaded Liana Gardner, the young woman who had tried to rescue her boyfriend, into the back of an ambulance. She had regained consciousness after the police arrived but still could not stand without tipping over.

Lexie turned from the entrance to Liana's partner in the crime—the lanky Forrester Ellis, aka William Turnbull, aka Lester Moreau. Two police officers stood over him as he waited, handcuffed and kneeling, in a corner of the store.

"He's been arrested for armed robbery, assault, kidnapping." Emile lowered his phone after reading off his priors. "He's a bad character."

The arrival of the police after her frantic 911 phone call had stopped Lexie's shaking, but the nervous, tense feeling—like she was going to explode out her skin—never eased. Super sensitive to every stimulus around her, she continually flinched at every loud sound. Her head remained a jumble of pictures from the attack.

Lexie rubbed her thumb over the nose of the dragon in her cane, praying for its soothing energy to settle her. "He was sent by someone who wanted me dead. He told me I pissed off the wrong man."

Emile's gaze drifted across the room to the handcuffed young man. "Let's find out who that is."

Emile took off toward the perpetrator. Lexie followed, feeling safer if she stuck close to the detective.

With the paint wiped away, the tattoos on Forrester Ellis's face made him appear even more terrifying. He had two black tears down his right cheek below the outer corner of his eye. Strange black symbols covered his face and neck. The same odd shapes tracked from his wrist all the way up to his shoulders. There was something about the marks that struck a chord.

"Emile, look at his tattoos. What do they remind you of?"

Emile took her elbow, making sure to help her over the broken glass on the floor.

"You think it's our spell?" he asked, guiding her toward Forrester.

Her eyes scanned the damage, the episode playing over again in her head. Her certainty about most things right now seemed a little shaky, but the similarity to the symbols she'd seen on Renee remained adamant.

"It looks the same to me."

Emile typed a message into his phone. "I'll have Central Lock-Up take pictures of everything on him and compare it to the photos

I have of our victims."

Forrester Ellis sneered. "I want my lawyer. I got rights."

His harsh voice vibrated through Lexie. *You pissed off the wrong man, Mambo*, replayed in her mind.

Emile never glanced up from his phone. "You'll get your phone call after you're processed and we take some photographs of your tats. They look familiar." He put the phone in his jacket pocket. "Same as a few murder victims I've had turn up. Those symbols were carved into their skin. You handy with a knife, Forrester? Or do you prefer Lester?"

"You can't pin no murders on me."

Emile crouched in front of his perp. "If those symbols on your face and arms turn out to be the same as what's on my victims, I could have a good case to get the DA to hold you on murder one. You know murder one, Forrester, you got out of it before. That witness turned up dead and you walked out of jail. Not this time. The evidence is inked all over you."

Forrester's eyes darted around the store. "I didn't kill no one."

"You tried to kill this woman." Emile motioned to Lexie. "Why?"

Lexie reached out with her power, anxious to see what the young man knew, but he wasn't easy to read. It was as if something blocked her.

She went to Emile and whispered in his ear, "Ask him what he knows about voodoo."

Emile hesitated and then raised his head to Forrester. "You like voodoo?"

Beads of sweat popped up on Forrester's brow. "I don't know nothing about it."

"But you know what a mambo is." He kept his eyes on his

suspect. "You and your buddy both called the owner of this shop mambo. How could you not know anything about voodoo but know about the mambo?"

The sweat trickled down Forrester's cheek. "The store's called Mambo Manor. I was calling her the same as the sign out front." He shifted his weight from one knee to the other. "I want to get out of here and call my lawyer."

Emile arched into him. "Whoever sent you to take care of the mambo knew those tats would link you to the murders I'm investigating. Someone set you up. They sent you here to silence the mambo, and then was going to frame you for the deaths of three other people."

Forrester's firmly pressed lips softened, his eyes rounded, and doubt lines creased his brow.

A shift occurred in the air. Whatever magic protected him flickered like a failing light bulb. For a split second, she got an indication that the strings someone had pulled to keep Forrester compliant were about to break.

Seconds ticked by. Lexie tapped into the waning energy around Forrester. He must have sensed it too because his cool façade shattered.

His hands twisted in the cuffs, but he never raised his eyes.

"He'll kill me if I talk. He'll kill my entire family."

The deadpan delivery surprised Lexie. Forrester was terrified of whoever put him up for the attack.

Emile sat back on his heels, his long slow sigh settling around them. "Let me get him before he gets you."

Forrester turned his head to Lexie. His sneer was back, along with his cocksure bearing.

"You got a powerful enemy, lady. He paid me to scare you.

That's all."

Emile edged closer, tensing like a tiger about to strike. "Who paid you?"

Forrester grinned with defiance. "After I get my lawyer and we cut a deal, then you'll get a name."

To wait for lawyers and litigators to work out a deal could take weeks, and she didn't have that long. If Forrester was meant to scare her, the next one coming after her would try to kill her. She had to speed up the process and get him to talk.

Emile stood, shaking his head. "Take him to central and get him processed. We're going for attempted murder."

Lexie stepped in, anxious to see if the crazy idea in her head would work.

"Can I try something?" Her voice carried over the shuffle of the officers helping Forrester from the floor.

Emile faced her, his mouth twisted into an apprehensive scowl. "Try what?"

"I can touch him and find out whatever you want. All his past crimes, his illegal connections, the stuff he won't tell you without a deal."

At first, Emile stared at Lexie as if she was out of her mind. She careened her head around to him, hiding her face from Forrester and the other police, and then winked.

Emile nodded, letting her know he understood. "Sure. Why not? You're the mambo of this city. You can probably get everything I need without getting lawyers involved."

"No, man." Forrester retreated, backing into the officers guarding him. "Don't let her touch me. She's got powers."

"Who told you that?" Emile took Lexie's elbow and ushered her closer. "Give me a name, and I can ask her to stay away from you, but without a name, I might have to let her do whatever she needs to do."

Lexie got into the act. She rubbed her hands together. "I won't hurt you. You won't even know I'm in your head."

Forrester raised his shackled hands. "Keep her away from me."

His brittle voice drew a few looks from the other officers in the store.

"I'll tell you what you want, but don't let her put no bad juju on me."

Emile rested his hands on his belt. "I thought you didn't know anything about voodoo."

Forrester's gaze darted back and forth between Lexie and Emile. Beads of sweat dotted his upper lip, and a flush rose up his neck and colored his cheeks.

"My grandmother's a priestess. She's warned me about the mambo. Says she's in league with dark spirits. She's bad for the city."

The officers next to him chuckled.

Lexie did not share in their laughter. For her, it was a sad reminder what mountains she still had to climb.

"If you want me to protect you from her ..." Emile curled his fingers, beckoning for him to give up his secret. "Give me a name."

Forrester shook his head and remained tight-lipped.

Lexie's frustration roused the black in her center. She could smell his fear, and the darkness in her wanted to exploit it. Perhaps it was time to put Kalfu's power to use.

She leaned into the young man, allowing the sinister side of her to trickle through her muscles and bones, spreading to her extremities.

She waved her hands in front of him, letting him see the

blackness taking over her fingertips.

Forrester's face dripped with sweat. His eyes bulged, and he had the panicked gaze of a man about to face a firing squad.

"If you know what I am," she whispered while dangling her blackening index finger over his hand. "Then imagine what I will do to your soul when I touch you."

Forrester recoiled, butting up against the police officers behind him.

"Harold Forneaux," he screeched, never taking his eyes off her finger. "He paid me five thousand to scare the mambo. He wanted me to rough her up, get her cane, and bring it to him." He rubbed his neck where Louis's teeth had left a red mark. "He didn't tell me nothing about no dog."

Emile retrieved his phone from his jacket. "Get him to lock up. I need both of you men to sign on as witnesses to his testimony."

The larger officer on Forrester's right gripped his shoulder. "You got it, Detective."

Escorted by two lawmen twice his size, Forrester left the store, his head hung low.

She faced Emile, hiding her hands. "What are you going to do?"

"Calling my boss to get a car to Harold's home and bring him in for questioning." Emile shifted his attention to the person on the other end of his line. "It's me. I'm gonna need you to pull in some favors."

Emile went to the side of the shop to continue his call out of earshot.

Magnus formed next to her.

"Interesting trick. Did our dark-hearted friend teach you

that?"

She wiped her hands together, forcing the black out and back into her center. "No. I guess I'm just getting the hang of his power."

He surveyed the police officers still gathered in the shop. "What will you do now that you know it was Harold?"

Lexie had no answer for her ghost. What else could she do but wait?

"You were pretty good when that woman, Liana, was about to go after Louis. I didn't know your powers had progressed so far."

"Neither did I." He avoided her gaze. "I only knew you were in danger, and I had to help."

Louis, who had been quietly sitting to the side, padded up to her.

She rubbed the big dog's ears, and the last traces of black retreated into her center. "And you were the best watchdog ever."

Louis barked and thumped his tail on the floor.

Magnus scanned the faces in the store. "Where's Will?"

Lexie bit her lower lip, her cheeks burning. "I tried to call but got his voicemail." She searched the shop. "I put my phone down and forgot to recheck it."

Magnus encouraged her to look toward the entrance of the store. "I think he got the message."

"Lexie!" Will came rushing up to her, not paying any attention to the mess in the store or the heavy police presence. He only had eyes for her.

She opened her mouth to tell him what had happened when he smothered her in a kiss.

The warmth of his embrace and the ferocity of his kiss took away the last traces of her shivering. She hadn't realized how much she needed him here until that moment. He was the only medicine that could quiet all the aches in her battered body.

"I'm an idiot." Will held her face in his hands, searching every inch of her. "I was tied up with clients and turned my phone on silent and then when I heard your message …" His arms went around her again. "I'm sorry, baby. I should have come right away. Please, forgive me."

For Lexie, there was nothing to forgive. He was there and that was all she cared about.

"Glad to see you made it." Emile returned, gripping his phone and brandishing a smile. "I was about to ask Lexie where you were."

After he let her go, Will looked at the red handprint on her neck. "Dear God." He touched the marks. "Are you okay?"

She took his hand and held it, so thankful to have him in her life. "I'm fine."

His face a deep crimson, Will spun around to Emile. "What the fuck happened?"

His choice of expletive shocked her.

Emile put a steadying hand on his shoulder. "Seems someone sent two thugs to rough up your wife." Emile's attention shifted to Lexie. "Took some talking with my superior, but once they get Forrester's statement, Harold will be brought in for questioning."

"Harold Forneaux?" Will motioned to her neck. "The voodoo priest you told me about? He's behind this."

Emile waved his phone at Forrester as he was being led from the shop by two police officers. "Harold allegedly hired that guy and his girlfriend to scare Lexie into giving up being mambo."

Will's arm fell from around Lexie's shoulder, and the cold pressed in on her.

"He wants more than that. He wants my shop. I believe

Harold is behind the murders of Otis Landry, Renee Batiste, and Gus Favaro."

"Whoa. Wait a minute." Emile held up his hands. "One step at a time, Lexie. Let me get Harold in for questioning on your attack. Then we'll look into the rest."

"Baby, how do you know this?" Will lifted her chin. "Is this a feeling?"

She folded her arms, the events of the evening settling over her. "More than a feeling. I've got a witness who has heard firsthand about his plans to take over buildings in The Quarter and how he means to get rid of everyone in his way."

Will narrowed his gaze on her. "Is this witness alive or dead?"

Lexie shot him a knowing glance, hoping she didn't have to spell it out.

His breath hissed through his gritted teeth. "Magnus."

Chapter Twenty-Two

Will administered first aid to Lexie's neck beneath the lights of the store's kitchen. A night chill wafted in the open door from the courtyard stirring the aroma of coffee. Lexie craved a shot of caffeine, but didn't want to exasperate Will, especially since she'd refused a dozen times to be checked out by a physician.

"When are you going to realize you can't tackle everything alone?" Will held a plastic baggie of ice against the red handprint.

"How was I to know I was going to be attacked?" Lexie gripped the sink. "I speak to the dead. I'm not a psychic."

He lifted the ice bag and checked the marks. "I want to rip apart the son of a bitch who did this to you."

"Emile has him in custody. Thanks to Louis." She motioned to the dog reclining on the kitchen floor, half-asleep. "He grabbed the kid by the neck and held him until the police arrived."

"And where was your ghost?" He tossed the bag into the sink.

"He promised to keep you safe."

"I was there," Magnus grumbled. "Did you tell him I opened the door so your dog could save you?"

"He was there. He helped me by getting Louis." She faced her husband. "What I do is dangerous. I never knew how much until that night I went to get you at that plantation, but I'm committed to this." She banged her fist on the sink. "I have to continue. I can't let Harold win."

"But are they going to be able to hold him?" He ran his hand through his hair. "If they let him out, and he knows your attacker talked. He will come after you again."

"Or he could be too afraid to strike," Magnus suggested. "Knowing if anything happens to you, he is the prime suspect."

She repeated his words to Will, who snickered at her ghost.

"Tell Magnus I doubt something as inconsequential as justice will stop a criminal like Harold Forneaux. Until he's behind bars, you're not safe."

"He heard you." She pointed to Magnus. "He's standing next to you."

Will rolled his eyes. "I prefer the dog to your ghost. At least I can see him."

Lexie touched her neck, wincing at how raw her flesh felt. The soreness had improved a little, but she didn't think she would ever forget the sensation of his powerful hands squeezing off her air. The panic welled-up again, but Will caressed her neck, examining the marks and her distress abated.

"I still say you need to go to the ER."

She moved away from the sink, terrified by the thought of needles. "No doctors. I'll get some fresh sprigs of comfrey from my atelier. I can make it into a salve at home. Best thing for a bruise."

He came up to her, lifting her chin. "Is this what you want? To be surrounded by people who want to overthrow you and hurt you? I know I said I would support you, and I will, no matter what, but we can pack up everything and move back to Boston whenever you want." He lowered his head to her. "Nothing can happen to you. I wouldn't survive it."

She ran her fingers down his askew black tie. "What about your business? You're just getting a name in this city. Big jobs are coming in. This is your dream."

He kissed her forehead. "You're my dream." He searched the kitchen. "Is he still here?"

"Tell him I left," her ghost said right before he melted away.

"He's gone."

Will wrapped her in his arms. "Good. Now I can give you a proper kiss."

In the courtyard, Magnus paced while the lights from the kitchen sent a warm glow to the fountain. The shadows of Will and Lexie sharing an intimate moment made him feel like a voyeur. He'd never been a fan of Will's, but the man's love for Lexie had swayed him.

"You're worried about her."

A dance of shadows came together under the balcony of Lexie's old apartment. A silhouette formed in the center and then the fog fell away, and a naked man stood beside Magnus.

A current of annoyance flowed through him. He'd hoped to observe the couple alone, eager to keep tabs on Lexie's safety, but there was another who now shared his duties. He still wasn't sure how he felt about the strange man/beast, but he would welcome his assistance, especially after the attack in the shop. His ghostly limitations could have cost Lexie her life had it not been for Antoine.

"If you are going to appear in your human form, we need to start arranging clothes for you."

"Only you will see me." His dark skin glistened when he stepped into the moonlight. "I won't show myself to her."

Magnus didn't understand his reluctance. "Why not? She would want to thank you."

A frown spread across Antoine's lips. "The last time I showed myself to a mortal they tried to kill me. People feared me in the swamps. I was hunted. I'm tired of running. Maybe with your master, I can have some peace."

Magnus inched toward him, understanding his plight. He, too, had hidden from the living for decades in his home. Afraid of what would happen. But Lexie had reaffirmed his faith in others.

"She wants you to stay. So does her husband. You proved yourself very useful. You can protect her in ways I can't."

"I've never seen a ghost move things. When you pushed that girl away … How did you do that?" Antoine went to the pond and sat.

Magnus glanced at the kitchen. Lexie and Will's shadows had moved away from the window.

"Lexie's power, the same power you felt in her, I share. It's because of it I can move things. And I have other talents."

The kitchen door opened and a warm yellow light flooded the paved ground.

Lexie's soft voice drifted into the patio. "Will, I'm fine."

Magnus was about to tell Antoine to hide when the man dashed for a shadowy corner.

"Fine?" Will's deep voice reverberated throughout the courtyard. "You have a handprint on your neck."

"I won't go into hiding until Harold confesses. I can't let him beat me like that. I have people who depend on me, and I have to show them I'm not afraid. What kind of mambo would I be if I ran away?"

They strolled together toward the pond. Will had his arm around her. Their faces remained hidden in the shadows.

Magnus sensed her jitteriness. She was doing her best to stay calm with Will, but beneath the surface, she was falling apart.

"Then you're never to be alone in this shop again. If I have to hire a security guard, I will." His adamancy added a tense energy to the air.

"We can't afford a security guard."

"Yes, we can," Will insisted. "You heard what Emile said. It's not safe for you to be alone."

Emile Glapion appeared in the kitchen doorway.

"We're all done here. You two can head home." He came out on the patio. "I have a patrol stationed outside your building. I can keep you guys under protection until we have Harold Forneaux in custody."

A fluffy black dog trotted out of the shadows and right up to Lexie. Antoine placed his head beneath her hand.

She turned to the dog and knelt. "There you are. You were such a good boy, Louis."

The dog's tail wagged, and for an instant, Magnus envied him. He could feel her emotions, sense what she was thinking, but he could never share with her what Antoine did—touch. He would never experience that sensation again.

"What if you can't keep him in custody?" Will patted the dog's head.

That made Magnus chuckle.

If he only knew what Antoine is.

Emile walked up to them. "Let's take this one step at a time. We have a confession. We can get Harold in for questioning and see what happens." He motioned to the dog. "In the meantime, I think you got yourself a pretty good security guard right there."

"He is, isn't he?" Lexie kissed Antoine's snout.

"And what was I?" Magnus asked.

She glanced up at him and whispered, "You know I couldn't do any of this without you."

"Let's get you home, baby," Will encouraged.

Lexie stood. "I'll just get the comfrey."

She walked across the courtyard to her small garden shed, the moonlight glistening on the tin roof.

Magnus was about to follow her when something urged him to stop.

The creak of the atelier door opening echoed around him. Then it quietly closed.

Below the rickety door shone a soft light.

Emile stepped closer to Will. "Did you speak to her about leaving?"

Will blew out a frustrated breath. "I tried. She's afraid it will make her look like a weak mambo."

"Find a way." Emile's strained voice sounded out of character. "I want her somewhere safe until I can get something on Forneaux."

Will lowered his voice. "And if you can't get anything on him?

How long before he sends someone else after my wife?"

Emile rubbed his hand across his chin. "I know how you feel, but I've got to follow the letter of the law with this guy. He's got a lot of cops and judges in his pocket. The slightest glitch and he will walk."

Magnus didn't want to hear any more. He had to convince Lexie to get out of the city.

He sent himself inside the little shed she used for private consults with clients.

A second later, he found her sitting at her workbench in her atelier. Two white candles burned on the table in front of her. She twirled a cutting of a green plant in her hand, staring at the broad hairy leaves.

"What is it?"

She never took her eyes off the cutting. "Will is talking about going back to Boston. He thinks I'll be safe there."

He approached the table. "I heard him, and I agree. You need to get out of this city, but not Boston. You already have a safe place to go—Kalila's."

"If I go there, you can't stay with me."

He sat next to her on the bench. "Emile is not going to be able to protect you from Harold and the Chez sisters. But Kalfu can. It galls me to say it, but I would rather have you alive under his roof than somewhere I can be with you."

"If I take Will there, Kalfu might insist Will leave, or do something to make him leave." She put the green comfrey to her nose and inhaled. "He warned me that allegiance to him makes every woman he possesses end up alone."

He dipped his head in front of her. "You will never be alone. Will would not leave you no matter what Kalfu does. And I am with you for life, dear girl. Fate has deemed it so. Even Kalfu can't break that."

She faced him, tears brimming in her eyes. "Thank you, but I have to find another solution. I can't risk losing Will."

A single black tear trickled down her cheek. Magnus wanted to rub it away before she saw it to spare her the painful reminder of what she'd given up to join with the dark spirit.

When she batted the tear away, she caught a glimpse of her hand. "I can never cry in front of anyone but you. You know all my secrets."

He smiled for her, wanting to ease her heavy heart. "And you know all mine." He glanced back at the door. "We should go. Emile and Will are waiting."

She wiped her face, appearing anxious. "One day I'm going to free myself of Kalfu. I can't spend the rest of my life living like this."

He waited as she stood and gripped the cutting in her hand. "But today, you need the protection of one monster to fight another. When all your enemies are defeated, then you can free yourself of his darkness."

"And when will that be?"

He reached into his center and summoned the energy to open the simple wooden door for her.

"I wish I knew."

Chapter Twenty-Three

Floating in darkness, Lexie lost herself in a happy dream world, where Will's arms kept her safe from all the evil beyond their bedroom door. But her confidence bristled when a strange spotlight shone down, appearing next to her bed. The gray beam carried an uncanny coldness. The threads of ice reached out to her, embraced her body, pulling her away from Will, and bound her in a tight cocoon. There was no air, no way to move, and as a scream climbed her throat, a finger touched her lips.

"You will not put yourself in harm's way. You're too valuable to me." Kalfu emerged in the light, and the cocoon melted around her. "Your ghost is right. You must move to the cottage. I can protect you there."

Lexie sat up, rubbing her head, not sure if she was awake or still asleep. "Why do I want your protection?"

A rumble of impatience slipped through her black center,

mirroring what she saw in his eyes.

"Because Damballah can't help you. You need my dark power to fight the dark magic coming for you."

He was right. And no matter how much he terrified her, she could not deny him. She would have to dance with the devil today so she could battle him tomorrow.

"I have to talk to Will about this."

Kalfu leaned over her, coming within inches of her face. "You will have to head out in the morning."

The darkness surrounding her bed closed in around him. Lexie sat back as his figure became engulfed in shadows. Then the blackness moved toward her. She pushed against it, fighting to keep it away, but it swept over her like a dense fog. She fell back, waiting to land on her bed, but instead, she floated, unable to see or hear anything.

Bright light accosted her eyes, overwhelming her. She winced as she slapped her hand over her face.

"Lexie, get up." Will's baritone voice mumbled in her ear.

She fought to open her eyes, but her lids were heavy.

"Why are you waking me? I'm exhausted."

"Baby, get up. We have to pack."

She opened her eyes and raised her head, her aching muscles protesting with every movement.

"What is it?"

He sat on the edge of the bed, still in his blue pajama bottoms. She glanced at the hazy shards of light coming through the windows and realized it was still very early.

"Emile called and woke me." He had circles under his eyes, and his hair poked up in places. "His men went to pick up Harold Forneaux last night. They found him dead in his home."

Lexie's pains forgotten, she bolted upright, startled wide-awake. "Dead? How?"

Will sagged into the bed. "Carved up like Renee and the others. Until he can get a handle on the killings, Emile wants us out of this apartment and out of the city. I've checked the flights to Boston. If we pack now and leave, we can make the early—"

"I'm not running away to Boston." She swung her legs over the side of the bed, remembering what Kalfu had told her. "We're staying here."

His sigh came out more frustrated than angry. "Lexie, screw the shop, your clients, and your followers. This is your life. I will not put it in jeopardy."

She wiggled her toes as fingers of sunlight stretched to them across the floor. "I have somewhere we can go." She glanced at her husband. "Kalila's place in the swamps."

"What? No!" Will stood, squeezing the phone in his hand. "We're not going out to the middle of nowhere. We're going where whoever is doing this won't find you."

She placed her hand over his. "But they will find me, maybe not next month or next year, but what I am will lead them straight to me. I have no choice but to stay and fight. And I can do that from Kalila's place. It has an energy that will protect me from anyone—"

"An energy?" He tossed the phone on the bed, his voice creeping higher. "Are you kidding me? I'm not going to put my wife's life in the hands of some bullshit energy!" He stormed across the bedroom.

"Will, hear me out." She went to him, touching his shoulder, desperate to get him to listen. "I need you to trust me. You can't protect me from what's happening. I have to fight because only I can do so."

His dark eyes cut into her, ripping out her heart. "What you are, what you can do … I admit it's beyond me, but people want to hurt you." He stepped closer. "I'm your husband. I have to keep you safe from whatever madman is out there. And I can do that better in Boston than here."

She curled into his chest, running her hands up his back, taking comfort in his warmth.

"When we went to the *haute défi*, and I challenged Bloody Mary, I had to confront her alone. You and Emile protected me, but I had to stand before the queen. Just me. And when I battled Emily Mann, it was the same—my fight. This is no different. It's my power someone is threatening. Let me tackle this foe the same way I fought the others. Stand by me, protect me, but I have to face this challenge. I can't run away."

He was quiet for a time. He held her, loudly breathing in and out through his nose.

"All right. We'll go to this house in the swamps. But I insist we bring an arsenal with us."

She eased back from him. "Guns? But we don't have any."

Will reached for his phone on the bed. "But I know someone who does."

"That's the dumbest idea I've ever heard!" Emile shouted, squeezing his mug of coffee.

His loud objection rattled around Lexie's kitchen.

"There's no point in arguing with her." Will sat next to him, a five-o'clock shadow brushed across his square jaw, and a cup of coffee in his hands. "I can't talk her out of it. That's why I called you."

"Even if I went with you, it wouldn't be enough to protect you." Emile banged his drink on the countertop. "You're vulnerable out there. There are too many places a perp could hide and even if we did sweep the area, by nightfall all that would be moot because we would not—"

"Emile, I have others who can protect me." She rested her elbows on the granite bar, dog tired, aching to go back to bed, but determined to make her friend understand. "Spirits who can do more than an army of cops."

"Spirits?" He rested his tightly folded hands next to his coffee mug. "Lexie, I just came from the morgue. Harold's body was cut up just like Renee's, Otis's, and Gus's. Spirits didn't do that. A person with a knife did. I won't stand by and let that happen to you."

She needed to get him focused on something else. Otherwise, he would never understand her reasoning. He might have been the nephew of a powerful priestess, but there were times Emile reminded her of Will—he could never comprehend something he could not see.

"What about the Chez sisters? Have you checked on their whereabouts? They were working with Harold."

"They're gone." His voice had an eerie flatness to it. "We sent a car to their place in the Marigny. The house we have on record for them is empty. It looks like it's been that way for quite a while. Everything was covered with dust and not a stick of furniture in the place. Neighbors claim no one has lived in the house for years."

Will sat up on his stool. "Are these Chez sisters dangerous?"

Lexie stepped back from the bar. "They must have killed Harold."

Will thumped his coffee on the counter. "Why am I hearing this now?"

"I don't want you going to Kalila's house. She was killed there, maybe by the Chez sisters." Emile pushed his mug away. "Those girls grew up in the swamps. They know it better than anyone."

Lexie eyed the dregs of coffee in her empty cup. "Reason enough for me to go. I'm meeting them on their turf, and when I win, this struggle for control will end."

Emile stood and retrieved his phone from his belt. "Let me have the state police go to their mother's old shack in the swamps and check it out before you run headlong into a real shitstorm."

Lexie brought the coffeepot back to the breakfast bar. "Where is their mother's place?"

"You didn't run into it when you went to the cemetery?" Emile arched his brows while opening his phone. "It's right next door to it—the Brown land."

"That name was all over the cemetery."

"Yeah, didn't you know?" Emile tapped his phone. "The Chez sisters are great-granddaughters of Julie Brown."

Chapter Twenty-Four

The glimmer of red, orange, and purple light from the evening sun flecked the swamp on either side of the car. Will maneuvered his car along the narrow road while the trees ahead parted, revealing the glistening light from the tin roof. The cottage seemed to welcome Lexie with open arms. The towering cypress trees and the muted gray clapboard around the house reminded her of a gilded cage.

"This is secluded." Will peered up at the house through the windshield. "Are you sure about this?"

Lexie caught a glimpse of Emile's blue Ford sedan in the rearview mirror. "It's the only way to end this."

Will slowed the car as they came to the circular drive. "End or begin? It seems to me whatever happens out here will only catapult you into another situation and another. I'm beginning to feel like these adventures will be a way of life for us."

She reached for his hand. "How do you feel about that?"

He held her hand and squeezed it. "I don't understand what you do, I don't want to, but I'll support you." He leveled his gaze on her. "But get your ass killed and me and Magnus will spend our eternities hounding you."

"Here, here," Magnus said from the backseat as he tapped his cane on the car floor. "I'm in total agreement with Will."

Despite the jumble of nerves in her belly, she laughed at her ghost. "You two have more in common than you thought, eh?"

Will parked his BMW beneath one of the tall trees next to the house and turned off the engine. "Kalila lived here? Alone?"

Lexie reached for her door handle. "She wasn't alone."

Her baton juju in hand, she climbed from the car. The rotting odor of vegetation from the swamp mingled with the evergreen of the cypress trees. The tail end of the sun sank behind the house, shooting red and orange rays into the trees. Lexie sensed the energy of the approaching night and feared the nightmares it would bring with it.

"Damn bugs." Will swatted at a swarm of gnats buzzing around his head.

Lexie thought it strange that no bugs bothered her, but perhaps Kalfu had arranged that too.

Emile's car pulled in next to them. He opened the door and stepped out.

"This is remote." He scanned the terrain.

Will went up to Emile. "We only have to worry about them coming at us from the road."

Emile went around to his trunk. "And by boat. This is the swamp, Will. Everyone and their momma has a boat. They can come right up to the shore without an engine, and we could never hear them."

Lexie pushed her front seat forward to let Louis out. "But he can hear them."

The dog jumped from the car and shook himself. Instantly, his nose was in the air, sniffing the wind.

Lexie also registered the change. A sudden chill surrounded her. She turned to the porch, following the pull of her black half.

Kalfu, without a shirt and only in his faded blue jeans, leaned over the railing and glared at her. Her center tightened into a dark, smoky ball. He wasn't happy.

"Titu's nephew must go. I will not have her blood here."

A brisk wind swept over the property, stirring the treetops. Black clouds gathered out of nowhere and blotted out the sun. The men didn't seem to notice.

"What did you get us?" Will approached Emile's car. "Anything we can use for self-defense?"

Emile popped open the trunk. "I got quite a few things."

While her husband was distracted, she hurried to the porch, Louis on her heels. She might have been his, bound to his power and his will, but she wasn't about to send the only person trained to handle firearms away. Will wouldn't let her stay without Emile.

"If you want me here, then Emile must stay. Will won't remain without him, and I won't stay without my husband. Considering what we're facing—we need him."

Kalfu's blue eyes rose to the darkened sky. "Send him away. That is not a request."

The wind swirled around her, lifting the hem of her white dress. She stood her ground as fallen leaves rustled across the porch steps. She refused to be intimidated, but the black in her bubbled and pressed into her chest. It was getting hard to breathe. Kalfu was angry, and he would hurt her if she didn't think of a way to soothe him. Something Damballah said came to her.

The devil likes you to think he is that strong, but you have the will and the ability.

"Emile has to stay until the Chez sisters are in custody. If he leaves, I will be in danger. You want me protected, then let him do his job."

His eyes turned an artic shade of blue, purer than any glacier. The air around her got bone cold.

"These signs of impertinence are distressing, Lexie Arden. Keep it up, and I will punish you."

Her right hand trembled, and she squeezed her cane to hide it.

"Punishing people is never the way to get them to do your bidding. You cajole, you sweet talk, and in the end, you reward." She moved closer to the porch. "You want to keep the Mambo of New Orleans in your pocket—keep her happy."

He chuckled and folded his muscular arms. "You can't bluff me. I feel your fear."

"Work with me. Don't patronize me, order me about, or treat me like your servant. Fear doesn't intimidate; it creates anger. And that anger could drive me from you. You want things, and I want things. We either work together, or neither of us will win."

He peered out at the men by Emile's car. "You forget who you're dealing with. I'm the reason you and your husband are alive. My power saved you, and it will save you again. I would appreciate more deference and less attitude."

Her cane responded to the threat. The white in it seethed, undulating with outrage. And in that fury, she found her strength. The jolt of energy rushing into her hand was unlike any other she had felt from the baton juju. The essence of white light in her center grew stronger, pushing the black aside. She sensed a presence with her—Damballah's beaming smile filled her head.

It was the first time she'd seen him, and it comforted her. He was with her, always.

"Part of me belongs to Damballah. I'm just as much his as yours. So stop with the intimidation tactics. It will only anger him, and me."

She turned her back on him and walked toward the men, her heart thumping; she'd never felt so powerful and so terrified. But as she walked along, no tightness grabbed her chest, no torrents of pain overtook her. No lightning bolts rained down from the sky, no sinkholes opened beneath her, spewing up molten lava, no eight-legged sea monsters rose from the swamp, wrapping her in their tentacles. Nothing happened.

And in that nothingness, she discovered Damballah was right. She had the power. She had conquered her fear and gained control.

"How many rounds?" Will asked as she came alongside him.

The pistol in her husband's hand sent a chill through her.

"What's all this?"

Emile had packed handguns, two rifles, a shotgun, and boxes of ammunition in his trunk. In addition, there were a few flashlights, Kevlar vests, and a pair of binoculars.

Will checked the sights on his 9mm as he pointed it at a tree. "We need to protect you."

She watched her husband, captivated by the firearm.

This wasn't Will. He'd never been into guns before coming to New Orleans.

"What we're up against won't fall to guns."

Magnus materialized. "I concur. It seems silly. What lives in

222

these swamps is already dead."

At the foot of the steps to the porch, Louis let out a long howl. The low, creepy sound rattled Lexie.

"Emile, just keep the guns out of sight."

She left the men and hurried to Louis. Before she could reach him, he took off around the house.

"He senses something," Magnus said.

Her instincts quickened, but she didn't feel anything, and that scared her to death.

At a fast jog, Lexie went around the back of the house, antsy to catch up. This wasn't like him.

Magnus floated alongside her, sharing her concern.

She let go a relieved breath when she found Louis on the back porch. The dog frantically pawed at the cypress boards, his whining deepening her worry.

Lexie slowly climbed the back steps. Afraid she might spook him, she approached the dog, speaking softly and holding out her hand.

"Hey, there. It's all right."

She rubbed his neck while the dog kept his eye on the house. Once she coaxed him away, a flash startled her.

An eerie greenish orb formed on the clapboard in front of her. Smoke snaked inside the sphere, and then a face broke through— a woman's scarred face.

"Get in here, Lexie Arden," Julie Brown ordered. "We have work to do."

Lexie almost dropped her cane.

Louis yelped and spun around. He ran at full gallop along the porch.

Lexie remembered what Kalfu had told her about Julie's

association with her dog.

Julie Brown's head floated across the boards, a glower adding to the frightening image.

"What did you do to him? He's terrified."

The wizened face of the old woman faded, but the malice in her eyes never wavered.

"I saved him. The same way I'm going to save you."

The last of Julie Brown dissipated into a cloud of black smoke.

The interaction between the dog and ghost raised Lexie's suspicions about Julie Brown's intentions. Perhaps she needed to do more research on how to rid herself of Kalfu and not trust her librarian.

Magnus stood next to her. "Will is coming to look for you."

Lexie second-guessed her decision to come to the swamp. Perhaps Kalfu and Julie Brown's dark magic wasn't the best choice to tackle the Chez sisters.

"I've got a feeling things are going to get out of hand very quickly."

Magnus raised his gaze to the swamp. "It already has."

The distress in his voice compelled her to turn around.

The flat, green swamp jutting right up to the porch behind them teemed with all things unearthly—the spirits of men, women, children. In an array of clothing, from old-fashioned nightgowns, richly embroidered ball gowns, tuxedos, and tattered overalls, the apparitions hovered above the water, their toes dipping into the algae-covered surface. Their gazes blank, they stared ahead to the house as if waiting for instructions. Some had ropes around their necks, others bullet holes in the temple or forehead. There were those with deep gashes in their throats or their faces partially torn off. Some, though, didn't look harmed at all.

A rumble rose from the water. The mouths of all the ghosts moved in unison. Their croaky voices lifted and called, "She is coming."

A wave of air rushed across the surface of the water and tore onto the shore. The strong gust of malevolent energy hit Lexie in her center.

She grabbed the porch railing, the energy squeezing her chest.

"What is it?" Magnus reached out to her, but his hand passed through her arm.

"Can you feel that?"

Magnus nodded. "And I hear them. It would seem Maman Brigitte is about to make an appearance."

"Lexie?" Will shouted, coming around the corner.

He bounded toward her, the butt of a gun sticking out from the waistband of his jeans.

"What are you doing back here?"

She glimpsed the swamp, but the spirits were gone. The evil presence, however, remained in her core, holding her in its powerful grip.

"I thought I saw something in the swamp."

Will glanced out at the water, his brow furrowed. "What? A boat?"

She patted his chest, not wanting to tell him about Julie Brown just yet. He had enough to deal with.

"No, probably just some turtles splashing around."

He put his arm in the small of her back. "Help me with your bags. You must have packed up everything you own."

"I'm right behind you."

Magnus leaned in front of her. "How long do you think we

will be here?"

She sucked in a breath, still uncomfortable with the dismal sensation closing in.

"I have no idea."

"But I do, Lexie Arden."

His voice rang in her head.

"Now that I have you here, I will never let you go."

Chapter Twenty-Five

L exie flipped on the recessed lights in the library, and a warm glow shone down on row after row of dusty books. The room reminded her of the one her grandmother had kept in her home. Filled with books on everything from herbs to dreams to spells, her grandmother's library had been where she'd gone to escape after her father's death. It was the one place her sister and mother had refused to enter. It was her safe place. And now she had found another.

"Are you sure you want to stay in here?"

Will stood outside the doorway, browsing the books, the pistol tucked into the waistband of his jeans. Louis was at his side, raising his nose into the air, but not venturing past the threshold.

She observed the dog, eager to get his take on the library, but he didn't appear as upset as he had on the porch.

"I want to do some reading." She walked up to one of the

bookshelves. "There's a treasure trove of spells here. I'm hoping I can find a few to help us."

Will smashed his lips together, not appearing impressed as he stepped inside.

She held her breath, waiting to see if he would sense anything odd. But he strutted across the room without the slightest hint of dismay.

"Leave the door open." He kissed her forehead. "Emile and I will be right down the hall in the living room if you need us."

"I will be fine in here. I promise."

With one last wary glance at the stuffed bookshelves, Will walked into the hallway. He stopped at the door and motioned to the dog. "Keep him with you."

Lexie was about to protest, thinking Louis would never stay in the room after what she'd witnessed before, but she didn't want to explain about Julie Brown.

After Will retreated into the house, Lexie dropped her gaze to Louis.

She patted her thigh and cooed to him, attempting to get him inside.

"Come on, boy."

Louis wagged his tail, but he didn't set foot into the room. Then he whined.

"What's wrong?"

She gazed into the animal's big yellow eyes, searching for something to help her understand why she had such a connection with the gentle beast, but there was nothing there.

A creak came from the floor behind her. Louis growled and bared his teeth.

Lexie turned to Julie's corner. A gentle wind brushed over her

SEIZE

bare arms, and the temperature dropped.

The library door slammed closed.

"Why did you do that?" Lexie demanded.

Julie Brown surfaced at the door; her black shawl pulled tight about her shoulders.

"Antoine can stay outside. I don't need that boy in here when we've got work to do."

Lexie's stomach dropped to the floor. She knew the dog was different, but how different? She twisted her hands, feeling naked without her baton juju.

"What did you do to him?"

Julie scrunched her face, making the scars disappear. "I'm surprised he let that boy and those men come inside. Kalfu don't like to share his women with no one."

"I'm not his woman." She stepped toward the closest bookcase. "Tell me about Antoine."

She pulled her pipe from the pocket of her long red skirt. "He worked in the city—red light district—for a madam with a mean streak. She did business with me." She puffed on her pipe and smoke rose out of the bowl. "Antoine came to me on a rainy night with a letter from his mistress, Lulu White. I was to kill him for turnin' down a customer—a male customer. You see, Lulu didn't care what sex you preferred, but when a customer asked, you put out no matter how you felt about it."

"For refusing to have sex with a man, you turned him into a dog."

She set her pipe in her teeth. "He didn't just refuse the man; he beat the man nearly to death. Lulu hung out with the social set and knew a lot of state senators. The boy angered one of her political friends, and she wanted me to kill him. But I took pity on

229

Antoine LaSalle. I was supposed to send back Lulu his severed cock, but I sent her someone else's. How she gonna tell them apart?" Julie's raucous laugh rolled around the room. "I made Antoine into the legend swamp people talked about since I was a little girl—the *rougarou*. I was only gonna let him learn his lesson and change him back. Let him start a new life somewhere other than the city. But then the storm came."

Lexie faced the door, a mixture of shock and anger coursing through her veins. A hundred questions ran through her head at once, but only one stuck out.

"Why have I never been able to pick any of this up? With all the power I have, I should have felt something."

Julie removed her pipe and limped to a bookcase, an indifferent smirk on her face. "That boy's lived on the run since the day I changed him. Hunters, tourists, those wantin' fancy pictures to put in the newspaper, been chasin' him down for years. And you think after all that, he would know how to hide what he is from you? You got to win him over, build his trust. Takes a lot to tame a *rougarou*."

Lexie's heart broke as she considered what Antoine had been through. The hardships of his life made hers look minuscule. But despite all his abuse and ridicule, his heart had stayed pure. That was what she had sensed from him—his goodness. It was what had comforted her. And now it was time to bring comfort to him. She had to right the injustice he had suffered.

"How do I change him back?"

Julie sucked in a deep breath of smoke and shook her head. "You can't change him back. I'm not human no more, and the power to change him back died with me. He is what he is—forever."

Lexie had become a mambo to help others, to make their lives easier, and bring comfort. To be told she could not perform her deepest wish was a blow like no other. She had felt inept as a mambo, weak, lost, and at times afraid, but never until this moment had she been useless.

She went to a bookcase and rested her hand on the dusty shelf, wanting to collect herself.

Julie floated up to her and hovered by her side. "Nothin' worse than havin' all the power in the world and can't help the ones you care about. I know how it feels. When I offered myself to Kalfu to free me of Maman Brigitte, she cursed my kin." Julie took her pipe out of her mouth and tapped it on the bookcase next to her. It didn't make a sound. "I've had to stand by as every girl child descended from me is bound to serve her. She possesses them at birth when they're weak, turns their minds like she tried to turn mine. My great granddaughters are her creation. There's nothin' resemblin' a soul left in either of them no more. But I haven't given up on freein' my family. One day it will happen."

Lexie realized what kept Julie Brown tied to the library. It wasn't fear of Kalfu, but blood.

And what about your family? What will he do to them?

She took in all the books, her desperation to be rid of him stronger than ever. "How did you cast Maman Brigitte out?"

Julie puffed on her pipe, ribbons of black smoke curling around her head. "I came up with a spell. I took pieces from a few spells I knew, powerful ones, like the Once Was spell."

Lexie recalled the horrid spell that had taken Titu. The memory of her maimed friend turned her stomach.

"I thought the Once Was spell was used to absorb power. How can—?"

"Once Was absorbs; mine repels." Julie pointed at a notebook tucked between two books. "What I created drains the power out of you."

A rush of optimism came over her. "Could it send other spirits away?"

"I only tried it on Maman Brigitte, but yes, it might work on another. But which one you sendin' away?" Julie lowered her gaze to Lexie's chest. "You got two of them in there. Might send Kalfu and Damballah away. Then what you gonna do?"

Lexie removed the fragile notebook from the shelf. "Start living my life again."

"Your life?" Julie came up to her, her black eyes swimming with pain. "Child, you're marked. All powerful souls are marked to serve. That's why you got the sight. Those born with it can only serve those who can't see. They can deny it if they choose, many do, but they will never be happy, never be fulfilled. It's what fate's decreed for you."

Lexie clutched the notebook, a dust cloud rising toward her nose. "But I have to be free. I have a good man, a loving man, and I want a family and a life outside of this chaos."

A softness invaded Julie's eyes taking away their black brilliance and turning them an earthy brown.

"Sweetie, what you speak of isn't meant to be, not for you. You're special, Lexie Arden. You're the chosen one. There can't be greatness without sacrifice."

Lexie angrily opened the notebook. "Then I won't have greatness. I want an ordinary life."

"And those living an ordinary life would choose greatness." Julie shuffled to the corner. "The irony of life—we always want what we can't have."

Lexie ignored her and rifled through the pages, reading the spells as she went. "What is your spell called?"

"The Seize." Julie sighed, her image fading. "Think carefully about this. When you drive out one spirit, another might replace it. The void left by one god can be seized by another. So choose wisely, child."

Julie dissolved, but the lingering sweet smell of her tobacco hung in the air.

Lexie didn't stop to consider what the ghost had told her. The lure of being free of Kalfu's stranglehold appealed more to her than the consequences.

She hurriedly gleaned the scrawled handwriting on the pages until she found a spell called The Seize. She brought the notebook under one of the overhead lights to read it.

> *To drain power from a god, you must first find what spirit animal they hold dear*
> *and render it useless. For me, it was the black rooster, symbol of Maman Brigitte's*
> *power. The cane she carries with her becomes the black creature when she manifests.*
> *I seized the opportunity to kill it. Kill the spirit animal of the god possessing you, and*
> *you will be free. Then a simple banishing spell was used to remove the last pieces of*
> *the spirit from me. But finding the spirit animal can be tricky. The gods hide such*
> *things from mortal eyes.*

Chapter Twenty-Six

Foggy from hours of reading in the library, Lexie walked into the hall, frustrated and worn out. She'd spent her time hunting the vast tomes for any information about Kalfu's spirit animal. It was the key to her freedom, but it seemed even the priestesses who had served him had no idea what it was. He'd never carried a baton juju, nor was he accompanied by any animal. Her search could take time; time she didn't have.

In the dim light, she made out Louis's furry outline on the floor outside the library door. Suddenly, her sorrows paled in comparison to his. She'd tolerated this ghastly world of light and dark for only a few weeks; he'd endured his horrors for over a century. Moved by his story, she ran her hand over his soft fur, understanding why he brought her so much comfort.

The dog raised his head and opened his yellow eyes. She regarded his features anew, no longer seeing an animal, but a man.

"Hello, Antoine."

His head popped up and his eyes rounded with fear.

She gave him a reassuring pat. "I know who you are, and I'll protect you. I promise."

He stood and leaned against her, a circle of warmth pervading her being. It lightened her burdens and made what lay ahead for her, Will, and Emile almost bearable—almost.

Then she remembered the husband and police detective she'd left alone for hours in the house.

I wonder what the boys have been up to?

She headed down the hall with the dog close on her heels. When she rounded the wall that opened onto the large living room, she discovered darkness. The house remained deathly quiet.

Antoine growled next to her, raising the hair on her arms.

She waited at the entrance to the living room, searching through the shadows for any signs of Will or Emile. "What do you hear, Antoine?"

Then the refrains of gentle snoring reached her.

She made her way across the hardwood floor, following the distinctive sound she knew well. Will's snoring had woken her sometimes at night.

She crept across the room to the sofa in front of the hearth. There she found the men fast asleep. Their heads tucked against the backrest, their feet propped on the coffee table. In Will's lap, his pistol. Resting against the arm of the sofa next to Emile was his shotgun.

"Their incessant chatter drove me mad."

His voice rumbled in her head.

"They're simply sleeping. I have not harmed them, yet."

The thought of either man under Kalfu's influence dug her

clenched fists into her hips.

"You shouldn't have done that."

She waited for his response, but all she heard was a distant deep chuckle.

That he had manipulated Will infuriated her. Her husband was not his concern. More and more, Kalfu overstepped his bounds. Influencing her husband's business, the house, car, and now this … She had to cut their ties, and quickly.

At the sofa, she brushed Will's hair from his forehead, touching his cool skin to check on him. He was fast asleep. Even Emile had a peaceful look on his face as if enjoying his repose.

She was about to head to the bedroom to find a blanket to cover them when Antoine went to the front door.

He stood there, tilting his head as if listening to something on the other side.

He whined and then pawed at the door.

"You want to go outside?"

Antoine wagged his tail and jumped about, showing his excitement.

Lexie smiled at him. Mystical creature or not, he still had needs and letting a dog outside to go to the bathroom in the middle of the night felt wonderfully normal.

The deadbolt clicked, and she glanced back at Will and Emile, but they didn't move. The door only creaked a little as she slowly opened it, peeking outside to see if the coast was clear before whispering, "Go on."

She held the door open, but the dog would not venture out. He looked up at her and whined once more.

Lexie didn't understand. She didn't feel comfortable with leaving the safety of the house, but she feared the anger Kalfu might vent if the dog peed on his floors.

She checked the porch once more, and then stepped outside, encouraging Antoine to follow her.

The pitch black beyond the house awakened a sense of isolation. The only solace she had was the chirping of crickets and loud calls of the night birds. But the strange noises did little to offset the discomfort the dark swamps gave her. Before she could stop him, Antoine went bounding down the steps, dashing into the brush along the side of the driveway.

Lexie cursed under her breath, but remained by the door, afraid to venture far from Kalfu's protection. Her edginess grew as she waited for Antoine to return. The starless sky offered no dots of light to search the surrounding brush.

"Antoine," she softly called.

A rustling came from bushes to the side of the drive. She took a step away from the door to get a better look.

"Would you come on? I want to go back inside."

Then the black and white ribbon inside her vibrated with alarm. Something was wrong.

Lexie's heart climbed in her throat. The crickets and the night birds had gone quiet. An uncanny silence surrounded her.

Bam. The front door slammed closed. Lexie wrestled with the handle, but the door wouldn't budge.

"You stupid girl."

The booming voice of a woman was all around her.

"Lexie, get out of here," Magnus shouted as he materialized next to her.

"Silence, ghost!"

Maman Brigitte strolled out of a pillar of light behind Magnus.

He opened his mouth to speak, fighting to get the words out, but nothing came.

Lexie turned to the dark spirit. "Let him go."

Maman Brigitte floated up to her, her black gown trailing bones as her rooster cane tapped the mist gathered around her feet. Lexie was held in place as if the weight of a hundred hands pressed against her skin, pinning her to the weathered boards of the porch.

"I will let your Mr. Blackwell go after I'm done with you. Pity you didn't bring your cane. It would have made everything so much easier."

The bushes rustled just beyond the cottage. Lexie searched for Antoine, hoping he could help her. But the dog didn't emerge from the thick green shrubs—men appeared.

Two dark skinned, towering individuals with milky eyes and stone-like faces came toward the porch. Lexie's heart raced as she spied the rope and large burlap sack in their hands.

Kalfu!

But the spirit didn't answer her. She couldn't understand why he stayed away. He'd wanted to protect her, but where was he when she needed him most?

Panic gripped her as the henchmen of Maman Brigitte climbed the steps. She tried to move, fought to break free of the invisible restraints. The men closed in, their ghastly eyes digging into her soul. Her panic morphed into hysteria. She tossed her head, sucking in air as her terror blotted out all reason.

When their icy hands touched her skin, she screamed, praying the shrill call for help would rouse Emile and Will from their slumber.

But in the middle of her shrieks, something was shoved in her mouth. The disciples forced her to the ground, slamming her face into the boards. The burn of rope cinching tight around her wrists and ankles brought tears to her eyes. Outraged, she thrashed about, but the men simply overpowered her, pressing her body into the hardwood. Hogtied and helpless, she screamed, but the rag stuffed into her mouth muffled her cry.

The spellbound men lifted her, and as the dark burlap sack covered her face, she called on her final hope.

Damballah, save me.

The white power in her chest remained quiet. There was not a ripple of acknowledgment.

All Lexie's spirits had abandoned her.

Chapter Twenty-Seven

Inundated with anger, Magnus remained lashed to his spot on the porch as Lexie screamed. The horrific sounds tore him in two. It was the most painful thing he had ever endured. More than killing Frances, more than losing Katie. To be forced to watch Lexie's torment made him feel useless. She was his charge, his to protect, and he had failed her.

The men carrying the sack climbed down the porch steps and then hurried to a break in the brush.

He waited, terrified, as they lugged Lexie. Picturing her bruised and battered, or worse, squeezed the last ounces of strength from him.

Maman Brigitte floated in front of him, her sinister grin churning the hatred in the depths of his soul.

"Tell the men inside, I have the mambo, and I mean to kill her unless they bring me her cane. She will be at the place of sacrifice where my followers will carve her up like Harold Forneaux and Renee Batiste unless they do as I ask." She lifted her cane, stroking the cockscomb. "And after I have the mambo, your soul will be mine. Enjoy these last few hours of freedom."

"Kalfu will have your head for this," he spat at her.

Maman Brigitte's laughter agitated the mist at her feet. It crept down the steps and out onto the shelled drive.

"You have a lot to learn about the spirits of voodoo, Mr. Blackwell."

A brilliant beam of light shot up from the porch and covered her. Then as quickly as it came, the light retreated back into the boards, taking Maman Brigitte and the mist with it.

Magnus stood alone. The silence around him gut-wrenching.

Then the crickets returned, and a new dilemma tore through him. He could appear to the men, but only after they got out of the house. How could he get to them in time to save Lexie?

There was only one person who could help.

Antoine came tearing out of the bushes. The dog flew up the porch steps and arrived at Magnus's feet.

The moment he sat down, his fur undulated and rolled. Specks of light danced around him, and then his figure changed. The light shot upward, and the fur receded revealing a man's ebony skin.

Antoine manifested into his human form, his face creased with anger.

"That bitch tricked me into coming outside. I heard their voices and urged Lexie to let me out." He scrubbed his face. "Her men caught me in the bushes, and she held me under her power. I couldn't change and come to help Lexie. I heard her screams and tried to howl or do something to wake the men, but I couldn't."

Magnus gestured to the front door. "You have to wake the men. They can get their guns and go after her."

"But where did they take her?"

Magnus could still feel the ribbon between him and Lexie trembling. Her fear was his, and that he could not help her devastated him. He had to do something to rescue the woman who had saved him.

"Maman Brigitte said something about the place of sacrifice."

Antoine rubbed his arms against the chill in the air. "I know where that is. It's close to the Frenier Cemetery. There's a house where Julie Brown used to live. Behind it is where they sacrifice to Maman Brigitte."

Magnus pointed the cane at Antoine's nude figure. "You will have to change back before you wake the men. I can't go in. He won't let me."

Antoine dashed for the door. He was not halfway to it when a glittering cloud of light overtook him. He hurried for the front door and turned the handle, and then his hand slipped. The door creaked open as his tall figure shrank behind the cloud. The massive black paw of a dog broke through the fog covering him, and then the mist evaporated.

The black dog bounded into the house.

A ruckus of raised voices and barking rang out. Magnus waited on the porch for the men.

In their wrinkled clothes, the men came charging out, guns in their hands. When he saw them, Magnus summoned the power given to him by Lexie.

He willed himself to appear, forcing his energy to take shape.

Emile froze, but Will rushed right up to him.

"Magnus, where's Lexie?"

He raised his head and faced Will, hiding his shame. "Two men took her and dragged her into the swamp. They mean to kill her unless you bring them her cane."

Emile clapped his hand over Will's shoulder. "I'll call for back up." He rushed back inside.

Will's eyes rounded with fear. "Where did they take her?"

Antoine came out on the porch, wagging his tail.

Magnus pointed his cane at the dog. "He can show us the way. He's been there before."

Will stared at the dog and then Magnus. "The dog can show us the way?"

Magnus's gaze met Antoine's. "He's an extraordinary dog."

Blackness was all around her.

Her wrists and ankles hurt from the rope cutting into them while the burlap scraped against her skin. The sack smelled like rotten meat. She tried to breathe through her mouth to avoid gagging. Sounds became distorted, and the men carrying her never spoke, which only added to her misery. Hearing something would have alleviated a smidgen of her anxiety, and possibly given her a clue as to her fate.

They weren't gentle as they plopped her on something hard. Water sloshed around her. Then the surface beneath her rocked gently. An engine rumbled to life—an outboard motor. She was on a boat.

Soon, water seeped into her sack. Her white dress got soaked, compounding her shivering. Cold, wet, and terrified beyond belief,

Lexie could not fathom how she had arrived at this hellish moment.

The boat bumped into something, and her head banged against the bottom. The engine cut out, then a faint and steady heartbeat came into the boat. It didn't take her long to realize what it was—drums. She gulped back the bitter taste of terror in her mouth. They had arrived.

Her captors lifted her, rather roughly, from the bottom of the boat. A small hole in the sack offered glimpses of the activity around her. The only flashes she picked up were the flickering of torches which came through the dense trees.

Her muscles ached, her hip throbbed, and she longed to see Will. She wished she'd had one more chance to tell him how much she loved him, and how sorry she was for involving him in such a mess.

The men lugged her on shore, their labored breathing barely drowning out the sound of the approaching drums. The smell of smoke came through the burlap sack along with the sound of muffled conversations. Whatever festivities Maman Brigitte had planned were close at hand.

Firelight danced on all sides of her sack. Lexie's heart lurched. At any moment, she could end up in the flames, or perhaps feel the cold stab of a blade jabbed into her belly. She curled into a ball, convinced she had come to the end of her journey.

"Bring the mambo!"

The coarse voices were unmistakable.

The Chez sisters.

Once hoisted over a man's shoulder, his bones cut into her diaphragm. She considered her options with each labored breath. How would she get out of this?

Black dots swam before her eyes. She would probably

suffocate before she discovered the fate the Chez twins had for her.

The men dropped her to the ground, and she landed on her sore hip. She bit her lip, not wanting to give the twins the satisfaction of hearing her whimper. She gulped in air through the woven mesh of the sack, thankful for the chance to breathe without restraint.

The tie securing the sack below her feet finally undone, a cold blast came inside. She shivered, frightened of what awaited her.

The ground beneath squished through her toes. Boggy ground. They weren't that far from the swamps. The sack got yanked over her head, brushing against her nose and cheeks, stinging as it went. The first thing she saw was the back of a rundown shack. Built of cypress and dented sheet metal, it had a rusted tin roof and a rickety back porch that sagged in the middle. She took in the clearing next to the shack, and any hope of escaping from her captors plummeted.

Men and women, dozens of them, wore ritual attire—white clothes secured with red sashes—and danced in a frenzy around her. Torches with bluish orange flames were set up in a ring outside of the dancers and fluttered in the breeze. The smoke-covered clearing was alive with the sound of drums and chanting.

Two men, their eyes glazed over and milky white, grabbed her hands and carried her across the clearing. Ahead were two roughhewed posts set in the ground.

They neared the poles and then she noticed the rope.

The men thrust her against the posts and stretched out her arms.

"Let go of me."

They didn't react as they secured her hands, one to each post. Her legs were splayed apart, and her feet were also fastened, making it impossible to move.

The burn of fear in her chest deepened as dancers with milky white eyes circled her like sharks. Their strange gyrations resembled what she'd witnessed on the banks of Bayou St. John. Some bent their heads all the way to touch their backs, others crawled like insects, and some looked so awkwardly contorted that Lexie was sure their spines would snap. One man scurried around on all fours, braying and eating at piles of straw left below each of the torches.

The drummers picked up the beat. The rhythm vibrated through Lexie, mesmerizing her but also ratcheting up her dread because she knew when the drumbeat reached a crescendo, her life would end.

Lexie tried to swallow, but her mouth was dry. Tears filled her eyes.

Outside the ring of fire, shadows, shaped like men and women, moved erratically, imitating the dancers around her. Their openmouthed expressions evoked images of pain and madness. Faces twisted into silent screams before melting into the surrounding night. Their suffering swarmed inside Lexie, slashing at her center like a knife. The agony zapped all her strength, and she collapsed. Her head fell forward, and her arms and legs stretched taut against her restraints. It was as if her power had deserted her.

"You're ours now."

A hand lifted her head by the hair. Lexie wanted to cry out but had no strength. The Chez sisters stood in front of her, wearing long black robes. Their fiery red hair kinked by the humidity, their pasty white skin, and their deep red lips gave them a fiendish appearance.

But it was their eyes Lexie found the most disconcerting. Bright blue without a hint of imperfection, they seemed better suited to a saint, not demented servants of a voodoo spirit.

"We finally have the great mambo at our mercy."

Helen and Corinne spoke together, but it wasn't their lips that drew Lexie's attention. It was the baton juju gripped in their hands.

Made of shiny black wood, it had the head of a rooster, with a cockscomb forming the edge of the handle and his sharp beak the point. Carved feathers traveled all the way down the staff. At the tip were two chicken feet, stretched downward and ending with sharp talons. The display of shiny feathers and the rooster's face was almost lifelike.

"Did Harold know you have Maman Brigitte's cane?"

One of the sisters grinned and stepped forward, letting go of the cane.

"Stupid man was oblivious to everything we did. We used him, made him believe we wanted him to gather the energy to please our lady, but he was just a front to keep our secret safe. Maman wants what you have, Lexie Arden. And she means to get it."

The other young woman holding the cane approached. "Corinne and I did admire your tenacity in the beginning, Mambo. The way you took the baton juju of Damballah from Bloody Mary was inspiring, but now it's our turn to reign, and we won't demand another *haute défi* to do it. The lady told us to take what we want. So, we're giving her you."

Lexie darted her gaze from one sister to the other, and then it struck her. Helen and Corinne—*H. Cory.* The name Mike had given her for his boss, the one interested in the haunted buildings in the French Quarter.

"You're the ones who came up with this plan to kill Renee and the rest. You hired Mike Le Breaux to research buildings you could use to your advantage. It was never Harold's plan."

Helen smiled, seeming impressed. "Very good. Shame we can't keep you around to work for us. Finding smart help is so hard."

Helen brandished a black-handled knife.

Every ounce of Lexie's attention stayed on the razor-sharp blade. "You two will never be accepted as mambo." She struggled against her binds, the rope cutting into her skin. "The queen must appoint you. I am the chosen one."

"The queen is dead. She holds no more power." Helen waved the knife in front of Lexie's face. "And when we have your baton juju, we will be more powerful than the queen ever was."

"Wasn't draining Gus, Otis, Harold, and Renee enough for you? You have their power. How much more do you need?"

Helen charged up to her, baring her teeth. "If we're to achieve greatness, much more. Your power will give us the real prize—the shadow spirits. Control the dead and you own the underworld."

The confession drained the warmth from Lexie's skin, deepening the horror of what lay ahead. The balance between dark and light would be upended. If the living controlled the dead, the checks and balances the spirits of voodoo adhered to would end. The sisters would rule as mambos of the city, and could eventually force their psychotic aspirations on the entire world.

"If you control the dead, Maman Brigitte can rule the underworld. Is that why she put you up to this? To oust Kalfu?"

Corinne came forward. Her graceful movements disturbed Lexie. She sensed this was the sister to fear. Her ambitions emanated from her like the stench of death from a rotting corpse.

"She's been wanting out from the yoke of Kalfu for ages. She would be free of her husband and your master. Free to take the underworld without men ruling over her."

"Ah, I knew the cow was out to get me. Not to worry, Lexie Arden."

The darkness in her rippled.

"He's not going to hand over his power to you." Lexie tugged at her ropes, hunting for any weakness in the coils. "Kalfu will never hand over what he is to Maman Brigitte."

Helen backed away. "When our festivities are done, he will bow down to the lady, so will your ghost."

The mention of her ghost took Lexie by surprise. "Magnus? What has he got to do with any of this?"

Corinne stepped up to her. "Dead is dead, and what Maman wants, she gets."

She tapped the cane on the ground three times and then stepped back, joining her sister a few feet away.

The drums stopped. The dancers fell to their knees, holding up their hands as if praying to the heavens. The clearing around her was silent. Not even the crickets chirped.

Mist billowed from the ground. The dancers hooped and hollered, shaking their hands and shouting in unison, "She is coming."

The mist thickened. Color blended with the smoky guise— shades of black on velvet material became visible. A woman's gown with crisscrossed bones and skulls in the skirt entered the picture. Then her creamy white shoulders, head, and beautiful face materialized. Green eyes stared at Lexie. Maman Brigitte let out a fiendish cackle.

"Mambo. So now you are on my playground." She crooked

her finger, motioning the twins forward. "Time to take your damned power for good."

The kneeling dancers began to chant. "Mambo, mambo, mambo."

Maman Brigitte tapped her cane in time with their chanting. The feathers carved into the wood changed. They glistened in the torchlight and then puffed up like a bird about to preen itself. The head of the black rooster in the handle moved. Its cockscomb fell to the side, remaining black. The bird's beak rose upward, and as the rooster arched its back, the traces of stiffness in the cane fell away. It stretched, and then flapped its mighty black wings, letting go a hellish crow.

The sound awakened the replica baton juju Corinne held in her hands. It vibrated, and the bird's feathers along the shaft ruffled in a wave from the tip to the handle. The animal's neck pinked and the skin plumped. The feet popped out from the tip, and the rooster flexed its toes, flashing its steel-colored talons. The rooster hidden in the cane came to life, moving and wiggling out from its prison of wood.

The followers around them cried, "She is here," all at once and then crawled toward Lexie.

They grunted as they approached on their knees, staining their white clothes with mud. Their milky white eyes stayed on her, sucking dry her last hope of seeing her husband again.

The air around Lexie thinned. It was hard to breathe. She fought harder against her restraints as the hunger for oxygen consumed her. Then the glint of something shiny whisked by her face. The blade of a knife came within inches of her cheek. Lexie's knees buckled.

Helen held the knife to her throat with a cold sneer. "By the power of light, the power of dark, I take all you are and claim it as my own. You have no will; you have no mind. I will devour all that you are." She raised the knife higher and looked toward the starry sky. "Grant me the power, spirits. Give me all she possesses."

"Do it," Corinne urged behind her. "Before the cock changes back, carve her up."

Helen's blue eyes seared into Lexie. Right before she brought the knife down, Helen's face changed.

Her mouth opened wide, her eyes rolled back in her head, her back arched, and her face turned toward the sky. Her body twitched, and the knife slipped from her hand.

"What are you doing?" Corinne yelled.

She darted forward to check on her sister.

Helen convulsed and fell to the ground, a shaking mess. White foam spilled from her lips, and her limbs never stopped shaking.

Maman Brigitte sniffed the air. The black rooster at her feet huddled close to the hem of her dress, its feathers quivering.

A brilliant beam shot up from the ground, blinding Lexie. She shut her eyes and then opened them when the glare lessened.

Standing in front of her in a white suit, black tie, and black cowboy boots was Kalfu.

"You didn't think I'd let them hurt you."

"You bastard!" Maman Brigitte came at him, shaking her fist. "This is my sacred ground. My ritual. You've broken our laws by coming here."

Kalfu faced her, and the black in Lexie bubbled up like hot tar.

"You attacked what is mine to steal my power. You have broken our laws, not me, you stupid bitch."

The venom in his voice surprised Lexie. She had never heard

251

such language from him.

"I will have my blood. The ritual has begun and cannot be stopped." Maman Brigitte snapped her fingers and smoke rose around the skirt of her dress. "Your mambo will be mine."

A gray cloud closed in around her, covering Maman Brigitte and her rooster until all that remained were the spirit's furious green eyes. She and the bird became lost behind the wall of fog. A breeze rushed in and swept the cloud away. All traces of the goddess vanished.

Kalfu turned to Lexie. "Any ritual against you can be changed to empower you—remember that."

Lexie tugged on her ropes. "Get me out of here."

He winked. "All in good time."

She wanted to scream. Then a loud *bang* cut through the din of Maman Brigitte's devotees.

That was a gunshot.

Lexie ducked, wanting to drop to her knees, but her restraints kept her from moving. Paralyzed with fear, she remained huddled against the poles.

Then a second *pop* whizzed by, sounding closer than the first.

Lexie scoured the clearing, desperate to find out who was firing. There was movement from the side of the shack. Two men hung in the shadows, their faces difficult to make out. A torrent of emotion came over her. She knew who the shooters were. And when a black dog ran out from the shelter of the shack, barking with exuberance, her desperation to be reunited with her husband renewed her attempts to break free.

Screaming men and women in white ritual attire ran in all directions. The ensuing chaos of blurring faces made her forget all about the pain of the rope cutting into her skin. She knew rescue was close at hand, but waiting for it was agony.

Two men participating in the ritual rushed past her. Lexie caught a glimpse of their eyes. They were brown and glistening with fright; the milky white had left them.

She searched the crowds. Maman Brigitte had abandoned her followers, leaving them dazed and confused.

Corinne tended to her sister, kneeling over her and patting her cheeks to get her to come around. The black rooster stood next to them, trembling as the rest of the believers ran for their lives.

Will jumped out from the side of the shack, a gun poised in his hand. Her heart swelled. Emile was at his side with Antoine sticking close. The two men took off into the clearing.

Will spotted her. Her eyes connected with his. She had never known such elation. He bounded across the open ground, dodging frightened worshipers, his anxious gaze locked on hers. But then her joy slipped as she noticed one face missing from her rescuers—the only one who understood the deepest reaches of her soul.

Where's Magnus?

Chapter Twenty-Eight

How did I get here?

Magnus peered down at the strange black mist twisting and circling him. The world of shadows where he found himself was not his. It held no warmth and no comfort. He didn't understand what had happened. Moments before, he'd been with Will and Emile at the side of the shack. Then a relentless gloom had enveloped him and brought him here.

His anger gushed. Who had dared take him away from—

"Welcome, Mr. Blackwell."

He knew that voice.

Magnus's indignation turned to sheer outrage when Maman Brigitte walked out of a wall of mist, her black gown of skeletons engulfed in the same smoggy swirls dancing around him.

"Why have you brought me here? I belong to the mambo."

The woman's disturbing cackle reverberated through the

realm of shadows, agitating the wisps of mist into a feverish dance.

"Cut the shit. This is where you belong, Mr. Blackwell—the world of the dead. I tried to show you that when I sent your family to coax you here. But you're just as stubborn as that bitch you serve."

Magnus went to charge her, furious for what she'd called Lexie, but he couldn't move, could not lift his hands. The haze around him held him in place.

She motioned to a wall of swirling clouds beside him. "I have someone who wants to speak with you."

The murky surface flattened to a smooth finish. Then, movement, indentations, and lines zipped across the expanse. Figures pushed through, creating outlines he didn't recognize. Soon the shapes changed. Faces jutted out, a silky sheet of white stretching taut over their features. Colors cropped up, flesh tones and glimpses of hair came into focus but sank back into the murky depths before Magnus could recognize anyone. Other faces pushed through, only to roll over and evaporate.

One face solidified, bringing with it memories of loss and pain.

"Come back to me," Frances begged.

Her lovely pink lips and the light in her honey-colored hair called to him, but Magnus didn't cave. He knew better than to believe any demonstration provided by the crazed voodoo spirit.

"Why are you doing this?" Magnus hardened his voice. "She isn't real."

Maman Brigitte sauntered closer. "But you want her to be real. Join me and she will be. They're all here: your brother, father, Frances, and your mother."

Then the one person he'd prayed not to see, the person whose face still haunted him, emerged from the smoke. Her blonde hair and sharp features were the same he'd idolized in his childhood. Emilia Blackwell's smile, the warmest he had ever known, lifted the careworn lines on her face.

"Magnus, honey, come home. It's time for us to be together. I've missed you."

He squinted at the apparition, aching for it to be real. "Momma?"

Maman Brigitte swooped alongside him. "Don't you want to be held by her again?"

His mother's face dissolved into the gray fog. The overpowering grip of grief, the same that had devastated him on the day she'd died, slammed into the center of his being. His mother had been the only person who understood him. During his lifetime, and in the solitude of his afterlife, he'd often wondered how different his circumstances might have been had she survived a little longer.

But then, a tug came from Magnus's chest. Lexie was searching for him, calling to him, but the shadows around him had blocked his ability to answer.

"Ah, there she is." Maman Brigitte came around in front of him. "Your master's voice."

"She's not my master. She's my friend."

"Friend? Do you think a modern woman such as Lexie Arden would want to associate with a man like you? We all watched you in the beginning, doubted she would stick with you, but she did." A devious smile swept across her lips. "But now that she has Kalfu and Damballah's power. She doesn't need you to protect her anymore. Leave her and come with me."

Her words awakened the doubts he sometimes harbored about

his place with Lexie, but his practical nature had refused to believe he wasn't essential to her. They were a team, even if they had grown distant since she'd embraced Kalfu.

"I will never leave Lexie."

"We'll see." She snapped her fingers and disappeared, taking the mist with her.

A forceful gale hit Magnus. He held up his hand to block the wind, and when it suddenly stopped, he found he was on the clearing behind the shack. Before him, a disorderly mob of men and women dressed in white ran in all directions, screaming and calling out to Maman Brigitte to save them.

He stared in wonder. He was back, and the men had launched their rescue of Lexie.

It did not take long to find her. Still secured to the poles, Lexie stared lovingly at Will, who was next to her, wrestling with the ropes around her ankles. Emile was there, his shotgun aimed at the Chez sisters, who cowered on the grass.

Magnus's anxiety ebbed. This was more than he could have hoped for. He'd missed the excitement, but everyone was safe.

Even Antoine was there, baring his teeth at the twins.

But when the warm rush of his reassurance faded, the dim outline of another spirit surfaced next to Lexie. In a tailored white suit, and his black cowboy boots floating above the boggy ground, Kalfu grinned at Magnus, his unholy eyes radiating their dark light.

The ribbon he shared with Lexie throbbed as if rejoicing in its master's presence.

Suddenly, Magnus's limbs became like lead, and he felt hemmed in by an unseen force. He couldn't move. His dread rose, and he reached out to Lexie, calling to her through the connection they shared. Before his thoughts reached her, a wall of smog cut him off.

Kalfu emerged from the clouds, drawing closer to Magnus.

"I will take care of the mambo from now on, Mr. Blackwell. You're to stay in a quiet place I have arranged for you in the land of the dead."

Magnus's horror took over. He fought with everything he had to free himself of Kalfu's grip, but he couldn't move an inch.

You manipulative bastard!

Chapter Twenty-Nine

Lexie's wrists throbbed, her ankles chafed, and the chill coming through her thin dress escalated her shivering, but Will's touch chased away her fears. The firelight from the torches illuminated the upheaval around her. Maman Brigitte's disciples had scattered, their shouts echoing across the field.

"Hold on, baby. I'll get you out of this."

Her husband furiously worked the knots securing her to the poles. She ached to throw her arms around Will and tell him how much she loved him.

Emile stood a few feet away, his shotgun pointed at the Chez sisters, who were on their knees before him. She relished watching Corinne and Helen quaking, their black robes stained with mud. After everything they had done, all the innocent people they had killed, she hoped they rotted in prison for the rest of their lives.

"That's not very kind."

She glanced over her husband's shoulder, to the man in the white suit, smiling at her.

Her hatred for Kalfu festered in her soul. For someone professing his desire to protect her, he'd sure seemed to be absent when she'd needed him most.

"Where in the hell were you when Maman Brigitte abducted me?"

"I was there," he said. "I saw it happen, but behind every action is a plan, Lexie Arden. My plans for making sure you're never challenged again as mambo."

He passed his hand in front of Will's face.

"I'm almost there, Lexie," Kalfu said to him.

"I'm almost there, Lexie," Will repeated in a deadpan voice.

Shock and panic churned within her. "What have you done?"

Kalfu came around Will's side. He rested his shoulder on the pole next to her as he studied the men.

"Let's say I guided them as they set out to come and get you." He snapped his fingers at Emile.

Emile lowered the shotgun. Antoine stood beside him, another statue.

"I wanted to make sure you were protected." Kalfu slid away, moving like a snake in the grass toward Corinne and Helen. "These two ladies, on the other hand, will no longer be under the protection of that cantankerous bitch, Brigitte. I've got plans for them."

"What are you—?"

Will stepped in front of her. He raised his head and then she saw his eyes. They were milky white.

Bile rose in her throat. She had volunteered to let the spirit into her soul, but Will and Emile were innocents and not part of

Kalfu's diabolical games.

Kalfu waved nonchalantly at Will. "Not to worry. The eye color isn't permanent. It's what happens when we take over the living. You've seen it before."

Will used the black-handled knife to cut her ropes. His stiff movements and vapid expression frightened her.

"Let him go."

Will freed her hands and stooped down to cut away the ropes away from her ankles.

"Not going to happen." Kalfu waved to the departing crowd. "We use people to do our bidding and then make them forget. Will, Emile, Antoine will have no recollection of this fiasco—only that they saved you."

Trembling, she cupped Will's cheek, but he didn't acknowledge her.

"Why are you doing this?"

Kalfu inspected the cowering girls. "I thought that would have been obvious. Do you want to explain to your husband why this is happening? Tell him about me, about us?"

She rubbed her sore wrists and faced the master of her dark half. "He knows."

Kalfu's wicked grin tightened her stomach into a knot.

"He doesn't know everything."

She wanted to destroy Kalfu at that moment. Rip his energy from her and be done with him forever, but she knew that could never happen. Will was all she had left, and she couldn't risk Kalfu taking him away.

When the last of her restraints had fallen to the ground, the girls huddling together whimpered.

Their trembling and fright-filled eyes moved Lexie. "What

will happen to them?"

Kalfu stepped closer to Will. Her husband didn't resist, didn't flinch as Kalfu took the knife from his hand. She could not stand to see his white eyes staring off into space. His paralyzed stance eviscerated her.

Kalfu put the knife in her hand. "Kill the black cock."

Lexie stared at the knife, not sure what was going on. Julie's journal had killing Maman Brigitte's spirit animal as a way to rid a person of her possession. But Lexie didn't belong to her. So why kill her chicken?

Kalfu grabbed her shoulders and spun her around to face the bird cowering next to the twins.

"You kill the cock and then Maman Brigitte will serve you on this plane. She will be unable to attack you again or to hurt anyone you love."

Lexie shrugged off his grip. "Why would you want her to serve me? What are you up to?"

Kalfu raised his head, the playful gleam gone from his eyes. "I'm saving your ass. If you think I'm cold and calculating, Lexie Arden, then you have no idea the shitstorm Maman Brigitte will rain down on your life. When she gets wind of what's happened, she will hunt your family down until she has carried out her revenge. You know what happened to Julie Brown's descendants. Do you want to risk yours coming under her influence?"

His words rocked her to her core. Confronted with the possibility of having a rampaging voodoo goddess possessing her family put things in a whole new light. She didn't have a choice.

"Hurry," he urged in a disquieting tone. "While the cock is manifested, she's vulnerable."

He shoved her toward the bird. She almost stumbled.

What am I doing?

The sisters screamed as she approached, holding out the knife.

"Quiet," Kalfu grumbled. "I will deal with you two in a moment."

He waved his hand over them, and the sisters fell mute. Their mouths opened, but no sounds came from them. Fear mushroomed in their faces as they tried to speak. Tears trickled down their cheeks—black tears.

Repulsed, Lexie concentrated on the rooster. She wondered if her fate would one day be the same as theirs: huddled in a grassy field, frightened out of her wits, and utterly helpless.

The cock rustled his feathers when his black eyes spotted her.

She wasn't sure what to do: lunge at it, or slowly creep up to it.

"It will stay with its charges," Kalfu said behind her. "It's bound to the sisters and cannot leave them, so it will not run. Stab the knife into its heart."

Lexie closed in, all the while trying to figure out where a chicken's heart would be. She knew it had to reside in the breast. She couldn't deal with killing an innocent animal, but a magical one—that was different.

The rooster kept its eyes on her, not moving as she drew near. When she raised the knife about to strike, the animal lowered its head, almost bowing to her.

"Do it now!" Kalfu shouted. "It's about to change back!"

Spurred on by his harsh tone, Lexie drove the knife into the animal's breast.

She buried the blade to the hilt, making sure to place it deep. A few black feathers touched her hand. They were so soft.

What have I done?

The god-awful screech the rooster gave dropped her to her knees. She covered her ears, appalled by the sound.

The knife fell out of the bird's chest. Black light shone from the wound. It grew, blanketing the bird in an unearthly glow. The creature pitched over, landing beak-first in the grass.

On its side, the animal stiffened. Its neck jutted upward and its head curved at an odd angle. Its feet came together, its toes pointing downward, and the body elongated into a staff. The feathers shrunk and became impressions carved into the black wood. The cockscomb rose upward, forming the top of a handle and the beak the tip. The baton juju of Maman Brigitte took shape.

"Take it." Kalfu gestured to the staff. "As long as you possess it, she will be dutiful to you."

She hovered over the black cane, still not sure if she wanted this.

With her right hand, she gripped the staff, closing her fingers around the black feathers carved there.

It started as a tingle, nothing as overwhelming as her dragon cane. But it was a pleasant sensation that zinged through her muscles. The black in her rippled with excitement, stretched upward and then settled.

That was it—no all-consuming chasm. No euphoria, no wild rush of energy. She wrapped both hands around the cane, waiting for more.

Kalfu dipped his head to her ear. "What Maman Brigitte's cane has given you is insignificant compared to what you already possess. You own her now. That is all you need to concern yourself with."

"How dare you!"

Maman Brigitte's voice thundered through the clearing.

"You had no right to take my baton juju!"

A clap of lightning tore through the sky and landed a few feet away from Lexie. The electrical charge in the air made her hair stand up and her teeth chatter, but she held on to the black cane.

This might not have been a good idea.

Maman Brigitte, in an aura of glowing light, walked out from the spot where the lightning had struck. Her fiery hair and green eyes ablaze, she held up her black rooster cane like a warrior queen.

But it wasn't Lexie she charged to meet, it was Kalfu.

"You deceitful shit! You lied to me."

Kalfu crooked his finger at Lexie, urging her closer. "You were the one who broke the peace by having your henchman kill several property owners in the city. You planned to collect shadow spirits to give yourself more power, didn't you?"

Lexie made her way across the grass, the blades tickling her feet.

Maman Brigitte hissed. "And who set those spirits free from the River of Shadows. Damballah wants them back, and he will make you pay."

"I have an arrangement with our dear Sky Father." Kalfu's spiteful stare honed in on Lexie. "Since we share the mambo, there can be no war between us. Whoever rules the mambo rules the world."

How was she the only thing keeping Damballah and Kalfu from fighting for control of the universe?

I'm just an interior decorator from Boston.

Maman Brigitte shook her fist at him. "All the gods know you tricked Lexie Arden, but you will never keep her. I will see to that."

Kalfu stepped around the wide skirt of Maman Brigitte's black dress. "Do your worst, Brigitte, but in the meantime, Lexie Arden will hold on to your cane to keep you under control."

The infuriated goddess of death went to the sisters, who were huddled together on the ground. "I chose these two to receive me, not your …" Maman Brigitte glared at her. "Plaything."

"Hey!" Lexie held up the black cane, angry at the inference. "I am not his plaything. I'm my own woman."

Maman Brigitte cackled. "You're the same as all the rest of his bitches. He will use you and toss you aside when another, more powerful one comes along."

Kalfu waved his hand down Lexie's thin nightgown. "There are none more powerful than her, Brigitte. Even your husband, The Baron, agrees."

"You two are always conspiring against me." Maman Brigitte furiously pounded her cane into the ground. Another bolt of lightning tore across the cloudless sky. "You have broken the agreement between us with this despicable act." She pointed her cane at the Chez sisters. "Return my charges to me."

Kalfu shook his head. "They have killed in cold blood and for personal gain. The punishment is clear."

Maman Brigitte's bravado faltered. The fire in her eyes dimmed. "No, you can't. They're just children. I was the mastermind. I urged Harold Forneaux to carry out the murders. He had his men carve up the victims."

Kalfu pursed his lips, seeming unconvinced. "And then had your charges kill Harold, taking the power he'd collected from the dead. They were going to continue your plans to secure the shadow spirits. And they had Lexie Arden brought here to drain all her power, my power, and give it to you."

Lexie glimpsed the terrified young women. "What will happen to them?"

Maman Brigitte raised her head, her beautiful face a mask of grief. "They will be taken to the bridge to blackness and cast to the other side. They will be banished from the world of the living and the dead, never to return."

Memories of the soul she had cast across the mystical bridge returned. The terror in Emily's face as the clouds of nothingness had engulfed her still tormented Lexie.

"They should be given to the authorities," she whispered to Kalfu. "Their fate should be determined by a court of law, not you."

Kalfu glowered at her. "Part of being a mambo is making decisions that hand out a justice not determined by your courts. Get used to it." He clapped his hands.

The girls jumped to their feet as if being helped up by an invisible force.

"Ladies, we must be on our way," Kalfu said in a cheerful tone.

Maman Brigitte gave the two young women a loving look.

The black baton juju in Lexie's hand vibrated. The shaking intensified. It became difficult to keep her grip on the cane.

"What's happening?"

Kalfu casually waved at Maman Brigitte. "She's upset. Her cock cane quivers when she's upset. Think nothing of it."

Lexie held the cane, wondering how she would manage with two such powerful pieces in her life.

Will is gonna shit.

She remembered her husband. Will's stone-like expression remained unchanged as he waited with Emile and Antoine next to the poles.

"What about my husband, Emile, and my dog?" she asked, turning back to Kalfu. "You have to free them."

267

Kalfu had his arms around the Chez sisters, one on each side. The terrified young women begged with their eyes for Lexie to help them, but she remembered her journey by boat, stuffed into a sack, and Helen's face as she'd held the black-handled knife against her cheek.

"You have the power to free them, Lexie Arden." His malicious grin stimulated her blackness. "Will them free. My power is yours."

Before she could ask him to change his mind about Helen and Corinne, he became consumed by a burst of blinding light.

"No!" Maman Brigitte cried out.

But it was too late. When the light dimmed, Kalfu and the girls were gone. All that remained was the green grass in the clearing and the chirp of crickets.

The black cane's shaking stopped. The wood warmed in Lexie's hand. It grew hot, almost too hot to touch.

"This is all your fault." Maman Brigitte wheeled around to her. "I will make you pay for this."

The spirit's cheeks burned bright red, but Lexie wouldn't be intimidated. She controlled Maman Brigitte's power now.

"You were going to let them kill me."

"You're going to die someday, girl, and when you do, you will come to me. I will enjoy making your eternity a nightmare."

Lexie held up the cane, satisfaction flowing through her. "But before that happens, you belong to me. Don't anger me again, or I will send you across the bridge to blackness myself."

The goddess grabbed the folds of her black gown. The jawbones of the skulls in her dress dropped open. A whirlwind of black smoke rose from the ground, covering her in seconds. Maman Brigitte's fiendish cry of, "Bitch!" echoed throughout the field as a funnel-shaped cloud ascended into the night's sky. The howling wind sucked the fire from the circle of torches and the tin roof of the fishing shack rattled.

Lexie arched against the tempest, struggling to stay upright.

A piercing whistle filled the clearing. Lexie covered her ears and turned away from the twister. And then, in an instant, the noise, the windstorm, and Maman Brigitte were gone.

Lexie stood in the quiet clearing. All that remained of the ritual was the circle of snuffed-out torches.

It all seemed like a horrible nightmare, but the painful red marks on her wrists told her it had happened. She debated how she could return to her life and pretend nothing had changed. For her, everything was different. She was not the naïve woman who had moved to New Orleans so many months ago. She had seen the dark underbelly of voodoo, and it had scarred her forever.

She hugged herself, the chill of the night closing in around her. Her husband and Emile remained like mannequins in a store window.

Across the clearing, movement tore her attention from Will. The ethereal creature bobbed across the grass, his blond hair and long black coat caught up in an undetectable breeze.

"Where were you?"

Magnus scowled as he inspected her wrists. "Kalfu kept me away. I was trapped by that shack and had to watch the entire affair."

Lexie bit her lower lip, disturbed by his news. "He's gone too far this time."

His gaze dropped to the black rooster-headed handle. "Is that what I think it is?"

Lexie held it up for him to get a closer look. "Maman Brigitte now bows to me. Unlike Kalfu and Damballah, I can tell her what to do."

"Careful with her. She means to hurt you."

Lexie set the cane's tip on the grass. "I can't swing a dead cat around here without running into someone who wants to hurt me."

He squinted at Will and Emile. "Why are they not moving?"

"Kalfu has them under some spell." She stepped up to her husband. "I don't think they know what's going on."

"How do you break this spell?" Magnus waved his hand in front of Antoine's snout.

"Kalfu said I have the power to break it. I'm not sure what to do."

"Lexie, do what you told me to do. Tap into your center of power, then think what you want to happen and it will. That's how I have learned to hone my ability to move objects. And occasionally people."

Magnus's reassuring grin restored her confidence. Funny how he could do that. Whenever he was around, she felt strong.

Lexie gripped the cane in her hand. The sharp cockscomb cut into her palm. The ripple of energy wasn't as strong as her dragon cane, but the effect was invigorating.

In her mind, she pictured Will and Emile waking up, embracing her and feeling energized by their rescue. The power in her center pulsated, as her desire to have the men return to her grew.

"Lexie?"

It wasn't Magnus's melodic voice. It was her Will.

The milky distortion had left his eyes. His arms went around her, and she kissed him, reveling in the peace he brought to her soul.

"I thought I'd lost you, baby," he murmured in her ear. He let her go and scanned the clearing. "When I saw you tied to those poles, with the Chez sisters about to cut you up, I was glad Emile brought all his damned guns."

Emile came up to them, still gripping his rifle. Antoine was at his side, jumping up and down and barking.

Emile embraced Lexie and kissed her cheek. When he stood back, he motioned to the cane in her hand.

"Where did you get that? That's not another baton juju, is it?"

"I can't wait to see how you handle this, dear girl," Magnus said with his usual sarcasm.

Lexie ignored her ghost and decided to stick to the truth as much as she could without frightening the men.

"Actually, it is a baton juju. It belongs to Maman Brigitte. I have it now." She held up the black rooster cane. "I'm going to hold on to it for a while."

She waited, holding her breath, to see what Will would say.

His eyebrows went up in a "who the hell is that" way. It was what he usually did when she spoke over his head.

"Maman Brigitte? Is she like Kalfu?"

The question reassured her. At least he was curious.

"She's not as strong as Kalfu in the underworld. Maman Brigitte protects graveyards."

Emile stared at her. "Does she know you have her cane?"

Lexie let out a breath and set the cane's tip on the ground. "Yes, she does."

Will eyed the rooster handle. "I like the dragon one better."

Her heart lifted. "So do I."

"Well done," Magnus added. "I'm proud of you."

"Dammit! Where are the twins?" Emile's voice sounded steeped in frustration. "We need to take them in for questioning."

What did she tell Emile? She struggled to come up with something that sounded as close to what happened as possible.

"Someone helped them get away. You guys were so into untying me, you didn't see when a man led them into the swamps."

Emile checked the chamber on his rifle. "We have to find them."

She stayed his hand over the gun. "They couldn't have gone far. They know their days are numbered. We need to get out of this place and head to the cottage. Then you can call for backup to help in the search."

Emile lowered the gun. "You're right."

Glad she had appeased the detective, Lexie went to Antoine, patted his head, and then hooked her husband's arm.

Will stuffed his 9mm in his waistband. "We need to get you out of those wet clothes and into a hot bath."

He guided her back toward the fishing shack. Lexie felt the weight of her new cane as she walked, wondering what secrets it held.

Almost to the shack, she glanced over her shoulder at Magnus, who remained by the wooden poles.

She opened her center and called to him with her mind.

"I'm with you, my dear." He floated away from the poles, swinging his cane as he went. "We are a team. Where you go, I go too."

Chapter Thirty

Raindrops dotted the sidewalk outside the front door of Mambo Manor, reminding Lexie of a Rorschach ink block test. But the intricate patterns did little to distract her from the police car parked outside her store—something Emile and Will insisted on despite her protests. She knew the Chez twins were no longer a threat, but their fate, along with her new cane, and her loathing for Kalfu, kept her preoccupied.

A zing crept up her arm. She glanced at her dragon cane, comforted by the weight of it in her hand. Maman Brigitte's distasteful rooster cane never gave her peace, only worry. She didn't feel as if she had earned the baton juju but stolen it at Kalfu's urging. For now, she'd left it in a locked closet back in her condo until she could figure out what to do next.

"Are you ever going to tell me what happened to you?" Nina was at her side, her arms folded as she gazed out the french doors.

"You take off for a few days, and when you come back, we have the police camped outside our door."

Lexie flexed her hand, her fingers stiff from holding the cane's handle so tightly.

"Emile is being overly cautious after my attack. He urged Will to take me away for a few days because I needed to recover."

"And he took you to the swamp?" Nina arched one eyebrow at her. "Not my idea of a romantic getaway."

The anxious trembling inside her returned. It had been there since the confrontation with Maman Brigitte. A sense that things were not over—not by a long shot.

"Are you ever going to tell me about that?" Nina motioned to the faded red marks around Lexie's wrist. "That isn't sunburn. And unless you and Will are into some kinky shit, I deserve an explanation."

Lexie made her way across the store to the glass counter where a selection of magic crystals and silver jewelry were on display. She stopped in front of Nina and raised her head.

"I got them at a ceremony. A voodoo ceremony in the swamps."

Nina glared at her, the suspicion brimming in her pretty brown eyes.

"Why don't you ever trust me? I know about your ghost, your dragon cane, your ability. Why not share the rest with me? I can handle it."

Lexie had grown very fond of her shopkeeper, but she felt it best not to trust her with her secrets—they might put her in more danger down the road. The only soul she ever confided in was Magnus. Perhaps it was a side-effect of who she was or a result of working in a world clouded with deception, but her faith in others had sharply deteriorated over the past few months.

"I know you can handle it, but what I am isn't very easy to explain. There are more sides to being mambo than doing readings or performing rituals on feast days. There's a darker side, and I prefer to spare you from that."

Nina went around her to the counter and picked one of the books displayed there.

"Since I started working here, I've done a lot of research on voodoo and the loa associated with it. Your cane belongs to Damballah. The dragon is his spirit animal. The person who possesses his cane holds his power." She nodded to the cane in Lexie's hand. "Which makes you a powerful mambo."

Perhaps she had underestimated the young woman.

"How much do you know about the sacred spirits of voodoo?"

Nina snickered and set down the book. "There are twelve recognized as powerful, along with several lesser deities."

"Can you name all twelve?"

Nina grinned, her confidence beaming. "There are the spirits of the underworld such as Papa Legba, Baron Samedi, Maman Brigitte, and the evil Kalfu. Then the others who oversee the land of the living like Agwe, Ogoun, Erzulie, Marinette, Loko, Ayizan, Mombu. The lord of light, Damballah, rules over them all."

Lexie knew from experience Kalfu's dark reputation was well-deserved, but she'd not encountered all his fellow spirits. Would they eventually appear seeking alliances, power, or revenge? The prospect terrified her.

The door to their establishment opened and Lexie turned away.

A family of four strolled in; two wide-eyed youngsters zoomed straight for a glass shelf displaying ceramic ornaments of landmarks such as St. Louis Cathedral, Jackson Square, The Cabildo, and Cafe Du Monde.

Nina eyed the little girls investigating the dolls. "I'd better go stop those kids before we end up charging their parents for damaged merchandise."

She took off across the room and skillfully distracted the children by guiding them to a shelf of cloth voodoo dolls.

"What are you thinking?" Magnus asked, materializing next to her.

Lexie admired how the little girls followed Nina. The way they skipped and giggled flooded her heart with sorrow. She would never see her daughter playing in the store.

"What to do next," she told her ghost, hiding her unhappiness. "If I rid myself of Kalfu, I will be powerless to stop Maman Brigitte or any of the other spirits from coming after me. To free myself of the darkness puts me, and everyone around me, at risk."

"I can't believe that. There must be something—"

The door of the shop flew open. Mike bounded inside. His blue button-down shirt was untucked, his gray suit rumpled, and the wild glint in his eyes gave the impression of a man on the edge of madness.

"Have you seen the Chez sisters?" He rushed up to Lexie, holding out his hands. "I can't find them anywhere."

Lexie quelled her desire to knock him to the ground with her cane. The danger he had put Nina in remained fresh.

"Is there a problem?"

"I have to find them," he said in a raised voice. "I've got some business with them. I've been texting, calling, and asking around in the voodoo community for them, but no one has seen them in days."

Lexie tapped her index finger on her cane, debating how to proceed. "What business could you possibly have with them?"

Mike ran his trembling hand through his hair. "Helen and Corinne asked me to put some deals together for them. I have attorneys and business people leaning on me for ..." He edged closer to Lexie. "Look, my reputation is on the line. If those two women are a no-show for deals I set up for them, I'll get slammed. This is my livelihood."

"You should have thought of that before you got yourself involved in their dirty business."

"Mike?" Nina approached, a worried frown on her lips. "Is everything all right?"

Mike twisted his hands together. "Ah, no. I can't find my clients." He pulled his phone from his jacket pocket. "I need to make some calls."

Lexie noticed Magnus floating across the store to the red door that led to the back of the shop. He pushed the door open, and Antoine trotted into the room.

Oh shit!

Lexie moved in front of Mike to block him from the dog's line of sight. "Why don't you get in touch with a few members of the—"

She didn't get to finish before Antoine's big black muzzle pressed into Mike's crotch.

The rumble of an angry growl carried through the shop.

Mike froze, holding his phone in his hand, splaying his legs to avoid touching the dog.

"Ah, what's that?"

"Guard dog," Lexie said with only a passing interest. "After I got attacked and Harold Forneaux turned up dead, my husband insisted I have twenty-four-hour protection."

A bead of sweat broke out on Mike's upper lip. "Yeah, I heard about that."

She admired Antoine's dead-eye accuracy for honing in on his balls. One wrong move and Mike would be losing more than his dignity.

"Maybe the same killer is hunting down all the people Harold associated with. You ever consider getting a dog, Mike? You might need one real soon."

The color drained from Mike's cheeks.

Nina eased closer to him. "Hey, you look horrible."

Antoine growled again, sounding more sinister. He raised his nose slightly upward.

"Ah, I should go." Mike inched backward, cupping his crotch. "I have some things I have to do."

Nina grabbed his hand, stopping him. "Oh, about tonight, I know you had tickets for that play at the Saegner Theatre, but I will have to cancel. It's inventory day and we will be here pretty late."

He shook off her grip and slowly backed into the display counter. "Sure. No problem."

Lexie's stomach tickled with curiosity. Why was Nina making up lies to get out of a date with a guy she was so head over heels for?

"I guess I'll see you around." Without even a second look, Nina went to check on the precocious girls.

The cool brush off made Lexie smile. She sensed Nina's ardor had fizzled.

That makes things much easier.

With a cocky sense of assurance, she turned to Mike, ready to send him on his way.

He remained pressed into the glass counter, more beads of sweat gathering on his brow. He pointed at Antoine.

The canine stood at attention, his eyes riveted on Mike.

"That thing looks as if it's about to eat me alive."

Lexie patted the dog's head. "He won't touch you … this time. But come back here again, and he'll make sure you never walk out."

Mike's mouth dropped open, and his eyes bulged. He took off, his leather-soled shoes slipping on the brick floor as he ran toward the entrance.

His comical retreat made Lexie smile. He deserved worse, especially after how he'd treated Nina. Perhaps a spell to make him impotent?

"That's my girl."

Kalfu's smoky voice oozed with charm.

"I'm rubbing off on you."

The statement irked the hell out of her. She would never be like him.

Mike leaped onto the sidewalk and slammed the door behind him.

Lexie's smile went with him. The blackness weaving through her soul brought her back the hopelessness of her situation.

Antoine nudged his nose into her hand as if sensing her distress.

"Why did you let him in here?" She scratched under his chin.

Magnus adjusted the right sleeve of his coat in a fastidious manner. "Our crooked real estate agent needed a gentle reminder to stay away. Just in case he planned on breaking into the shop again."

Lexie glanced at Nina, who was still with the children. "He won't be back. Nina's done with him."

"Or the Chez sisters' spell on her has ended." Magnus cocked an eyebrow at her. "I wouldn't put it past them. The relationship made things easier for Mike to get access to your store."

Lexie wanted Mike to pay for what he had done to Nina. No one she cared about should suffer such disregard.

"Perhaps I should suggest Emile subpoena his records. He might find a few things there to incriminate him in the murders. Maybe tie him to the Chez sisters. The families of the dead need a scapegoat—something to ease the pain of their loss."

Magnus directed his gaze to Nina, and how she entertained the two young girls with a few toys from the shop's shelves. "I would leave him be. Fate will find a way to make him pay for his crimes."

"You sure about that?"

He turned back to her. "My dear woman, look at me."

A shrill scream ripped through the store. Lexie grabbed her chest and spun around, searching for the source.

A frazzled Nina came scurrying up to the counter, her arms around the two young girls. The children had tears in their eyes, their lower lips trembling.

Lexie went to the children. She held their cold hands, overcome with worry.

"What's happened?"

Nina knelt beside Lexie, appearing as terrified as the children. "There's something in the rear of the store. I was showing the girls a toy drum, and this black thing—like a shadow—came out of nowhere. It was a man with no face. It floated right in front of us on the wall." Nina lowered her voice. "It's not the first time I've

SEIZE

seen it in here."

Lexie stood, gripping her cane. The shadow spirits. They had remained in the background in the past, and had never scared her customers before.

The parents of the young girls arrived at the counter and hurried them out of the shop, soothing their whimpers with hugs and kisses.

Lexie followed them to the entrance. The police officer stationed outside was already at her steps, his hand on his gun. She smiled and motioned for him to return to his car.

Nina came alongside her, watching the policeman climb back in his cruiser. "We're getting a lot of phone calls from people seeing those shadow ghosts. Residents in the city have been stopping by the shop asking how to get rid of them. Whatever is going on, it's getting worse. Is there anything you can do?"

"You have to see to this," Magnus asserted, gliding up to her. "Your time with the Chez sisters kept you from tackling this problem, but it can't wait anymore."

The escalating situation trouble with the shadow spirits reignited her dedication to protect her followers. "You're right. I need to get rid of them."

"What was that?" Nina turned from the door. "I didn't hear you."

Lexie debated what else she could do. There weren't a lot of options. She needed to find the spell to send the spirits back. Her troubles with the council would return, and the respect for her position as mambo would suffer if she didn't do something and fast.

"I need to go somewhere, Nina. Do I have a lot of sessions today?"

Nina went behind the counter and checked the appointment book. She dragged her finger down the open page.

"You have back-to-back readings this afternoon." She sighed and leaned against the counter. "They're all people having the same trouble with these black spirits as we are."

Lexie reached for her purse under the cash register. "You can handle things for a while, right?"

Nina frowned. "Where are you going?"

Lexie gave Magnus a knowing stare. "The library."

Chapter Thirty-One

On the hardwood floor of Kalfu's dusty library, Lexie sat with her legs tucked under her white dress, hungrily gleaning the book in her lap. Her red turban and cane were on the floor, while the overhead lights shone down on the array of leather-bound books scattered around her. She twirled a lock of her blonde hair around her finger as she tried to make out a few faded words on the yellowed pages.

"Why you in such a rush to get rid of these shadow spirits?"

Julie floated along the bookcases, dragging her finger across the dusty spines.

Lexie sighed but didn't glance up. "Because if I don't people will start to discredit me. I've already had one member of the council challenge me because I haven't sent these spirits back. I'm afraid the others will rise against me too."

Julie stopped and read the title of a book, tilting her head to get a better angle. "And people are seein' them all over the city?"

"Yep." Lexie turned the page on the book balanced on her right leg. "I have to find some way to put them back, or chaos will return to the city."

"That city has always been in chaos." She tapped the book on the shelf she was interested in, and it magically eased out from between two others. "Ever since they murdered Simone Glapion, that place has never been right."

Lexie raised her head. "You knew her?"

Julie pointed to the book on the shelf. "Look in that one. I remember it had somethin' about a spell for sendin' spirits back to their place of origin."

Lexie climbed from the floor, wiping her hands on her dress and leaving a dark smudge of dust.

She went to retrieve the book while Julie took a pull on her pipe.

"I did business with Simone—voodoo business. Not her kind of business. I was sad to hear about her dyin' in that fire. She was a good soul."

Lexie remembered the details of Simone Glapion's death, the way she'd been beaten to death with the dragon cane and left to burn in the fire. She'd seen the horrific details through the eyes of the woman's killer—Magnus. Her murder had been the turning point in his life—the one that set him on the road to her.

She opened the tall black book and scanned the pages.

She came to an earmarked page, bits of black candle wax stained it.

"Is this it? Banish to darkness spell. Used on dark spirits, to send them back to their world."

"Could work."

Julie didn't sound convinced, and that perturbed Lexie.

Shouldn't she know this stuff?

"But you need to test it first," Julie insisted. "Never conduct a spell without doin' your research."

Lexie frowned, feeling like a schoolgirl told to do her boring homework. "Titu used to tell me the same thing. But time is a bit of an issue here. I need to send the spirits back before all hell breaks loose."

"You said those pesky shadow spirits were in your store. Try it on them. If it works, you have found your spell."

It sounded like a good plan, but something about it nagged at her intuition. "Perhaps I might do that."

"But drivin' a spirit back to where they come from isn't just about the spell. It's about havin' the right amount of power to overcome their attachments to this plane. And you got plenty of that, child." The ghost examined the dragon cane lying on the floor. "You got Damballah's cane. Use the cane in the spell to give it power. That ain't written in the journal you hold. It's just somethin' all priestesses know."

Lexie had used her cane before in spells. Its power could help her with this one. She remembered Maman Brigitte's cane but decided to keep it locked away. Best if no one knew she had it just yet.

Julie glided toward the baton juju. "It ain't like before when Simone had it. You got one black eye and one white. I won't ask how that happened. None of my business."

Lexie went back to her spot on the floor and sat. "It represents the powers I carry—Damballah and Kalfu."

"But you ain't got Kalfu's baton juju." Julie traced the dragon's teeth with her finger.

Her fingers tingled. Here was her first clue in ridding herself of him.

"He has a baton juju? Have you seen it?"

Julie shook her head and shuffled back to the bookcases. "No one has. And you best be careful of that boy. He makes all kinds of promises but delivers on none. By holdin' on to his cane, he keeps control of his power and the one who wields it. He can manipulate you in any way he likes." She chuckled and glanced at another row of books. "Get his cane, and you have a way to get rid of him."

Again, the nudge of suspicion rose in her center. Could she trust Julie? It seemed everywhere she turned these days someone or something was out to get her. Perhaps she should do some more digging.

Lexie reached for her phone and checked the time. She would have to head back to the city for her afternoon appointments.

"I need to take this spell with me if I'm going to test it."

Julie blew a few smoke rings in the air. "Nothin' can leave here."

Lexie eyed her phone. "I've got an idea."

She took a picture of the page, hoping her technology would outsmart the curse. In the privacy of her atelier, with the herbs and supplies she needed to conduct her magic, she would give the spell a test run.

After she checked the photo, she closed the book and regretted having to leave. There was so much she could learn from the library. She wanted to spend her every free minute in the small room, getting lost in the pages from the past.

She put the last book back into its slot on the shelf.

"I envy you, getting to stay in here and read all day long. I was always happiest lost in a book as a kid."

"Be careful when you speak such desires." Julie put her finger over her lips. "The spirits are listenin'."

Lexie went back to gather up her cane. "Yeah, I know." She picked up her turban. "Kalfu is always in my head."

"Ah, yes. I used to have him in my head too, before …" Her voice trailed away.

"How exactly did you end up bound to this place?"

Julie rested her elbow on a bookshelf. "After I freed myself of Kalfu, he wanted retribution, but the mambo who received his power and this house hid me in this room. She's the one who made it so he couldn't come in here and take me away. It was supposed to be temporary until she could negotiate with him, but she died before that happened. I could never leave this room. When the storm hit, I died here, and discovered my soul could never leave."

"Who was the mambo? Someone from the swamps? Maybe we can find her spell and reverse it."

Julie lowered her head and shuffled to her place in the corner, avoiding Lexie's inquisitive stare.

"No, there's no record of that spell in here. Simone performed it and she never kept journals of her magic. She's the only priestess of Kalfu you'll find no mention of in this room."

Lexie squeezed her cane, holding herself steady, rocked by the news. Of all the past mambos Lexie wished to learn more about, Simone Glapion was at the top of her list. Time after time, her destiny intertwined with the woman.

There were no coincidences in voodoo.

Magnus paced the white shells on the driveway, anxious to head back to the city. The more time he spent among the tall cypress trees and murky water in the swamps, the more he hated them. And the bugs, by God, they were everywhere. Black ones with hideous legs, flies the size of a quarter, and mosquitoes that looked large enough to lift small animals off the ground. He had never been so glad to be a ghost.

A cloud crossed over the sky, blocking the midday sunshine. The gray rose around him. But instead of moving on, the fog lingered, remaining stationary—an unsettling chill shot through his soul. The bright sun shone down on the ground outside his dusky perimeter. Magnus knew then the occurrence wasn't natural. A powerful spirit was close by, waiting to appear.

In the shadows of a cluster of giant oaks, the branches of the trees parted like welcoming arms, making a path. Maman Brigitte walked determinedly from the darkness beneath the trees, pounding her cane as she went. She reached the road, and white dust rose from the shells she crushed under the tip of her baton juju.

"I should have guessed it was you." He glanced up at the sky. "Dark clouds seem to follow you."

"And you as well." She rested her hands on her rooster-headed handle. "Have you considered my offer?"

He chuckled, impressed by her determination. "Nothing will ever entice me away from Lexie."

Maman Brigitte dipped her head. "Then how about an incentive? You come with me, and your little mambo gets out from under Kalfu's clutches."

Magnus stiffened, unable to move as he considered her offer. It was what Lexie wished for most of all.

"How could you do that? Lexie has your cane; Kalfu controls her. He will never allow it."

She tossed her head back and cackled. "I don't need a cane, boy, to get what I want. There are others who would help me. I told you before that bastard Kalfu has angered many in our realm. If you were to agree to give up your human, then the other gods would join forces to stop Kalfu and free your mambo."

Freeing Lexie meant everything to him, but if he agreed, he would never see her again. He wasn't sure he had the strength to go through with it.

"But why do you need me?"

Maman Brigitte floated backward, dimming as she moved away. "Because you're the sacrifice the gods of voodoo require of the mambo. She must give up her most trusted spirit guide to free her soul of darkness."

He took a few steps, following her to the trees by the side of the driveway. "And if I consent, what then?"

She raised her gaze to the cloud blotting out the sun. "The wheels of fortune have already been set in motion, Mr. Blackwell. Don't fight your fate. It only makes things harder. We will meet again soon."

"Magnus?"

Lexie's sweet voice came from the porch of the cottage.

He turned to her, but when he glanced back, Maman Brigitte had vanished.

"Did you find anything?" he demanded, determined to appear steadfast.

"Might have. I want to try it when I get back to the shop."

He stared at the spot where the nightmarish woman had been. The cloud above had evaporated. Only bright sunshine carpeted the ground.

Lexie came up to him, a spring in her step. "You okay? Forgive the pun, but you look like you've seen a ghost."

He wanted to laugh, but the humor of the situation eluded

him. "I guess the trials of the past several days have worn me out."

"Let's just hope the worst is behind us." She pulled her keys from her purse.

Magnus admired the play of sun on her hair, wondering if he could go back to an afterlife without her.

"I have a feeling everything will be better soon."

Chapter Thirty-Two

The aroma of fresh-cut thyme wafted past Lexie while she worked at the faded and scratched table in her work shed. Shards of early afternoon sunlight crept through the cracks in her flimsy wooden door, reminding her of the hour, and the appointments she had waiting inside her store.

But the bay leaves, chamomile flowers, mugwort, and damiana leaves piled on her table could not wait. The freshness of the sprigs, mixed with the Van Van and calamus oil—essential for guaranteeing luck and success with any spell—were at the height of their power.

She lit the candles next to the mass of herbs—one black and one white. She double-checked everything on the picture on her phone. The last thing she had to do before speaking the words to drive the spirits in her store back to the River of Shadows was to lay the dragon cane across the table as per Julie's suggestion.

The moment the cane touched the concoction of herbs, the vibe around the table changed. Something was off.

Magnus sat next to her on the bench, quirking his lips into a strange grimace.

"Why does it feel like you forgot something?"

"Everything is here. This is what the spell calls for."

"And what makes you think it will be limited to the shadow spirits in this building? What about the other spirits, like me?"

She closed her phone. "It only works on dark spirits. You aren't a dark spirit."

He furrowed his brow. "I'm half dark just like you."

She rubbed her hands together, summoning her power. "Yes, but you are bound to me. That is different."

He held his hand over the pile, appearing to test the energy. "Perhaps you're rushing this. You should check with another priestess, like Cecily Henri."

Lexie spread her hands over the mix of herbs and oil. "Cecily has no power to help me. And all the other priestesses I know, I don't trust. Well, they don't trust *me* yet. You saw what happened in my shop today. I have to try this. I have to know if it will do anything."

Magnus sat back on the bench. "Let me be the first to say this is a bad idea."

"It will be fine. Stop worrying."

He folded his arms and glared at her. "That you're not worried is what worries me."

She closed her eyes and concentrated on her center. The black and white ribbon awakened and flowed outward and into the room. She guided it to Magnus, building their connection and fusing his energy with hers. The power surged within her, giving her a growing sense of euphoria.

It began as a tickling in her chest and grew to a hard tug, almost lifting her off the ground. Her power was ready, balled into a beam to direct wherever she wished to send it.

The words she'd memorized floated in her head, then she recalled what Titu had taught her about the emotion needed when evoking a spell. She sucked in a deep breath and put her heart into the recitation.

"By my command, by the powers inside me, I send you back, dark spirits. Return to the River of Shadows. I remove the bonds and free you from this side of life's plane. Return from whence you came."

The table beneath her hands moved. Lexie's eyes flew open, and then the cane on the table vibrated.

The shaft of the cane bent slightly, and then the scales carved into the marbled wood undulated as if struggling to come to life. The dragon head stretched, sticking out its long neck and then tilted from side to side, keeping its one black eye and one white on Lexie. The rest of the cane slithered as the creature came to life. A pointed tail whipped around, and the dragon's chest expanded. It rose higher, its red tongue darting in and out.

With the god fully awake, Lexie was ready to proceed.

It's time.

She slapped her hands into the mixture on the table, sending a waft of dust into the air. A jolt of electricity zinged up her arm. She peered into the dragon's eyes, connecting with its power, and then, unexpectedly, the pearl eye closed. The black onyx eye radiated, bathing the shed in an unworldly glow.

That's not supposed to happen.

Lexie was about to pull her hand out of the herbal mixture to stop the spell when the ribbon connecting her to Magnus violently twisted. It dragged and bucked like a kite caught up in a hurricane.

Magnus stood, clutching at his chest. "Lexie? What is happening?"

"I don't know. This wasn't in the spell book."

He shook, his whole body overtaken by spasms. He rose off the floor, pulled upward by his chest, grimacing in pain.

She yanked her hands from the table and reached up to assist him. A loud *snap* echoed throughout the room. A thrust against her chest slammed her back into a shelf of herbs. She toppled to the floor, stunned.

"Lexie!"

Magnus lifted higher, propelled upward by some invisible force. A beam of light pierced the tin roof. A brilliant white ball engulfed him, snapping him up like a frog eating a fly.

He fought against the light, punching at its edges, attempting to free himself, but it was pointless.

Lexie struggled to her feet and grabbed for him, but her hands went through his ethereal form.

"You can't stop this."

Kalfu's voice infuriated her. She summoned her power, tapping into the dark and light, but it refused to comply. It seemed to feed off what was happening, throbbing with energy. Panic gripped her and the more she tried to clear her mind and hone her ability, the greater the blackness became.

The light ball immersed Magnus. His struggling lessened as if he had given in.

The sight of him, limp and powerless, terrified her.

"Magnus, don't you dare give up on me!"

But he did not even raise his head to her.

Helpless, she stood by as he rose into the beam. He floated into it head-first. Then his red vest and black coat disappeared until eventually, all she could make out were his black boots.

When the last of him ascended into the light, a sound like a banging door carried through the shed.

Lexie stared at the roof, dumbfounded—there was no Magnus and no luminescent beam. She touched her chest and pictured the ribbon she shared with her spirit guide. It floated aimlessly without an anchor. There was no Magnus on the other end, only darkness.

The sensation sucked the air from her lungs. What the hell had happened? Had she screwed up? That was nothing like the outcome she'd expected. Titu had taught her that rushing to perform a spell could create problems. But this?

She had to do something. She scrambled to collect her phone and then noticed her baton juju on the table. The serpent had returned to its wooden state with both eyes open.

The wink.

The open black eye had not been part of the spell. Someone had interfered with her magic. There was no other explanation.

Enraged, she reread the instructions pictured on her phone a dozen times. She had done everything right. This wasn't getting her anywhere.

She had to return to the source.

Batting back tears, Lexie barreled out of the atelier, and slammed the door behind her. The streaks of afternoon sunlight caressing the courtyard's vibrant green plants had not changed since she'd gone into her shed. But the idyllic setting no longer felt warm and cozy. Her world was empty without Magnus. The heaviness of the humidity in the air around her matched the oppressive sensation she fought to ignore in her heart.

She squeezed the baton juju in her hand, forcing herself to stay together. She couldn't lose it—not yet. Lexie had to fight to get him back.

Her obstinacy growing with every step, Lexie marched across the courtyard for the back door of her store.

"I'm going to find out what happened, Magnus. I'm gonna fix this. I promise."

She was gone.

The ribbon connecting Magnus to Lexie no longer existed. The earth-shattering loss took every ounce of energy he possessed. The tattered edges flapped in his center as he glided without any sense of direction. He floated along, contained in a sort of bubble, unable to influence where it took him because he could no longer summon Lexie's power. He was at the mercy of his surroundings.

How can this be happening?

The light around him faded. Black fingers rose from the bottom and streaked upward cutting into the bright light. He didn't like the sensation the black projected. It was bitter and unforgiving.

His boots touched down on something solid, giving him some reassurance that he might have returned to Lexie's world. Then the black embraced him.

"So very happy to see you, Mr. Blackwell."

Magnus strained to make out a figure coming toward him in the darkness, but he knew the woman's throaty voice.

The white of the skeletons in her dress showed up first. The sway of the stiff material made a swishing sound as Maman Brigitte approached.

She tapped the black rooster cane on the ground, the uneasy vibration resonated throughout the dark place, sounding like thunder.

Adamant, not to show any fear, Magnus casually adjusted the cuff of his jacket. "Where am I?"

"My world." She came to a halt in front of him. "Welcome. You will be here for eternity."

He clenched his fists. "I belong to Lexie."

"No, you belong to me. Lexie cast you out. She sent you here."
The spell.

He'd sensed something was wrong before she'd cast it. Someone had taken advantage of her inexperience as a priestess, knowing the sorcery would send him to Maman Brigitte's land of the dead.

"Why?" He held his head up high, determined not to show how losing Lexie gutted him. "Lexie will be just as powerful without me. There was no need to bring me here."

"Ah, but there was," a voice called from the edge of the darkness.

He strutted forward, his white suit arriving before the rest of him. Kalfu's infernal grin reeked of his contempt.

"I wanted you out of the way, Magnus." Kalfu stopped next to Maman Brigitte and clapped his hands together. "You're a real pain in the ass. You're interfering with my ability to control the mambo had to come to an end. I don't need you being Lexie's conscience. I can do that."

The reality of what had happened hit Magnus. He and Lexie had been set up, but the worst part was she had not realized the betrayal. The spell had been rigged by Kalfu to send Magnus here. But what hurt more was the guilt his disappearance would thrust on Lexie. She would blame herself and her impatience.

"Haven't you taken enough from her? She wanted children; you robbed her of that."

"She will have children, I assure you." Kalfu examined his fingernails, appearing bored.

Maman Brigitte brought her cane down hard on the mist-covered ground. "Our deal is done. You have the girl, and I have the ghost. I owe you nothing else. Now give me back my cane."

"And give up control over you? Not a chance." Kalfu faced her, flourishing a cruel grin. "Until she is all mine, Lexie will keep your cane."

"You bastard." The skeletons in Maman Brigitte's gown quivered. "That wasn't our deal."

"So, complain to Damballah." He baited her with his cool gaze. "You will do as I say. And when I require your services again to get rid of the mambo's husband, you will do it."

"No!" Magnus tried to rush the spirits, but an unseen force held him in place. "You can't hurt Will. Lexie will be destroyed."

Kalfu chuckled, his blue eyes twinkling with delight. "And then she will have me to help her, to console her."

"Damballah will be pissed." Maman Brigitte waved off Kalfu's threat. "He'll fight you when he finds what you have planned. He never wants us to manipulate the living."

"I've had enough of that passive giant with no stomach for interfering. Soon, I will be more powerful than him." Kalfu's clenched fist rose into the air. "And when the time is right, I will take what he has. I have a mambo and a large amount of power. He can't stop me."

Magnus feared what lay ahead. An uprising in the voodoo world would claim many lives. He had to find a way to warn Lexie.

Maman Brigitte snickered at Kalfu. "And how do you plan to get that bitch of yours to comply? She hates you."

Kalfu stared right at Magnus. "I will give Lexie Arden something that will bind her to me forever. Something she wants more than anything."

"Lexie won't go along with this." Magnus's soul burned with murderous intent. "She will fight to get me back. And she will defeat both of you."

"You're a fool, Mr. Blackwell," Maman Brigitte chided. "A dead and useless fool."

She cackled and floated away, the sound of her repugnant laugh following her into the blackness surrounding them.

Kalfu remained, his head tilted, studying his newest acquisition.

"It's a shame you aren't still living, Magnus. I had such fun manipulating you during your lifetime. You were one of my more delightful endeavors."

Magnus's anger strained his voice. "You didn't influence me."

Kalfu's eyebrows went up. "Really, my good man? Who do you think whispered in your ear to kill Simone Glapion, encouraged the evil in your heart to grow? Can you not see the planning that went into this? Think about it. You're here because of me."

He turned on his heels and sauntered away.

The dark grew colder and closed in around Magnus. It was something he'd not experienced before—iciness. It clung to him, chiseling away at his resolve.

He went to move but a force like a thousand chains squeezed

at once, not letting him go. He wrestled against it, but he was trapped. He didn't like the sting of panic taking over his soul—he had to get free, or he would go mad in such a horrid place.

The frigid temperature kept dropping. Before long, it permeated every ounce of him. He opened his mouth to call out, but his lips didn't move. The realization amplified his terror. Inside his mind, he let go a ferocious scream.

I have to get out of here. I have to get free. I can't stay like this.

Magnus fought to regain his sense of calm, but knew it wouldn't last long. It was only a matter of time before he lost control of his reason.

No spirit could survive such a hell—not even one as irrepressible as Magnus Blackwell.

Chapter Thirty-Three

L exie shoved open the front door to the Acadian cottage, letting it bang on the inside wall. With the afternoon light accompanying her, she stomped across the living room's hardwood floors. She wanted Julie Brown to know she was on her way, and she was angry. She'd pictured ripping the ghost apart on the drive to the house. But as she proceeded to the hallway and eyed the door to the library, she thought that too good for her.

Unexpectedly, the library door creaked open, beckoning her to enter.

The invitation gave her pause.

"Bring her to me. I will find out what she did to your ghost."

His voice only fueled her rage. "No, she's mine."

Lexie stormed into the room. Once she flipped on the lights, she headed to Julie's corner.

"What did you do? You gave me the wrong spell."

Lexie's blackness still throbbed. She squeezed her dragon cane while the hairs on the back of her neck stood up. The ghost was there, watching her. There was a hint of smugness coming from the old priestess.

"No, I gave you the right spell. It was meant to banish your Mr. Blackwell." Julie materialized, her corncob pipe jutting from her smashed lips.

Lexie squeezed her cane, picturing Julie's skinny neck in her hands. "Why send Magnus away?"

Julie shuffled forward, tugging at her shawl. "Simple. I gave up your ghost's freedom so I could get mine."

The comment blindsided her. "But you're trapped in this library. You told me you couldn't leave because—"

"Maman Brigitte made me a really good offer." Julie took the pipe from her mouth. "I help her get your ghost, and she would set me free."

"But I have Damballah's power." Lexie's words tumbled from her lips, while the fury in her belly ignited. "I could have set you free."

She tapped the pipe against her hand. "His power ain't gonna do a dark spirit like me no good."

I'm going to destroy you!

Lexie went after her, standing over her figure, wishing she could beat the living shit out of her with her cane.

"Where is Magnus? What did Maman Brigitte do with him?"

Julie ignored Lexie's posturing and floated across the room to a bookcase.

"He's in her world of the dead. Where else would he be?"

Lexie followed, the black taking over her reason. But amid the chaos, she found clarity and a way to fight back.

"Why are you still here? Magnus is gone but Maman Brigitte hasn't come for you."

Julie faced her, not appearing concerned. "She will."

"Are you sure about that?" Kalfu's smugness oozed through Lexie, empowering her. "I could stop her with a wave of my hand. Then you would be trapped here for as long as I desire."

The light in Julie's black eyes changed.

Lexie could almost see her confidence siphoning out.

"Maman Brigitte promised she would come for me."

Lexie raised her dragon cane and gripped the staff firmly in both hands. "When did she make this promise? Before or after I stole her baton juju?"

Julie's mouth fell open, and her pipe dropped to the floor. Before it hit the hardwood, it vanished into a smoky haze.

Lexie had her answer. "Maman Brigitte is under my control. She can never let you out of here unless I approve. And I will make sure you rot here forever."

The betrayal meant Lexie could never trust Julie again, but she could still be useful. It was about time she started using all the damn power she'd collected and enforced her will on those who hurt her.

"I will teach you never to double-cross me again."

Lexie raised her cane above her head, the black and white eyes of the dragon shining into the room. The power of Kalfu and Damballah in her center came together in a tight ball. The baton juju vibrated, excited by what was to come. A tingling sensation erupted in her chest, shot down her arms, and passed into her hands. Her body pulsated in time with the cane, resembling two hearts beating as one. An explosion of white heat in her center radiated out to the room. Her hate for the ghost fueled her determination to make the bitch pay for what she had done.

"I bind you to this library, Julie Brown. You're to remain here until I let you go."

"No!" Julie rushed toward her, falling to her knees. "You can't! You mustn't!"

The pain in her voice did nothing to sway Lexie.

"You are to do my bidding, appease my will, and gather any information I may require from these books." Lexie lowered her cane and came right up to Julie's face. "And if you do not help me get Magnus Blackwell back, I will cast you across the bridge to blackness where you will remain for eternity."

The streetlights jutting through the sides of her warped atelier door urged Lexie to go home and be with her husband, but her guilt would not let her leave. On the work table, a collection of the rarest voodoo books she owned were opened to a variety of pages all sharing one topic—how to bring the dead back.

Candles flickered at the ends of the table and all along shelves. She'd even put on the overhead light Will had installed when he'd built the little workshop for her. The converted greenhouse had proved useful for private spiritual sessions with her clients, but she doubted she would ever conduct another. Without Magnus, what was the point?

Not hearing his gravelly voice, or seeing his cruel grin would turn her duty into a chore. He'd made her smile, and occasionally giggle, and his presence had reminded her of how special she was—how unique they were together. And the friendship she shared with him, his constant companionship and advice, would be missed deeply. Without Magnus, she would be incomplete.

But getting him back was the crux of her problem. According to the books, the living could never set foot in the world of the dead. She'd searched for rituals, spells, amulets, and herbal concoctions, but nothing would be strong enough to keep him like before.

Frustrated, she flipped through the old books, not caring if she damaged the pages. Her center ached. She rubbed her breastbone, and a glimpse of her torn black and white ribbon flapping without a connection flickered in her head.

I can't go on as mambo without him.

The door to her atelier creaked open, letting in the noise from the city. The music blended with the laughter of people on the street. Their joyful voices intruded on her grief.

She glanced at the open door, about to snap at Nina for checking on her again when the gray Maine coon cat sauntered in. The white energy in her fluttered. Before she could say anything to the feline, the mist seeped up from the floor.

It circled her ankles and blotted out her white sneakers. It engulfed the fluffy cat, which sat patiently at the entrance. Soon, his green eyes became hidden behind the smoke.

The dense fog climbed like a winding vine, plumping as it shot up, twisting into different shapes until it reached the height of a man. Something solidified inside the smokescreen. When the cloud retreated, Damballah's bald head and smiling face loomed over her. The thick haze eased down the sides of his white suit, eventually sifting into the cracks in the cement.

Damballah rested one hand on the lapel of his suit jacket.

"I told you before to be careful, Lexie Arden. The spirits in the land of the dead are not to be trusted." He motioned to her dragon cane resting against the side of the work table. "Kalfu likes to trick his priestesses, making them do his bidding. You won him Brigitte's cane and her power, but she will have her revenge."

"She already has." She stood from the bench and picked up her baton juju. "She took Magnus from me."

He pointed at her chest, and the shreds of the ribbon that used to connect to her ghost slithered out. Like the torn edges of a wind-ravaged flag, they flapped, reaching out to his hand.

"I know." He lowered his hand, and the tattered ribbon retreated. "I felt it when he went away. She keeps him in the land of the dead. A vile place from what I hear."

Lexie clasped her cane, suppressing an urge to break it over her knee. "Can you help me get him back?"

Damballah cupped her face. His warmth reassured her and the black in her soul retreated.

"I can't help you. This is your task. You must prove to the universe that the bond between you and your ghost is unbreakable. Win him back, and none of the gods will ever be able to take him away from you again."

Lexie wilted in his hands. "But how? I've looked in my books and searched the spells in everything—"

His baritone laughter vibrated the walls of the shed. "There are books, Lexie Arden, and then there are books. The library in your cottage by the swamp is much more than a library. It's a doorway. All you have to do is find the key."

"A doorway? Where do I—"

He went to the bench and picked up her red turban. "Learn. Study all you can in Kalfu's library and you will find the key."

She shook her head, disheartened. "Magnus was right. All you spirits speak in riddles."

"Riddles are clues, my dear girl," he said in his throaty voice, mimicking Magnus. "Remember what I said, *the job of a spirit is to guide, to coax, to influence but never to do. The actions of the living are their own to make.* Those who do not abide by my rule eventually pay the price." He put the hat back on the table.

A thousand questions crowded her head, but only one pushed to the top.

"What about getting rid of the shadow spirits? Is that something I have to figure out on my own too?"

"You're a fast learner, Lexie Arden. You were a wise choice for mambo."

"Was I?" She set the dragon cane aside. "I'm not so sure. I meant to send the spirits in my building back to the River of Shadows. Instead, I banished my spirit guide. I feel like a failure."

His green eyes twinkled as he studied the dragon cane.

"Kalfu has a cane, very much like yours. All the gods of voodoo do. Each is carved in the image of the spirit animal we hold dear. Find a way to Kalfu's world, and you will find his cane. Then you will have the means to free yourself and return those pesky spirits to my river."

Lexie saw the glint of the black and pearl changeling stones. The image of the dragon winking at her with its one black eye as she'd banished Magnus sent a chill through her.

She rubbed her hands up and down her arms. "I'll need his dark power to get Magnus back, but how do I live with it inside me until then? It's like a sickness weakening my resolve to stay good. I get angry, I yell at people I care about when it takes over. How do I keep it under control?"

Damballah set the dragon cane next to the black rooster. "You need something to remind you of the light inside you. To remember the beauty of your soul and why you were chosen to be mambo. Your capacity for love will keep you from being overrun by the darkness."

She swayed on her feet, utterly drained. "I'm sorry, but I don't feel full of love at the moment. I want to kill those who took Magnus from me."

Damballah tapped the tip of her nose. "You need to stop thinking so much. Let what is inside of you guide you."

A strange light came from his fingertip. Her face flushed and a tantalizing heat permeated her body. She became bathed in the uplifting, protective light.

"Remember the love you hold in your heart is your greatest power. Never give up on it."

His singsong voice acted like a lullaby, soothing her doubt, calming her anger. Her eyelids drooped, and no matter how hard she struggled to keep them open, the warmth surrounding her, and the peace Damballah created sent her drifting off to a deep sleep.

"Rest, Lexie Arden. When you wake, your world will change."

Chapter Thirty-Four

Coasting on a puffy cloud and wrapped by sunshine, Lexie's soul hummed with contentment, a happy change from her consuming worry. In a place without a sky above or the ground below, she lost herself in her dreamlike surroundings. More white clouds gathered, bunching together and floating alongside her.

This had to be a dream. But when had she dozed off?

Who cares? Enjoy it.

She relaxed on her cloud and let her hand hang over the side, feeling the air below rush past. Then, something wet and cold brushed against her hand.

What the hell is that?

"Lexie, baby."

Her eyes popped open.

The clouds disintegrated, and the tin roof of her workshop formed. She turned her head, groggy as hell. The shelves on the walls, cluttered with pots of herbs, books, and the tools of her trade, were there—the candles she had lit still flickered.

Will's face came into focus. He stood over her bench, gazing down and smiling.

"You were fast asleep when I walked in here."

Something cold and wet touched her hand.

She glanced down. Antoine lay under her bench, nuzzling her.

"What are you doing here?"

She sat up, holding her head, feeling the effects of whatever Damballah had done to her. The tranquility from his touch vibrated in her bones.

Will settled on the bench next to her. "I called the store when you didn't pick up your phone. Nina told me you'd been out here for hours after you canceled all your afternoon appointments. She said you were upset. I thought I'd better come down here and check on you."

"You came to see me?"

The gesture melted her heart.

She rested her hand against his blue pinstripe suit jacket. She tried to tell him about Magnus, but instead of words, tears came.

"Now, what's so bad?" He held her to him. "You've been hiding out here all evening, haven't you? You only hide when you're upset."

She sniffled against him. "Magnus is gone."

"Gone? What do you mean gone?" Will held her back. "He can't have—"

He stared at her face.

"What's wrong with your eyes?"

The tears.

She remembered her black tears and frantically wiped at her

cheeks, hurrying to come up with some excuse.

He took her hands. "Lexie, what is this? Is something wrong with you?"

She sagged on the bench; all the peace Damballah had given her drained away.

"When I told you I had given myself to Kalfu, some things changed inside me. I have black tears because of him ... and there are a few other adjustments he has made."

Will took her hand. "What else has he done?"

She tried but could not tell him. The fear of losing him outweighed her need to reveal her secret.

"Your success. My success. He had a hand in that."

Will chuckled. "No matter how powerful this Kalfu is, we're the ones who worked long hours to build what we have; not some spirit. I can't believe everything we have is attributed to him."

He was still the same ole practical Will. She should have known he'd refuse to accept Kalfu's influence in their lives. But after everything he'd witnessed with her, why did he remain so resolute?

"Now tell me about Magnus. Where did he go?"

The crushing pain in her heart transformed into a sharp stab. "I'm not sure. But he's gone. The tie we shared, the ribbon that connected us, has been cut."

He squeezed her hand. "How did this happen? You two seemed inseparable."

She wiped the sleeve of her white dress across her face. "I performed a spell meant to send other spirits away, and it sent him away instead. It's all my fault."

"Hey." He caressed her cheek. "Whatever happened, it wasn't your fault. I know it, and I'm sure Magnus knows it too."

She sniffled, encouraged by his assurance. "You think so?"

"He'll come back. You can never get rid of that man." His thumb brushed away a black tear on her cheek. "So, Kalfu did this to you?"

She clenched her hands hiding her shaking. "Everyone committed to the dark side of voodoo has black tears. I should have told you earlier, but I—"

"It's all right, baby. I can't understand your world, but if you want this, then I want it too. But if the day ever comes when you want out, then that's fine with me. Just be happy."

He let her go and stood. He spotted the books on her table and leaned over to read from an open page.

She stood, anxious to soothe the awkward vibe in the air. "I know this is all way out there, but it's my world. You don't have to understand it, just know it is a part of who I am now."

He picked up the book on top of the pile. "Perhaps I should start doing a little reading of my own, so I know something about what you do."

"You would do that?"

He frowned while flipping through the pages. "I'd better start getting to know your world. It sounds a lot more complicated than mine."

She wrapped her arms around his neck. "Thank you."

He put the book back on the table and took her in his arms. "How can I help you? What can I do to make you feel better?"

She rested her forehead against his chest, convinced she'd hit rock bottom. "You can't help me. I have to find a way to get Magnus back."

"You're not alone." He nuzzled her cheek. "I may not know the difference between a Kalfu and a Maman Brigitte, but I'll fight off any bad spirits if you need me to. I'm here for you. And no matter where this path leads you, I'll be right by your side."

It was just what she needed to hear. Knowing she wasn't alone, and that the man she loved was with her, meant everything. It patched the crack in her heart and reignited the tenacity in her soul.

She hugged him tight, never wanting to let go. "I'm going to get Magnus back."

"I know you will, baby." He kissed the top of her head. "You set your mind on something and no voodoo god can stop you."

He kissed her. The warmth of him chased away all her sadness. And when Will pulled away, she coaxed him back to her, not wanting their moment to end.

He brushed his fingers against her cheek. "What is it?"

She gazed into his eyes. "You make me happy. When my world has gone to shit, you always manage to keep me going."

He brushed a wisp of hair that had fallen from her ponytail. "You always did have a way with words."

She laughed, letting go of her stress. His support on one of her darkest days endeared her to him even more.

"How did I get so lucky to find you?"

"It was fate."

Her arms went around his neck. She admired his five o'clock shadow, the curve of his square jaw, and as she basked in the romantic candlelight around them, Lexie wanted to lose herself in Will.

She kissed him again, encouraging him. She thought he might be hesitant to make love in her little shed, but as she coaxed the jacket off his shoulders, Will undid his tie, an eager grin on his lips.

"Are you sure?"

She nodded, taking his tie and easing it from around his neck.

"I just want to feel you next to me."

Will lifted her from the floor, but there wasn't enough room for them on her work table. After ushering the dog outside, he spread his jacket on the floor.

His frenzied kissing she'd not expected. It reminded her of something teenagers did after sneaking out of their homes to steal a few moments alone. Maybe it was the place—somewhere anyone could walk in—that escalated their passion. Lexie wasn't sure, but she went with it.

She helped him out of his shirt and trousers, and caught glimpses of the potted plants and voodoo books around her, feeling slightly guilty. She should be helping Magnus. But her dark half urged her to forget about her ghost and enjoy her husband's attention. Her white power remained eerily silent.

While Will wrestled her white dress over her head, she giggled at his clumsiness. The dress tossed aside, he joined her laughter. Soon, they were naked on the floor, their hands roaming each other's bodies.

His touch chased away the last of her sorrow. The magic between them, the one that kept them together through the craziness, still burned brighter than any voodoo spell.

His hunger for her came through with every caress, kiss, and nip of her skin. Tonight, he was rougher than usual, and she was glad. His arms held her tighter, his hands skidded brutishly over her curves, and when he thrust inside her, it was what she needed.

The aroma of his faint cologne blended with the musky smell of his skin transported her back to their first nights together. His hot breath on her cheek, the feel of him inside her, heated her frozen soul.

The change in the air around her was slight, but she detected something different. It was as if a smidge of electricity touched her skin, and for a second, she got a whiff of freshly cut grass.

No, it can't be.

Her eyes flew open. She wanted to stop Will, to check the shed, but the yearning of her body, so close to coming, drowned her reservations.

When she moaned as the rush of ecstasy raced through her, Will reciprocated with a loud groan.

They lay together on the floor, the flicker of candles dancing on the tin walls.

She sniffed the air again. The perfume of sweet grass was gone. There was only the essence of sex and smoke.

But I did smell it. That bastard!

"It's been a long time since we did it like this." He rolled over, taking up a curl of her blonde hair in his fingers. "The last time was on that Fielding job. In the living room of their unfinished renovated living room."

She nestled into his chest, wanting to forget about Kalfu's intrusion. "You said we needed to christen the house."

He wrapped her in his arms. "I seem to remember we christened a lot of houses together." Will raised his nose in the air. "You smell that?"

She tensed. He smelled it too.

"Tandoori chicken." He sat up. "Unmistakable."

Disappointment ran through her. He was talking about food.

"It's the restaurant a few doors down. They must be cooking for the dinner crowd."

Will got up and reached for his pants. "Why don't I go order some dinner to take home? Then I can help you lock up the store and we can pick up the food."

She sat up, feeling a bit let down. "I'm glad I at least come in slightly ahead of food in your mind."

He zipped up his pants as he kissed her. "You know how I love to eat."

She gazed up at his carved abs, muscular chest, rope-like arms, and broad shoulders. "And where you put it, I will never know."

He shrugged on his shirt. "Get dressed and finish up whatever you need to in the store. After dinner, we can christen the floor of the living room. We haven't done it there, right?"

He grabbed his jacket, stuffed his tie into the pocket, and rushed out the flimsy wooden door.

Lexie climbed from the floor and stared at the books still spread out on her table.

I should be finding a way to get him back.

But she needed time with her husband—a few moments of happiness to soothe her pain.

Later, after Will went to sleep, she could hit the books once more.

She dressed and blew out the candles. When she stepped outside, the night air caressed her hot skin. Still glowing from their interlude, she strolled across the courtyard, thinking of Will ... and Magnus.

Antoine was at the pond. He padded up to her, whining.

"What is it?"

"He doesn't like me," the smoky voice said.

Kalfu stepped from the shadows beneath her old balcony. Back in his jeans and snug T-shirt, he reeked of his usual cocky confidence.

"Antoine always was a stubborn shit."

The dog growled and bared his teeth. Lexie moved in front of

316

the creature to protect him from Kalfu's wrath.

But the spirit wasn't interested. Instead, he motioned to the shed.

"Such a touching moment between you."

Her cheeks burned. "I never took you for a pervert."

He came up to her, his grin churning the acid in her stomach. "I always keep my eye on you. Now more than ever."

An uncomfortable twinge zigged through her belly. "What's that supposed to mean? Nothing has changed between us."

He touched the center of her chest. The black ribbon in her bucked and swayed.

"But it will."

A black wave of energy hit her. It was like drowning in a pool of tar.

Lexie stumbled backward until she ran into the edge of the pond. She clung to the cement with her fingernails, waiting for the deluge to wash away.

Antoine was at her side, his cold nose against her cheek, his warm fur cuddling her right side.

When she could look up to where Kalfu had been, there was no sign of him.

She sat on the ground, her back against the pond, regaining her wits. The dog stayed with her, his head in her lap, his yellow eyes never straying from her face.

She searched her center, mindful of any changes in her being. Nothing registered.

"What was that for?"

"*To remind you that you are mine,*" came back in her head.

"Okay, I got a little of everything on their menu."

Will strolled back into the courtyard.

When he saw her on the ground, he rushed to her side.

"Lexie! What happened?"

She let him help her up while wiping the film of perspiration from her face.

"I got a little dizzy."

He touched her brow. "When was the last time you ate?"

"Ah, breakfast. I've been too preoccupied to eat."

She thought the lie sounded good enough. There was no point in telling Will about her encounter with Kalfu. She didn't need to worry him.

"Let's pick up our dinner and get some food in you." Will put his arms around her, holding on to her. "You're doing too much."

"No, I'm fine," she told him while he walked her toward the gate to the street.

The flutter of nerves tweaked her stomach.

What did he do to me?

Chapter Thirty-Five

Thunder rattled the french doors in the back of her shop. Lexie sat at her kitchen table, books spread out in front of her, while the aroma of coffee teased her. She studied the trickle of raindrops on the window panes of the doors, wishing Magnus was with her.

For the past several days, she'd combed through every book she had at her disposal. But the books, and the internet searches, brought her no closer to the answer of how to get Magnus back.

She'd avoided returning to Kalfu's library. Their last encounter had angered her, and whatever blackness the arrogant god had added to her soul stuck with her in the form of a lingering cold. She'd not been able to shake the aches and chills hounding her. Until she had exhausted all her references at the shop, she refused to set foot in the library.

She also didn't have the stomach for another confrontation with the disloyal Julie Brown. Lexie needed to have her energy back and her wits about her before tangling with the former priestess.

Nina waltzed into the kitchen. She stood by the table, impatiently tapping her foot.

Lexie glanced up from her pile of books.

"Madame Henri is out front. She said you called her."

Lexie sat back, struggling to remember when she had called the woman. "Ah, yes, I did. Can you tell her to come back here?"

Nina set her hands on the table, a scowl on her face. "When are you going to snap out of this? You've been canceling client appointments, avoiding the store. People come here to see you, to see the mambo. Clients are beginning to spread rumors around town that you're avoiding them. You need to fix whatever is going on with you."

Lexie reached for another tissue from the box she kept with her day and night. "I have to figure something out first. Fix a problem before I can deal with other peoples' issues."

Nina pointed at the tissue box. "You can start by seeing a doctor. You look like crap and have been walking around this place like you're in a coma."

Will had the same complaints. But she knew what was wrong with her, and no medical doctor could help her.

"It's just a cold."

Nina stood back from the table. "Seems more like the bubonic plague to me."

Lexie waved the tissue in her hand at her assistant. "Just tell Madame Henri to come back here."

After Nina left, Lexie blew her nose again. Antoine sat up from his spot on the floor next to her chair. He put his head in her lap.

He'd been doing that a lot lately. She figured he sensed how much she missed Magnus. Animals detected the sorrow of their owners and tried to comfort them. Or at least that was what she'd read once in a magazine.

Cecily Henri walked into the kitchen wearing a black dress trimmed with lace. Her gaze went to Antoine.

"I recognized the *rougarou* at our council meeting. Glad to see Antoine has a good home."

Lexie dropped her tissue in the wastepaper basket under her table. "I suspect you know him from your days in Kalfu's house."

Cecily had a seat across from her, gleaning the pile of open books. "He told you I once lived there."

"Julie Brown told me."

Cecily folded her hands in her lap. "Watch out for her. She's a trickster. She knows every spell, every incantation, every ritual in that library, and she'll use them against you."

Lexie picked up her cell phone. "Yeah, I learned that the hard way. She gave me a spell to banish the shadow spirits back to their river. I ended up sending Magnus away." She handed over the phone open to the spell's picture. "She gave me this from one of the books in the library."

Cecily held the phone out at arm's length, squinting to read the text.

"That's a banishing spell. For spirits haunting a person or place." She handed the phone back to Lexie.

"Is there a way to reverse it?"

Cecily gestured to the books on her table. "There's always a way to reverse a spell; you have to find it. Whenever you set out to change something, you must always make sure you have the spell to change it back. Sort of like a voodoo safeguard. Didn't Titu teach you this?"

"She died before we got to that." Lexie shook her head, missing her mentor more than ever. "Sometimes, I ask myself what

I'm doing here. I must be a pretty big disappointment as mambo."

Cecily patted her hand. "Nonsense. No one knows everything there is to know about voodoo, and every priestess makes mistakes along the way." She winked. "Even a mambo can't be right all the time. Give yourself some credit for trying. Not many people would have taken on this challenge. What makes a mambo is heart, not spells and rituals."

Lexie eyed the dragon cane leaning against the counter. "Can I get Magnus back?"

"Certainly. But be careful. Maman Brigitte can be a real backstabbing bitch when you mess with her underworld. I heard you have her cane and she will want it back. Use that as leverage."

"How do you know Maman Brigitte has him?"

Cecily stood. "I may not have the power anymore, but I can still pick up when changes occur. You made her angry, and that ripple has gone out to every priest and priestess who has the gift."

Lexie reached for another tissue. "Thank you, Cecily. You've given me hope."

The older woman put her hand to Lexie's brow. "You look awful. Perhaps you should be home in bed."

Lexie sniffled. "I can't rest. I can't sleep. I can't do anything until I get Magnus back."

She rested her arms on the table, bracing herself to stand. The quivering in her muscles made her silently vow to lay off the coffee until she got some food into her system.

But when Lexie rose from the table, a funny, lightheaded sensation came over her.

"Lexie?"

Cecily's voice sounded far away.

Her legs buckled. She felt herself going down and was unable to stop it.

But she wasn't afraid. The ribbon in her center rippled with excitement, and she knew everything would turn out okay.

She kept telling herself that as the black spots closed in around her.

Everything will be fine. Soon, life will be perfect.

Crisp air-conditioning tinged with a sickly antiseptic aroma roused her from her sleep. Lexie didn't like that smell. It meant needles and hospitals. Anxiety sped up her heart, and then an unrelenting pounding started in her head. Forcing herself up, she opened her eyes. Bright overhead lights made her wince.

"What the fuck?"

"Mrs. Bennett?"

She cracked her eyelids to get a look at who had addressed her by her married name.

After the blurry vision passed, a pretty middle-aged woman in teal scrubs smiled at her.

Behind her was a small exam room with shelves of medical supplies against one wall and a sink next to a closed door.

"You with us?"

She rubbed her eyes. "Where am I?"

"Tulane Medical Center. ER. You passed out at your place of business. An ambulance brought you here."

Something damp rested against her head. Lexie reached up and felt a wet washcloth.

"Is my husband here?"

"Mr. Bennett is in the waiting room. I think he's about worn a hole in our floor."

The nurse raised the head of her bed. Lexie wasn't sure if that was to make her feel better or worse. The change in altitude brought on a bout of nausea.

"I'll go get him for you." The woman walked out of the room.

Lexie closed her eyes again. Her mind went into overdrive exploring the possibilities of what had brought her to the ER. She'd chalked up the illness to Kalfu's tampering, but perhaps it was something more. Never one to look up her symptoms on the internet, she now wished she'd paid better attention to what was happening to her body.

"Lexie?"

Will's woodsy cologne enveloped her, then his arms wrapped around her. Suddenly, she felt better. It was bad enough being in the ER, but she could handle it with him by her side.

He sat on the edge of the bed, inspecting her features. "You scared the crap out of me."

Lexie eased up on her elbows. A tug on her right hand stopped her. She looked down and saw an IV.

"Is that a needle in my hand?"

Her chest tightened, and her heart rose in her throat.

Will brushed a few blonde hairs from her face. "The doctor says you're dehydrated and weak. The IV was to make you feel better."

She flopped back on her pillow. "I hate needles. Take me home."

"No way. The doctor ran blood tests to see what's up with you." He gripped her hand. "I told you to go back to Dr. Paulson and get checked out. You should have listened to me."

Returning to George Paulson was right up there on her to-do

list with wrestling grizzly bears in Alaska.

The door to her room opened, and a short man with a broad chest and receding hairline strolled up to her bed. He wore a long white coat with the green, diamond-shaped Tulane Hospital emblem over his right chest pocket. His smile seemed sincere, if not a little crooked.

"I'm glad to see you're back in the land of the living, Mrs. Bennett. I'm Dr. Carl Brubaker."

Will stood. "She's got her color back." He turned to her. "You were white as a sheet when they brought you in."

"Yes." Dr. Brubaker grabbed a stool at the foot of her bed. He eased it around to her side, forcing Will out of his way. "Made me think you were suffering from anemia, so we drew a whole lot of blood work to see what's up."

Lexie waited, her stomach doing cartwheels. "And? What is it?"

Dr. Brubaker took a penlight from his lab coat pocket and flashed it in her eyes.

Lexie batted his hand away. The bright light only made her headache worse. "Just tell me what's wrong so I can go home."

The physician sat back on his stool. "Nothing's wrong. You're a little anemic and dehydrated, but that's to be expected. You're going to need to take it easy for a few days. After that, everything should be fine."

Will came around the doctor and held her hand, the worry lines in his forehead adding to her frayed nerves.

"Is it just a cold?" he asked.

Dr. Brubaker stood. "No, not a cold. But it is something that will go away in about nine months." He grinned. "Congratulations, Mrs. Bennett. You're pregnant."

Chapter Thirty-Six

Nestled under a mound of blankets, Lexie sat on her sofa, a steaming mug of chamomile tea in her lap while she stared out the windows at the churning, muddy water of the Mississippi River. Her head throbbed, her muscles ached, and her heavy heart sank to the lowest depths of hell.

"I have chicken soup in the fridge, along with lots of juice and popsicles in the freezer." Will came up to the sofa, slipping on his jacket. "I will be no more than an hour or two at the office. I have to get these clients out of my hair, and then we can spend the evening together. I can pick up some takeout, and we can veg on Netflix, or talk, or whatever you want." He smiled, beaming at her. "I still can't believe it."

Lexie was utterly numb. "Neither can I."

"See? All this time we were both thinking you had a cold, and you were pregnant." He chuckled, sounding almost giddy. "We have to remember this next time you get pregnant, so we can save ourselves another trip to the ER."

He laughed again, but the sound found its way to the stabbing pain in her brow, twisting it tighter like a garrote.

"You'll need to make an appointment with Dr. Paulson ASAP."

She put the mug on the coffee table and pushed away a few of the blankets smothering her. "I think I want to find another OB. I wasn't impressed with him."

"Really?" Will adjusted his collar. "He's the best in the city."

"Will, if I'm to have this baby, I want to pick out the obstetrician."

He held up his hands. "All right. You do whatever you want. I'm gonna make this as easy as possible for you."

Lexie tried not to laugh. Easy? If he only knew.

He checked for the keys in his jacket pocket. "I'll call you when I leave the office." He kissed her cheek. "I love you, baby."

The slam of the front door was a welcomed relief. She couldn't think with Will around planning baby names or debating the pros and cons of Lamaze. What she needed to discover was who had given her the baby.

The encounter with Damballah was the first thing that had come to mind after the ER doctor told her the news. It made sense. He had touched her, and the sleep she'd fallen into had been heavenly.

Kalfu had touched her too, but her reaction to his power had not been as pleasant.

Antoine came across the living room to her sofa and placed his head in her lap.

She rubbed the scruff of his neck. "You knew, didn't you? You knew the moment it happened, and you know who did this."

She tried to read what she saw in his yellow eyes, but nothing came to her.

"I wonder what Magnus would make of all this."

She ached to share her news and her concerns with him. He would have helped her, told her how to handle it. He was the only one who knew her secret, and she missed having his confidence.

"Fuck!" She tossed the rest of the blankets aside and climbed from the sofa. "I can't do this without him."

Lexie marched to the table by the door and found her purse and the keys to the Cadillac. Then she remembered the damned car remained in the parking lot near her French Quarter shop.

She pulled out her phone and hit her Uber app.

Antoine came up to her, carrying his new leash in his mouth. "You have to stay here."

But the fluffy black dog would not be put off and pushed his muzzle into her crotch as if to say, "I'm going too."

Lexie finished with her phone and took the leash from him.

"This would be a whole lot easier if you would just appear to me."

The dog barked, sounding adamant.

Lexie sighed and then slowly nodded. She clamped the leash to the black leather collar she had bought for him.

In a way, Antoine brought some comfort. She didn't feel so alone with him by her side.

She opened the front door and gripped his lead, a tingle in her belly.

"Get ready, buddy. We're going to the swamp, and we're going to find a way to get Magnus back."

Lexie slammed on the brakes of the Cadillac and skidded to a stop in front of the Acadian cottage. She stormed from the car to the porch, hellbent on getting revenge.

Antoine followed her up the porch steps, a line of hair from his back to the base of his tail rose until it stood upright. Before she reached the front door, the dog growled.

"What is it?"

A frigid breeze blew past carrying the aroma of fresh-cut grass.

"I hear congratulations are in order."

His voice cut across her heart like surgical steel.

He strolled across the shelled driveway, not making a sound.

"Why are you here?"

"It's my house. I could ask you the same question."

She banged her dragon cane on the porch boards. "According to the state and the federal government, it's my house. I'm paying the taxes on it."

He lowered his gaze. "Where's Brigitte's baton juju?"

"I left it at home. I like this one better."

He nodded his approval. "It suits you, but Brigitte will want hers back, so you must guard it carefully."

An idea struck Lexie. "Will she give me Magnus in exchange for her cane?"

He came closer, pointing at Antoine.

The dog lay down, resting his head on his paws.

"She did not take Magnus. You sent him away. You will have to find a way to get him back." He rubbed his fingers across his brow. "She will try to stop you. Your ghost is a great prize. Holding the spirit guide of the mambo gives her some leverage over you."

Lexie wasn't in the mood for his games. "Well, not for long. I'm going to find a way to get him back, no matter what it takes."

"Is that wise?"

She sized up the handsome man, guessing why he didn't want Magnus back. Kalfu had been pushing her ghost aside for quite a while.

"Why do you care what I do? Magnus is my problem."

He eased closer, a speck of concern in his elusive eyes. "You are with child. Should you be challenging powerful gods and goddesses, and draining all your energy. You ended up in the ER because you taxed yourself. You shouldn't risk your health again for Magnus. Consider your baby."

"Yeah, about that." She rested both her hands on the cane, attempting to stay calm. "Any idea how I got pregnant?"

He gazed into her eyes. "Perhaps the child is a gift."

"Damballah came to me before you did that night. He was kind to me and touched me." She tried to read the baby growing in her womb, but she could not sense it, feel it, and certainly not tap into its power. "Perhaps he gave me this gift."

"Did he?" He leaned closer to her and whispered, "Think again."

She stumbled backward, but the railing behind her blocked her from getting away. How could he have impregnated her? He'd touched her, just once. And even though it had overwhelmed her, it couldn't have made her pregnant.

Kalfu folded his hands, appearing entertained. "I told you I would give you a child when the time was right. Well, it's time."

"You're the father?" Lexie bent over, retching at the thought of carrying his child.

"Now, now. None of that." He knelt in front of her. "I am the baby's creator, dear lady. The child will resemble you and your husband, but her tendencies will be mine."

She wiped her mouth, pushing herself up with her cane. "*Her* tendencies?"

He bowed his head. "Another mambo to take the reins after you've grown weary of the position."

Lexie's maternal regard for the child siphoned out of her. If the baby turned out to be like the cold, devious manipulator before her, how could she love it?

She hardened her heart against the nightmare of raising his child. But she could not let him sense her disgust. He would destroy her with one thought if he knew.

Lexie raised her chin, showing him the defiant mambo with which he preferred to spar. "You should have given me a choice. Asked me if I wanted this."

Kalfu's smug grin fell. A dark shadow crossed his features, and the evil glow in his eyes burned into her.

"It wasn't your choice. It was mine."

The fury in his voice silenced all her arguments. She'd pushed him far enough, for now.

She pictured her life with Kalfu's spawn. When she thrilled in killing small animals, or tormented classmates, or conjured black clouds in her bedroom—how would she explain any of this to Will? Perhaps she could get rid of it before he figured out the child wasn't his.

His wicked smile returned. "Not to worry, Lexie Arden. Your husband will be happy with the child no matter whose personality she exhibits. Parenthood blinds people to ugly acts. And you will not consider aborting my child again. Try, and I will punish you."

He waved to the front door. "Go get what you came for. Magnus Blackwell is waiting."

She wanted to argue with him, but the visions of her future robbed her of the strength. Emotionally waylaid, she used her cane to keep from falling while she hobbled toward the house.

Before she put her hand on the doorknob, she glanced back at the drive.

He was gone.

Antoine came running up to her, his long black coat shining in the light. She waited for the dog to join her before she stepped inside.

The lock clicked, and the door creaked open.

"A gentleman always gets the door for a lady." Kalfu's voice hung in the air.

Once she and Antoine were inside, she shut the door and set the lock. It seemed silly, but it made her feel better.

She rested back against the wood, taking in all that he had told her.

A girl. A daughter for Kalfu, and a nightmare for Lexie.

She dreaded the day Will found out. For as long as she lived, she vowed to keep the child's conception from him.

And the child? This time, the voice was her own.

She pushed away from the door, desperate to stop thinking. "There's no time for this. Magnus needs you."

At the door to the library, she put her hand on the handle and debated how to deal with Julie. She'd been cruel and tied the woman to the room the last time they had met. Would she help her?

Lexie eased the door open.

There's only one way to find out.

Dust scintillated on the shelves under the overhead lights. The books she'd removed before were where she had left them in a pile on the floor. The corner Julie occupied remained drenched in shadows despite the glare of the lights.

Lexie stepped into the room, ready to face the treacherous ghost once more.

She motioned for Antoine to stay at the entrance. The fluffy dog sat and followed her with his soulful eyes.

When she reached the center of the room, Lexie browsed the bookshelves, wondering where to begin. She tapped her dragon cane on the floor and opened her center, ready to use her considerable power to make the spirit help her.

"Julie Brown, come to me."

A ball showed up, floating in the corner, slowly growing brighter. A shining beam shot out from the middle and ran from the floor to the ceiling. Small particles danced inside it until they came together to form a shape—the hunched over figure of a woman. The beam contracted into Julie Brown's center. Like an old television warming up, the color of her dress, her corncob pipe, and her black shawl sharpened.

Once again a part of Lexie's world, Julie shuffled out of the corner, a stream of black smoke coming from her pipe. She kept her eyes lowered, hiding her gaze. She crept closer, and the sweet smell of tobacco wafted past Lexie.

"I'm here, Mambo."

Antoine yawned and made himself comfortable by the open door.

Lexie went around the tentative ghost, debating if she had made the right decision in coming to the house. But without Julie's knowledge of the library, Lexie's search for the spell to save Magnus could take years.

"I'm here to save my ghost. Betray me, feed me false information, or send me on a wild goose chase, and I will give you to Kalfu." She leaned into the ghost. "But help me, and I'll consider letting you out of this room."

Julie's hands trembled as she pulled at her shawl. "I will do whatever you want. Just don't send me to him. You have no idea how sadistic he can be."

She stood back, hopeful that Julie's fear of Kalfu would ensure her loyalty. "I need for you to find the book with that banishing spell. The one that sent Magnus Blackwell away."

Julie went to the bookcase across the room. She pointed to the black leather-bound book left out on a shelf.

"I knew you would come back. I wanted to show you how sorry I am."

Lexie approached the shelf, not believing a word. She'd learned a valuable lesson: trust no one—except Magnus.

Lexie set her cane against the bookcase. "Since you're the mistress of this library, I suspect you already know how to reverse this spell."

"It ain't that easy. You can't just say a spell and get your ghost back."

Lexie opened the book, searching for the banishing spell. "Then what do I have to do?"

Julie raised her head, her dark eyes narrowed on Lexie. "Your ghost is in the land of the dead. You want him back, you've got to fight for him."

Lexie glanced up from the pages, wrinkling her brow. "How do I do that?"

Julie slinked closer and pointed at the book.

An undetectable wind fluttered the pages. Suddenly, the flurry of activity stopped. The book opened to a section with dark red ink.

Lexie closely examined the handwriting. *Is that blood?*

Julie poked a map in the middle of the page. "You have to go to Guinee."

"Where is that?

"Guinee is the land of the dead."

Epilogue

Clinging to his last sliver of hope, Magnus scanned the curtain of black around him for any hint of life—mortal or spirit, he didn't care. The nothingness was agony. Occasionally, he swore he saw movement in the form of floating wisps of smoke. They would tease him and make him believe he wasn't alone. Perhaps madness had finally won.

He continued to float in the blackness. He wasn't sure how, but something held him there. He kept reaching into the abyss with his ability, but all that came to him was emptiness.

When not hunting for others like him, he thought of Lexie. The memory of her giggle, her smile, her trust in him gave him the strength to go on.

She must have figured out what happened to him by now. Even though he had no sense of time in his weightless world, he was sure she would find her way to him.

"What if she's happy that you're gone?"

The voice wasn't his. It was hers.

"I would love to rid myself of all spirits." It was Lexie's voice coming from the everywhere around him. *"They have ruined my life, my chance at happiness. I get so tired of the dead and their demands."*

"Still believe your mambo wants you back?"

"Stop it, you bitch. That's not her. Lexie would never say that."

"Are you sure?"

He wrestled against his binds. He could never believe anything he heard in this place. The voices were all part of Maman Brigitte's mind games. She tortured him by raising doubts about Lexie's devotion to him.

Up ahead, in the blackness, Magnus detected movement. It had been so long since he'd seen anything, he questioned whether this was real.

It began as a slight change in the light. A grayness blended with the black. An unidentifiable shape came closer, swaying in the darkness.

The faint aroma of rum and cigars drifted by. He couldn't believe it.

Where have I smelled that before?

"Good to see you again, Mr. Blackwell."

The deep baritone voice seemed to echo all around him. A black curtain of smoke formed in front of him. It rustled like fabric in a breeze, and then parted in the center. A tall man in a top hat, black tailcoat, dark glasses, and cotton plugs stuffed up his nose sauntered up to Magnus. The same spirit of the dead he had met at Holt Cemetery ages ago.

"Ah, Baron Samedi."

Relief coursed through Magnus. He wasn't mad, after all.

The Baron carried his long-marbled cane carved to represent a human backbone. The blood-red stones in the eyes of the skull handle radiated a peculiar crimson light, illuminating the space around him.

The glow let Magnus study his world, and as soon as he did, he wished he hadn't. He was in a cell with grimy stone walls and no windows. He floated above a black lake suspended by rusty chains.

He peered into the smooth water. Something white bobbed on the surface. He squinted to get a better look. Then Magnus jerked away.

Bones, hundreds of them, polluted the lake. A skull beneath him glanced up. Its jaw slackened, and the black water came through creating the illusion of a gaping black hole between the rows of perfect white teeth. A garbled shriek came from it. Horrified by the ghastly sound, Magnus fought against his restraints.

"The lake of the dead." The Baron turned his freakish amber eyes to Magnus. "Where the souls of those not fit to return to the land of the living are kept. Dregs of society in that place."

Magnus closed his eyes to the black soup of bones, fearing his fate. "Is that why I'm here? To be added to that?"

Baron Samedi touched the tip of his cane to the lake. The bones sank, and the water glassed over to form a smooth surface. Soon, a black stone floor replaced the lake.

"You must forgive my wife, but you've gotten on Brigitte's bad side. She's always a surly bitch when crossed."

Baron Samedi waved his skeletal cane over the shackles holding Magnus's wrists and ankles. They fell away and disappeared into the wall.

He set his feet on the floor, thankful to be able to stand. He took in the rest of the room, wiping his hands.

"Am I to remain in this cell while your wife decides what to do with me?"

The Baron grinned and tapped the ground with his cane.

The walls swirled as pigment dotted the black. Paneled rich oak replaced the stone and rosettes cropped up along the seams. The black above him washed aside to reveal white plaster with a vine of roses circling the border. White and peach floral sofas, chairs, and heavy wood tables sprang up from the floor. A mantel formed on one side of the room, decorated with more carved rosettes, it had a framed portrait above it.

Magnus recognized the likeness. It was him, wearing his long black coat, red vest, high cut black boots, and holding his prized dragon cane. His thick, dirty-blond hair was as he currently wore it, and his flashing green eyes looked out over the room. The painting was the same that had hung in his living room at Altmover Manor, but the subject was not how he'd seen himself since aligning with Lexie. The malice in his scowl and the distrust in his eyes had faded long ago. The artist had recreated Magnus Blackwell, the man, but had not captured the ghost.

"This was my living room at my old home."

Baron Samedi went to one of the chairs and ran his hand over the upholstered seat.

"You had excellent taste."

At the mantel, Magnus admired the picture he had prized in life. "To what do I owe this?"

Baron sat in the fancy chair. "I have news for you. Your mambo is with child."

Magnus reached for the edge of the mantel and squeezed. Shock resonated through him like a church bell on a Sunday morning. It wasn't Will's, of that he was sure.

"Who's is it?"

Baron shrugged and sat back. "Whoever it is, they're very powerful. More powerful than my wife or me. The child will be very strong, perhaps too strong for the mother. Lexie Arden will need you."

Magnus's optimism swelled. He released his grip on the mantel.

"Are you letting me go?"

"Not quite." The Baron caressed the skullcap on his cane's handle. "Your mambo will have quite an ax to bury with my wife. She has her cane. Brigitte will need it back, but I also do not wish to offend the Mambo of New Orleans. She's become powerful, and with her baby, dangerous. There must be a compromise."

Magnus rubbed his chin. Of course. When power was up for grabs, compromise was the tool of choice to get one's way. His father had taught him that. It seemed what rang true in the world of the living still resonated in the land of the dead.

"What do you want?"

He rhythmically tapped his finger on the skull, his gaze glued to Magnus. "By rights, you should remain with me. Guinee is my world. You are dead."

Magnus rested his elbow on the mantel. "But I also belong to Lexie."

The Baron rose from his chair. "All the spirit world knows Damballah arranged your binding with the mambo, and only he can break it. I wish no ill will with him, but I also do not want to cross my wife."

Magnus's patience waned. "What are we to do?"

The Baron's booming voice reverberated throughout Magnus's living room. "Your mambo must come here. She must win you back and convince my wife you belong with her. If she does that, you can go free."

He walked up and patted Magnus's shoulder. His features melted into nothing but haunting black eye sockets and white bony crevices. When he tilted his head, his dark skin, full lips, and disturbing eyes were back in place.

"But she will have to jump through a few hoops to get to our world. There are many trials she will have to best, many of my brethren she will have to finesse." He raised his eyebrows. "She must be very convincing to raise the dead."

Magnus knew it was a setup, but he had to go along with whatever Baron Samedi was after. He would do anything to get back to Lexie.

"Can I trust you to help Lexie on this journey? Make sure she's kept safe. I would be grateful if I knew she was being cared for by one who knew this world."

Baron Samedi's smile widened. "It will cost you."

Ah, here it is—the reason for his visit.

"What do you want, Baron?"

"A soul, Mr. Blackwell." The skull with the bottomless black holes for eyes reappeared, obliterating his human features. "If you leave my world, you must replace your soul with another. Balance must be maintained."

Magnus stepped away from the mantel. He considered what the spirit was asking.

"Are you suggesting I take a soul from the living?"

"The universe has deemed you can't take a life, but the mambo can." His jaw slackened, offering a glimpse of his white teeth gleaming like shark fangs. "If she wants you, she will have to pay the toll. A soul for a soul. Otherwise, you will remain here, for all eternity."

Magnus stumbled forward, horrified, and gripped the back of a chair to keep upright. He could never allow Lexie to suffer the hell he'd endured for taking the lives of Simone Glapion and Frances. He had accepted his fate, but he would not let her repeat his mistakes.

"I won't have Lexie kill for me. She is too good to be stained with such a sin."

Baron Samedi lifted his cane and expertly twirled it with one hand. "Judgment is a merciless mistress, my good man." He stabbed the tip of the cane into the hardwood floor, and the walls shook. "Sometimes true redemption only comes by watching those you love suffer for your sins."

Magnus sank to his knees, destroyed. He could not picture a world where he and Lexie shared such a dastardly deed. She was goodness, light, and all he had never been. If she took on the heavy mantle of his sins, he would never forgive himself.

If he had to suffer eternity under Maman Brigitte's yoke to spare Lexie such a fate, he would do it.

Magnus hardened his heart and prepared himself for the ultimate sacrifice—never seeing Lexie Arden again.

About the Authors

Alexandrea Weis, RN-CS, PhD, is a multi-award-winning author of over twenty-seven novels, a screenwriter, ICU Nurse, and historian who was born and raised in the French Quarter of New Orleans. Having grown up in the motion picture industry as the daughter of a director, she learned to tell stories from a different perspective and began writing at the age of eight. Infusing the rich tapestry of her hometown into her novels, she believes that creating vivid characters makes a story moving and memorable. A member of the Horror Writers Association and International Thriller Writers Association, Weis writes mystery, suspense, thrillers, horror, crime fiction, and romance. She lives with her husband and pets in New Orleans where she is a permitted/certified wildlife rehabber with the Louisiana Wildlife and Fisheries and rescues orphaned and injured wildlife.

www.AlexandreaWeis.com

 **Lucas Astor** is a multi-award-winning author from New York. He has resided in Central America, the Middle East, and traveled throughout Europe. He lives a very private, virtually reclusive lifestyle, preferring to spend time with a close-knit group of friends than be in the spotlight. He is a writer and poet with a penchant for telling stories that delve into the dark side of the human psyche. He likes to explore the evil that exists, not just in the world, but right next door behind a smiling face.

www.LucasAstor.com

"A dark story of passion, revenge, and a Faustian pact ...
a guilty-pleasure read that kept me captivated." ~ *New Orleans Magazine*

HELL HAS A NEW MASTER
BLACKWELL
A MAGNUS BLACKWELL NOVEL: PREQUEL

Alexandrea Weis With Lucas Astor

BLACKWELL

A MAGNUS BLACKWELL NOVEL: PREQUEL

HELL HAS A NEW MASTER

In the late 1800s, handsome, wealthy New Englander, Magnus Blackwell, is the envy of all. When Magnus meets Jacob O'Conner—a Harvard student from the working class—an unlikely friendship is forged. But their close bond is soon challenged by a captivating woman; a woman Magnus wants, but Jacob gets.

Devastated, Magnus seeks solace in a trip to New Orleans. After a chance meeting with Oscar Wilde, he becomes immersed in a world of depravity and brutality, inevitably becoming the inspiration for Dorian Gray. Armed with the forbidden magic of voodoo, he sets his sights on winning back the woman Jacob stole from him.

Amid the trappings of Victorian society, two men, bent on revenge, will lay the foundation for a curse that will forever alter their destinies.

www.MagnusBlackwell.com

SOME MONSTERS NEVER DIE

DAMNED

A MAGNUS BLACKWELL NOVEL: BOOK ONE

Alexandrea Weis with Lucas Astor

DAMNED

A MAGNUS BLACKWELL NOVEL: BOOK I

SOME MONSTERS NEVER DIE

Over a hundred years after the death of Magnus Blackwell,
Altmover Manor sits abandoned. Lexie Arden and her fiancé,
Will Bennet, are determined to rescue the neglected Mount
Desert Island landmark. They want to make Altmover Manor
their home. But Magnus has other plans.

A spirit bound to his former residence, Magnus finds himself
inexplicably drawn to the young woman. She has a supernatural
gift; a gift Magnus wants to exploit.

As Lexie and Will settle in, secrets from Magnus's past begin to
surface. Compelled to learn all she can about the former owner,
Lexie becomes immersed in a world of voodoo, curses, and the
whereabouts of a mysterious dragon cane.

Magnus's crimes won't be so easily forgotten, and what Lexie
unearths is going to change the future … for everyone.

YOU CAN'T ESCAPE THE DARKNESS

BOUND

A MAGNUS BLACKWELL NOVEL: BOOK TWO

Alexandrea Weis with Lucas Astor

BOUND

A MAGNUS BLACKWELL NOVEL: BOOK II

YOU CAN'T ESCAPE THE DARKNESS

Magnus Blackwell's past is about to catch up with him.

An evil force has seized New Orleans. Pestilence, suffering, and darkness cloak the city. The citizens are scared and need their mambo to guide them, but Lexie Arden can't help anyone. A diabolical presence has taken Lexie's power and severed her ties with the other side.

Magnus Blackwell is fighting demons of his own. Torn between his devotion to Lexie and a spirit from his past, Magnus's loyalty is put to the test. He must revisit his sins to uncover the key to the hatred ripping the city apart.
If he doesn't, Lexie's reign as mambo will end.

Their search for answers leads them deep into the darker realms of voodoo—until a desperate Lexie does the unthinkable, and Magnus can do nothing to spare her from her fate.